THE PRETTY BEACH WAY

POLLY BABBINGTON

SPRING IN THE PRETTY BEACH HILLS

Fancy a trip to my new happy place?

You'll love it in the Pretty Beach Hills.

Spring in the Pretty Beach Hills is the first of four books based in the hills of Pretty Beach. And you thought the town was nice. ;) We have a new character to fall in love with, there may be a shirtless man on a bike (oh. my. gawwd.) and the house is utterly swoon-worthy. Then there are the two pubs, the stream, the hills, and let us not forget the cottages and the window boxes. If you're a Babbette (if you know you know) you are going to die.
Love Polly x

Spring in the Pretty Beach Hills

***

A Polly Babbella.

A beautiful spring day.
A chance meeting.
A love story in the Pretty Beach Hills.

Get ready to fall in love.
You're going to utterly adore it.

Jam-packed with all Polly's much-loved unique trademarks - a divine coastal setting, gorgeous female characters you'd just love to chat with and liberally sprinkled with a healthy dose of Polly's special blend of escapism by the sea.

'Polly really is like my secret best friend in a book. I knew I was a goner by the end of the first page.'

PRETTY BEACH

Welcome to the world of Pretty Beach.

A sweeping, sparkly blue inlet town surrounded by water, crisscrossed with sweet old laneways, filled with wonderful characters, and overlooked by a quaint old blue and white lighthouse.

1

The smell of the sea, comfort, and books cocooned Lotta as she sat in the library room in Pretty Beach to the Breakers surrounded by her things. She'd spent days there, lodged in the very same spot, curled up on the sofa. It had been her favourite sort of time off – one full of reading, more reading, and copious cups of tea. There may have been the odd pink gin, and there had definitely been a roast chicken. The only time she'd really left the snugness of the library room was when she'd gone for dinner with Jack.

Things were going along quite nicely with Jack, it had to be said. Since he'd taken her on a surprise date to the manor house where they'd first met, she'd been amazed at the upturn in her very existence. It was as if her life had zoomed around a corner, had a quick perusal at the two different forks in the road, popped itself into fifth gear, and cruised along on a high. This was Lotta's kind of high. A high where little parts of her life that had been festering in no-man's-land were suddenly starting to come together. It had been a long time coming. A very long time.

As she sat gazing at the shelves full of books around her, she pondered what had happened before she'd moved to the coast and where her life was going now. She felt as if by taking up residence in Pretty Beach to the Breakers, the old house on the corner by the sea, someone somewhere had waved a magic wand and given her an opportunity. She mused her new position further. It was all very promising. It was now time to take all of it – the house, Jack, her new job, and her newfound stability – and ensure that it was all tickety-boo. She was sitting on top of a very nice pink, fluffy cloud, and she wanted to stay there for pretty much the rest of her life. Thank you very much.

Lotta was going to take her run of good luck and make sure it didn't go anywhere anytime soon. It was, in fact, time for Lotta Button to roll up her trouser legs and put a plan into action for this – her new and very accomplished life. She would write lists, start spreadsheets, and formulate things so that she and her existence were a competent, together, on-the-ball powerhouse of success. Yes, she would run her life like a well-oiled machine. Umm, just as long as she could actually take her nose out of a book, pop a spot of oil in the machine, and get on with the life in question instead of living a secondary life in a book.

A waft of warm air came through from outside, bringing with it coastal scents from the sea, and she smiled. This was the house, Pretty Beach to the Breakers, she'd decided she was going to stay in and call home. The place where things in her life would not unravel in front of her and leave her in a heap, but rather, a place where she would finally be in control. There would be no man-child, no start-up, no second job through the night, and most definitely no design of apps.

She mulled it over as she sat thinking about everything she had to do in the next few weeks to continue with the transformation list she'd started. Now it was time to expand on the list – she had more to succeed at in her fresh new start in life. She had to get ready to begin her new job, she was determined to sort out her finances, and she was going to start thinking about budget renovations for Pretty Beach to the Breakers. Bing bong.

She sat with her feet tucked up under her on the library room sofa and went through what she had to do. First things first, her new job needed preparation and organisation. With a breeze coming in from the sea, she reluctantly put down her book, opened the notes app on her phone, and began making a list of the things she would need to do in order to be ready for her start at work. She wanted every part of her new position, every part of *her*, to be successful. She was more than determined to be competent, knowledgeable, well-informed, perfectly presented, and ready to take on the job at hand. Lotta Button was not going to let anyone, least of all herself, down.

Making a bullet point list, she underlined 'perfectly presented' and gazed out at the garden with the end of a pen in her mouth, thinking about what that actually meant. She mused about her first interview and the subsequent times she'd seen Anne Fisher, the woman who had recruited her, at the arcade in Newport where everything and everyone had been impeccably turned out. This was not a job where one could turn up in leisurewear and hope for the best. There was no place in the Corchrane company for fur-lined slipper boots, messy hair, and no bra.

As she noted down a few things on her checklist, it was quickly and sorely obvious that her work wardrobe was in need of a helping hand. Most of her good clothes had been sold on Poshmark after her ex, Dan, and the start-up of his ridiculous app had needed more and more of their money. Her actual work wardrobe that was leftover from those days was now a scant collection of clothes she'd worn to interviews over and over again. It was all a bit tired and jaded. None of it filled her with any confidence or joy.

Listing her work days and flicking over to the first week's schedule in the email Anne had sent her, she gulped. She was in at the deep end from the end of week one with fifteen CEOs from some of the most successful companies in the country booked in for a think tank on Success with VCs. She inhaled and breathed out slowly as she wondered what a think tank consisted of. It sounded all way above her head, but she was determined, even if she was the walking talking version of imposter syndrome personified, that she would appear as if she knew exactly what she was doing. When really, she so did not.

She scanned over the schedule further; this was no job for shirkers. There was a lot to learn and a lot to take on. She quickly ascertained that there was a reason it was so well paid. The following week was just as busy and high-end, with a small (and highly skilled, the email told her) group of surgeons at the top of their game who would be attending a two-day course to fulfil some of their yearly medical education criteria. Lotta swallowed as she read through some of the names of the attendees. A bottom of the ladder job in publishing answering social media comments, this was not.

The more Lotta reread the comprehensive background and training documents from Anne Fisher, the woman who had recruited her, the more she fell down a deep well of nerves. There was no way on earth she was going to be able to do the job! What had she been thinking in accepting it? She was a nobody who'd not even been able to make it at a mediocre level in the publishing world. She'd spent the previous few years contract cleaning offices as a second income. She felt, almost, as if her brain no longer functioned as it once might have done. She spiralled into what ifs and whys and shook her head as anxious thoughts zoomed around her mind.

After going around in circles, she'd fussed about all sorts – her organisational skills, her competence, and sitting underneath it all; what in the name of goodness she was going to wear. After deep breathing to try and keep everything in perspective, she decided that first off, she needed her attire sorted. On top of everything else, she did not need to be worrying about her presentation. She made a quick list of the clothes and accessories she would need and the grooming routine she should follow in order to look her best. A few minutes later, she was looking online at one of her old favourite shopping places when she'd buzzed around Bloomsbury with her fancy coffees and a head full of even fancier ideas. In about thirty seconds of browsing the website, she'd determined that her days of shopping there had probably disappeared at around the same time as Dan had asked her to work a second job.

Once the list of outfits or lack thereof was in place, she began a note detailing a plan of action to start establishing herself in the workplace; she'd read in one of her books that half the battle in a new job was being clued-up with a little bit of background information and knowledge on industry jargon. Lotta decided that she wanted to hit the ground running from day one; she listed a few goals, such as reading up on industry developments and trends and researching the fifteen CEOs who would be attending the think tank. She also made a plan to ensure she was prepared for the surgeon's two-day course and began sifting through information on surgical practice, regulations, and more. By the time she was ready for her mid-morning coffee, Lotta was surrounded by notes on an actual notepad, notes on her laptop, and notes on her phone. She'd given herself so many things to do, it was as if she'd started a job to start her new job. It was not for the faint of heart.

Sitting cross-legged on the sofa, she tumbled head first down a long tunnel, immersing herself in industry news and trends, brushing up on current affairs, and reading about the fifteen companies in attendance at the think tank. As she got herself deeper and deeper, opening a trillion tabs on her laptop, she began to wobble. There was wobbling in all sorts of places. By the time she'd got up to make her mid-morning coffee, she'd backed herself into a pickle, imagining herself in all manner of scenarios. She would become tongue-tied in the presence of scary, super-successful CEOs, she would have a gigantic case of imposter syndrome and not know what to do, say, or behave, and she would mix things up all over the place, delivering presentations to surgeons meant for CEOs of transport companies.

Getting up, taking off her glasses, stretching, and wondering what she'd let herself in for, she went to make a coffee. Walking back into the library room with a steaming cup, she video called Liv. Liv was sitting in the breakroom at work with a KitKat in her hand.

'Oh, dear. By the look on your face, something is wrong.' Liv chuckled.

'What if they don't like me?' Lotta blurted out.

'I presume you're talking about your new job?' Liv clarified.

'Ahh! Yes. I've started preparing, and now I'm thinking I'm way out of my depth. What was I even thinking? Liv! This job is no walk in the park. No wonder it pays well. I need one of my degrees just to get through the training document.'

'I'll tell you what James always says,' Liv replied as she took a sip from a mug and snapped one of the fingers of the KitKat.

'I'll take anything right now, whoever says it,' Lotta stated seriously. 'I'm so nervous. Maybe it would have been better for me to stay in the dark. I thought I was doing the right thing by preparing.'

'James always says to just focus on the positive and what you know. Have faith that you'll be fine. You just have to trust yourself,' Liv stated seriously. 'I was the same before I started my new job.'

'Wow. That's some husband you've got there.'

'I know. You've told me that many times before,' Liv joked. 'Just be yourself, and it will all be okay.

'What if I make a terrible mistake on my first day? I've just gone over Anne's notes and the training document. Honestly, I

THE PRETTY BEACH WAY

feel like I'm *way* out of my depth. I literally have no clue about CEOs or surgeons. I'm much happier with the world of books. Ahh!'

'Calm. You're going to be fine. And for the record, CEOs and surgeons are no different to the rest of us. Just imagine them sitting on the loo.'

Lotta's voice was trembling. 'What if it's too hard for me? Why did I think I could do something like this? I literally have no clue what I'm doing.'

'Take a few deep breaths, Lott. You can do it. Plus, Anne clearly thinks that. You're just having a bit of, what is commonly known as, first day wobbles.'

Lotta let out a huge sigh. Her mind went over every sort of bad scenario she could think of. 'But what if I'm not cut out for this at the end of the day? What if I mess up? What if they don't like me?'

'You'll walk it, Lott. Trust me.' Liv smiled. 'You're just having pre-new job nerves, that's all.'

'That's an understatement! I'm so nervous! I feel like I'm going to fail at this, just like everything in my life. Just like everything that happened with Dan. It's going to happen again. I feel like I'm too scared to be happy,' Lotta catastrophized.

'Oh, dear. I get you. That's sad, though, about the Dan thing. I'm sorry you feel like that.'

'And Liv! My clothes. I have, like, two blouses, both of which are via St Evangelines.'

Liv looked solemn as she stuffed another piece of KitKat into her mouth. 'Yeah, can't help with that. Fashion – so not my department. You'll need Timmy on the case.'

Lotta raised her eyebrows. 'Nope. I'm not getting him involved. Absolutely no way. You know he doesn't step foot out of the bedroom unless he's in designer. He'll make me feel worse. I've made a bit of a list involving a uniform comprising nice trousers and blouses and the odd skirt. I just need to hunt

7

for the blouses and possibly get a new pair of heels, oh, and a blazer. It all needs to be on a budget.'

'Well, there you are then. If you have a list, that's a start. Just go to the supermarket. Honestly, you can't go wrong.'

'Hair, what about hair?'

'Neat and tidy for this, I reckon. Lott, you're overthinking this. You know how to be presentable. You always are.'

Lotta looked at herself on the screen. She was in reading mode, meaning her hair was scrunched up on the top of her head in a huge messy bun, and she was ensconced in her softest, cosiest tracksuit bottoms and a slouchy grey sweatshirt that had been washed so many times it felt as if it was an old friend. She pointed to her hair and chuckled. 'So, you're thinking this won't cut the mustard.'

'Nup.' Liv shook her head. 'Don't turn up as Lotta the Reader. They won't let you in the door, from what you've told me about the arcade. You need to turn up as Sorted Lotta. The one who flitted around before she met Dan. The one we've all missed.'

Lotta nodded. Liv, as per usual, was so very correct. All she had to do was find the woman Liv was referring to. The one before she had been revoltingly scarred by a man with a start-up, way too many air plants, and an app.

2

The next day, Lotta was again in the library room. Hearing a car engine, she got up from the sofa and looked out onto the driveway to see Jack parking his car. She observed as he took his jacket from the back, grabbed his phone, looked over towards the window, and waved. Crossing back over the library room and hallway, she pulled the old double-width front door. The cronky hinges creaked as Lotta pushed the door fully open and stood on the step. On the drive, she could see Jack in jeans, a navy-blue polo shirt, a bit of a tan, a pair of sunglasses on his head, and his jacket draped over his arm. He stood with one hand leaning on top of his car and smiled as he saw Lotta. He was not looking ugly.

'Hello! How are you?' She smiled.

'I'm good. I sailed through the weekend traffic coming into Pretty Beach. I thought I was going to be stuck for ages.'

'Good to hear,' Lotta replied as he approached. From the doorstep, she hugged him and kissed him on the cheek. She inhaled the Jack smell, and as she had so many times before, she counted her blessings that they'd met. She was still so pleased that their paths had crossed in the lobby of a country manor. 'I've really missed you.'

'What have you been up to?' Jack asked. 'Actually, why am I asking? No doubt you have been reading. Am I right?'

'How did you guess?' Lotta laughed.

'It's not hard to work out. How is your TBR pile?' Jack asked as he followed her into the breakfast room.

'I'm slowly but surely getting through it,' she replied, waving her hand around at the pile of books beside her bed in the alcove. 'As you can see, it's slowly depleting. Don't hold your breath though, it will just as quickly fill up again.'

'Goodness! You have been busy, or not busy as it were,' he said as he put down his phone on the breakfast table. 'Righto, no more reading for you today,' Jack said, nodding over towards the alcove. 'I hope you've got your old clothes at the ready.' He winked.

'Err, what?' Lotta replied. 'Why would I be needing my old clothes?'

'I have a surprise for you in the car,' Jack said without a smile.

'A surprise that includes me wearing old clothes. Is that my kind of surprise? It sounds like work to me. What are you up to?' Lotta giggled. 'I have enough on my plate with work and my new job already. I don't need more work in my life.'

'Yeah, sorry, but this surprise *does* involve work. You'll enjoy it, though.'

Lotta raised her eyebrows and chuckled. 'I thought it might be something romantic. You know, like a *romantic* surprise.'

Jack's face was straight. 'Yeah, umm, no. I don't think I do romantic very well.'

Lotta thought about the first night Jack had spent at Pretty Beach to the Breakers. She'd thought then he'd done very well at romantic. *Works for me*, she thought. 'Hmm, yep, you need to raise your game a bit or I might get snapped up by the many suitors of Pretty Beach lining up at my door. I'm surprised you could make it up the path.'

Jack laughed, and Lotta swooned inside. 'By the end of the day, you're going to either love me or hate me,' he said seriously.

'What have you got?' Lotta asked, knowing that she already loved him, so that part was easy enough. Two minutes later, she was standing by the boot of his black SUV with her hands placed firmly on her hips, looking into the boot. A drop cloth lined it, and it was stuffed with tins of paint neatly stacked up in rows, window blinds in plastic boxes, and what looked to her like an industrial vacuum cleaner. She side-eyed before picking up a packet and then exclaimed, 'Disposable suit! Why would I be needing one of those? This is looking like something from a horror movie.'

Jack didn't laugh and picked up a box full of paintbrushes, rollers, and drop sheets and handed it to her. 'I am no longer prepared to sleep off a kitchen in a tiny bed.'

Lotta took the box. 'It's an alcove off a breakfast room.'

'I don't care. There are more than a few perfectly good bedrooms upstairs with more than nice views. I'm not squashing up in that bed, surrounded by piles of books, and waking up looking at a kitchen cupboard any longer.'

Lotta joked, 'You've stayed over like twice.' It had been many more times. Many, many more. He'd more or less moved in.

'Twice too many in that bed,' Jack bantered back. 'By the end of the weekend, you are going to be installed up there.' He nodded his head up towards the window to the left of the front door, which looked out over towards the water.

Lotta stuttered, 'But what about the carpet? The disgusting curtains, the fireplace, the old cupboards. All of it is grotty and ugly.'

Jack inclined his chin towards the paint. 'Cupboards will be white, these blinds are for the windows, and I'll sort the fireplace.'

'Blinds?' Lotta looked at him with doubt plastered all over her face.

'Yes. Bamboo matchstick blinds. I've been reliably informed they go with any decor.'

Lotta screwed her nose up and looked further into the full boot. She could make out the square plastic tubes with the blinds neatly stacked along the back. 'Show me.'

Jack rummaged in the back and then held a box up in front of her, opened the end, and pulled out the top third of a blind. Lotta turned her mouth upside down at a natural bamboo blind looking back at her. 'Not bad, actually. I can work with that.'

Jack's face didn't crack as Lotta watched his eyes flick to his watch. 'There are things coming later, if the delivery window is correct, which will be a miracle.'

'What the...? What sort of things?' Lotta asked incredulously. 'When did you do all this?'

'Things to make this place a bit comfier. You may like being surrounded by books and sleeping in a tiny bed, but I think it's time for some improvements. My back cannot take the sleeping arrangements in Pretty Beach to the Breakers any longer.'

'But I'm on a *seriously* tight budget,' Lotta spluttered as Jack headed to the front door. 'I can't afford any of this!'

'That's good, because I've already paid for everything. Right, less chatting, more working. Less whingeing. The first thing we're going to do is get rid of that God-awful carpet in that bedroom up there.'

Lotta trailed after Jack and thought about when he'd first come around to Pretty Beach to the Breakers, and she'd gulped at his fine form as he'd made short work of carpet removal. As he started informing her of his plan, she could hardly keep the smile from her face; she'd been here before, and she loved his strong presence as he took charge. Jack squared his shoulders as he finished bringing everything in from the car, and she felt herself relax. It felt very nice to have someone in command.

After the entrepreneur she'd pandered to for years, it was a breath of fresh air and then some. She could eat Jack the Worker up for breakfast as far as she was concerned.

Upstairs, in what Lotta and Jack had deduced was the master bedroom, there was a smell of musty fabric, and the walls wore an unhappy shade of dingy green. Faded, dusty, discoloured carpeting ran wall to wall, sagging in some places and coming away from the floorboards in the corner. Lotta looked on and tried to remain positive as Jack busied around, but all she could think about was her small bed looking lost in the huge room and how, despite the room's view and lovely old fireplace, it didn't feel comfy to her at all. She just couldn't see herself in the room, tucked up under the quilt with her books. She was much more comfortable in the alcove.

Jack picked up on her feelings as he threw her a packet with a disposable suit inside. 'Put this on. This is going to be great.'

Lotta looked at the carpet with doubt. 'I don't know. I think I'll just stay downstairs. Honestly, I'm fine down there. Come on, I'll make us a cup of tea.'

'Even if you do stay down there, this is gonski,' he said, pointing down at the carpet. 'Trust me on this. It's going, and today.'

Lotta was doubtful. 'Can we make a deal?'

'Depends on what it is.' Jack's face didn't crack.

'If we work on it and I still don't get the right vibes, I'm leaving the bed where it is downstairs. Deal?'

Jack half-smiled. 'It's a deal. You won't stay down there once today is over. Or at least, I won't.'

Lotta frowned at the look on his face. 'What? What do you know? I can tell you're up to something more than just this.'

'I told you. *Things* are arriving. You'll want to be up here by the end of the weekend. He checked his watch and grimaced. Right now, though, we need to muscle. We really need to get on with this.'

Lotta inhaled and shook her head. 'Okay, but I'm just telling you now, I'm quite happy with the alcove and living downstairs. I don't want you to waste your time with all this.'

'After today, you'll change your mind on that,' Jack promised. 'Trust me on this, Lott.'

~

A few hours later, the carpet, curtains, lampshade, various junk that had been in the cupboards, and an old plastic chair were piled up on the landing. Lotta went down to make a cup of tea, and bringing it back up, she handed one to Jack, and they then stood by the enormous open windows. Jack pointed at the view. 'Now we can actually see something, it's better in here already.'

'True,' Lotta replied, looking doubtfully at the rest of the room. She squinted at the yellowed paint on the architrave. 'The paintwork is so yellowed. It's been a long time since this place saw someone giving it a bit of love.'

Jack chuckled. 'You are going to be that person.'

'Me.' Lotta frowned, looking at him blankly.

'Yup. I'm going to whoosh over these windows with a hand sander, then do the same on the other one and the skirting boards. Then I'm going to use that industrial vacuum. After that, while you start rolling the walls, I'm going to go around these floorboards removing every last gripper rod and nail.'

Lotta looked down at the floor. 'You'll be a while, then. Whoever laid that carpet loved a gripper rod.'

Jack ignored Lotta's despondency. 'Then after I've sorted the chimney and the mantel, we start on the woodwork.' He checked his watch. 'Which will hopefully leave enough drying time...' He let his sentence hang in the air.

Lotta squinted. 'Leave enough drying time for what?'

'For the surprises arriving this afternoon.'

'I still have no clue what you are up to.'

Jack nodded. 'I think you're going to love it. All of it. At least, I hope you are.'

～

Jack's planning and Lotta's following had done wonders for the master bedroom. Removing the carpet alone and pulling down the awful curtains had flooded light into the room and removed years of dust and dirt. Lotta had made them a quick sandwich, and she was sitting on a gigantic paint tin by the sash windows with a mug of tea, looking around at the now whitewashed walls. Jack was perched on the bottom step of a ladder, eating his sandwich.

'I have to say, you were right,' Lotta admitted.

'Mostly I am in life,' Jack deadpanned. 'It's sometimes tough being right all the time.'

'Ha ha.'

'What am I right about this time?'

'This room. It's turned out well. I'm surprised at how much a quick coat of paint can do.'

Jack put his sandwich down and laughed. 'It's like one of those makeover shows. Only in this one, the results are actually nice and there's no man with gigantic shirt cuffs and hideous feature walls.'

Lotta chuckled. 'What's next on the agenda?'

Jack pointed to the matchstick blinds stacked up beside Lotta. 'Those blinds need to go on those windows if you want to have any chance of sleeping in this room. Then, the curtain poles need to go up.'

'I'll need to go out and find some curtains. The blinds will do for now.'

'I may have sorted that,' Jack stated as he took another bite of his sandwich.

'Right. Wow. Okay,' Lotta said, hiding a gulp. Jack was lovely, but she wasn't too confident about his interior design skills. She hid a grimace at the thought of what the curtains might be like. Just as she was finishing her tea, there was the sound of an engine outside. She jumped up and peered out the window.

'Err, there appears to be a very large van from the Cotswolds reversing onto the drive.'

Jack turned his wrist over and looked at his watch. 'A miracle has occurred in Pretty Beach! The delivery is actually bang on time.'

Lotta's hands flew to her mouth, and she felt a flutter of anticipation as she watched the delivery van inch its way closer and closer to the house. She was not used to furniture deliveries, nor was she used to surprises, or being spoiled. A few minutes later, she'd bolted down the stairs and was standing on the drive.

'Afternoon,' a portly man with bright red cheeks and a happy smile greeted her. 'You're not looking like a Jack to me, or maybe you are?'

Lotta beamed. 'Nope, but you're in the right spot.'

'I should say so,' the man replied, gawping over towards the sea and then up at the house. 'Pretty Beach to the Breakers, is it? Right address?'

'Yes, yes, you're in the right place.' Lotta smiled.

'Okay, we have a big 'un for you.'

'Ooh.'

'And we've been told there are a few turns in the stairs. Is that right?'

'Yes.' Lotta nodded.

'Well, I'd better get the lads to get this show on the road.'

An hour later, Lotta was practically jigging around the bedroom in happiness. Paint fumes and newness filled the air, along with a super-king sized, velvet-covered, sleigh bed. Alongside that were gorgeous bedside tables, huge ginger jar lamps, boxes full of homewares, a large double-width dresser with a stripped pine top and a wide, tall, oversized mirror leaned up on the wall.

Lotta just kept looking around and shaking her head. The bed, in a deep petrol blue velvet, was juxtaposed against the freshly painted walls, and as far as she was concerned, was ready and waiting to be slept in. Jack finished stuffing reams of plastic covering from the new mattress into a cardboard box, and Lotta moved to the window, stood with her hands on her hips, and looked back at the room.

'Happy?' Jack asked as he looked up from the cardboard box.

Was she happy? Was she ever. Lotta's breath caught in her throat. 'It's gorgeous. All of it. Every single thing,' she whispered, barely able to contain herself. 'I legit can't believe you've done this for me.' She shook her head over and over again. 'Thank you.'

'I told you, you needed to get out of the alcove and that tiny bed,' Jack said, smiling. 'Correction; *we* needed to get out of that alcove. I should say *I* needed to get out of it. I just made it happen.'

Lotta couldn't believe her eyes as she continued to just stare at the gigantic bed. She hadn't expected the surprise. She definitely hadn't expected him to nail it. She couldn't believe it. It was the kind of nice gesture that happened to other people in films and books and stuff.

Lotta swallowed and shook her head as her mind raced back to when she'd first arrived in the house. In that first week, it had been freezing cold and there had been a scary scraping sound from the sitting room. She'd fantasised for weeks about spending a night in a luxurious bed in a hotel. Now it appeared that the luxurious bed had arrived, and it was in her very own bedroom. She couldn't get her head around it. All of it was blowing her mind.

The bed was nothing short of magnificent. The turned legs,

the sleigh shape, and the tufted velvet suited the room to a tee. She walked across the room, ran her fingers along the edges of the bedframe, and then dived head first onto the mattress, giggling and splaying her legs in the air. 'I love it! I loooooooooove it! Thank you so much. I can't believe you've done this for me.'

'I did it for my back,' Jack deadpanned.

'Lol.'

Lotta sat up and looked towards the windows. 'What a view to wake up to. I am, like, totally spoiled. Oh my gosh! Thank you,' Lotta gushed.

'It sure beats waking up to the view of a kitchen cupboard,' Jack joked.

Lotta raised her hands up to the ceiling and wiggled her hands around. 'I cannot wait to read here. This is so exciting!'

'I thought you might say that.'

'I could *live* in here. If I didn't have to go to work and actually have a life, I could just exist in my books and this bed.'

'You would actually do that too,' Jack said, shaking his head.

'It's all so nice, Jack. *So* nice.'

Jack inclined his chin to the cardboard boxes on the floor. 'Matching curtains are in there, and we'll be done.'

Lotta sighed, almost purring in pleasure. 'I think tonight we might have to christen this bed.'

Jack chuckled. 'Sounds like a plan. Very happy to make that happen for you, ma'am.'

3

Jack and Lotta inched their way along the wet, winding roads of Newport, following the faint orange glow of the streetlights. A sheet of light drizzle washed the windscreen as they pulled into a parking space adjacent to a secluded Italian restaurant tucked into a quaint cobblestoned row of shops.

Lotta, in a pale pink balloon-sleeve jumper, dark wash jeans, and with her hair pulled away from her face into a low side ponytail, stole a glance at Jack. She felt her heart miss a beat as she noticed how handsome he was and felt for about the millionth time like she was an imposter in her own life. Who even was she? Was she really here with him, going out for dinner? Was she really in a happy, normal relationship? Was she going out to eat and doing nice things? She pushed her glasses up her nose as she looked over at him and then quickly looked away, embarrassed by her soppiness.

Sensing her gaze, Jack reached over and patted her on the leg reassuringly. Warmth radiated from his palm and settled on her leg. He gave it another gentle pat. 'All good?' he asked.

'Yep,' Lotta answered, trying to pretend that she wasn't

totally gushing inside at being with him. Instead, on the outside, she aimed to be, and sound, nonchalant. The nonchalance was in direct contrast to her heart, which was jumping around on a balance beam, doing all sorts of strange things. 'Just looking forward to eating out. I hope this place is nice.'

'Same. It's been a long day,' Jack replied as he turned off the engine and picked up his phone.

Lotta hopped out of the car, sighed contentedly, and looked up at the dark night sky as cool, drizzly rain hit her face. She peered over at the restaurant and smiled. She'd been reliably informed by both Suntanned Pete and Holly from the bakery, both important townspeople of Pretty Beach, that the restaurant was renowned for its homemade pasta dishes. Not only that, Holly had said its cosy ambience and old-school decor made it hard to beat. As Lotta squinted over at the restaurant on first impressions, she felt she had to agree.

'It's been a long time since I've been to an Italian restaurant,' she said as Jack joined her on the pavement. Her voice was heavy with nostalgia as she remembered her early days in London when she'd found little Italian delis in backstreets near where she'd worked. Days and locations when she'd been young and buzzy and happy. Places now that seemed so very far away.

Jack smiled. 'Same here. Have to love a nice pizza or a huge bowl of pasta any day of the week.' He peered towards the restaurant. 'Looks cosy.'

Lotta grabbed his hand and they walked past the restaurant window, their steps echoing on the tessellated floor in the little nook going up to the front door. As Jack opened the lace curtain-backed half-glass door, a full restaurant greeted them. Couples and families were tucked away on tiny tables, and chatter, Italian music, and laughter floated across the air. The place was abuzz with a hum of clinking glasses, conversation and happiness. The warmth invited a sit-down, a plate of pasta, and a glass of something cold.

A man with a beaming smile and huge moustache greeted them and escorted them to a small table tucked into the far side of the restaurant near a tiny bar rammed with optics, glasses, and bottle upon bottle of wine. Lotta and Jack settled into old-fashioned bistro chairs with buttoned cushioned seats and happily took menus as the man with the moustache informed them of the specials of the day.

Lotta gazed around at the gorgeous old restaurant where tables layered in white linen were full of people, not an empty chair to be seen. High up on wraparound shelves, a jumble of old books and paintings haphazardly spilt towards the edges. Dark-panelled walls were strung with party lights, and tiny fabric-covered lamps adorned every available surface. Everywhere Lotta looked, it appeared that things had been chosen and collected with care; Italian books and block candles, jugs and china jostling for space beside tables and knick-knacks tucked into every corner.

Lotta could barely take the smile off her face as she scrolled down the menu and lost herself in a world of homemade pasta. 'Holly and Pete were right. This place is fab!' she gushed. 'If the food lives up to the ambience, we're in for a treat.'

Jack glanced up from his menu and smiled. 'Yep. There's nothing like a recommendation for a good old-fashioned Italian restaurant. Love it.'

'I got the impression from Holly that she's in the know about everything and everywhere around here.'

Jack frowned. 'She's the one who lent you the necklace for the ball, isn't she?'

'The very one,' Lotta replied and then waved her hand in front of her face. 'She and her mum, Xian, are totally hilarious! When they arrived that day with the jewellery, Xian was doing some share deal on her iPad. She's really funny. I mean, *really* funny. She carries some sort of drink with her in a little flask, too.'

Jack wrinkled up his nose. 'What sort of drink? What, like an alcoholic drink or what?'

'I don't know what it is. Holly said it's disgusting. They call it her "special drink". It's amber in colour.'

'Right. Sounds, umm, interesting.'

'She legit whips it out of her bag and pours it into her tea. I should say she *lugs* it into her tea, actually.' Lotta chuckled. 'She secretly left some for me when she popped over.'

'Sounds like I need to get my hands on some,' Jack deadpanned. 'Or do some kind of trade in it.'

'The other guy, Pete, who seems to be on every corner, said it's revolting and advised me never to try it. Holly reiterated that.'

'Never say never,' Jack replied. 'I have strange taste.'

Lotta's phone lit up with a notification. She glanced at it with mild interest.

Jack followed her gaze. 'So, what's the story with your social media stuff?' Jack asked, sliding his menu away from him. He nodded towards her phone. 'It's like your phone has been alive since we left the house. It's been buzzing away merrily to itself. What's going on?'

Lotta smiled; her eyes lit up, but she brushed it off somewhat. 'I put my latest book review up just before you arrived to pick me up, and it's taken off. I must turn the notifications off on my phone. It gets annoying.'

Jack's eyes widened. 'Sounds good. Sorry, remind me how many followers you have again.'

Lotta felt a tad embarrassed. 'Umm, like loads.'

Jack frowned and then squinted as Lotta picked up her phone and turned the screen towards him. When he registered the huge amount of followers Lotta had, his eyes shot to the top of his forehead. 'What the? You didn't tell me it was that many.'

'You didn't really ask. I just said it was a "substantial" following.'

'Hang on. Fill me in on this a bit. When did you start it? And why?'

Lotta's book reviews had initially started as a blog. 'It just started as nothing, really. I wanted to share my love of books because I couldn't find anyone who did reviews the way I wanted to read reviews, if you see what I mean. So far, it's just been a bit of fun. I never in a million years thought that people would be interested in it. I've always thought my views on books were something that only I would understand.'

Jack frowned. 'I don't see what you mean. What's different about your reviews?'

Lotta considered for a second. 'Mine are more a conversation. Some of the book club ones are, how can I say? Stilted and sort of boring. They answer pre-determined questions and try to make it, umm, I don't know. Yeah, so anyway, it's a bit of fun. A hobby.'

Jack nodded, his face glowing with interest. 'That's a lot of followers for a bit of fun. You need to monetise it somehow.'

'You think so? I don't think I can be bothered.' Lotta waved her hand in dismissal. 'Too much on my plate, as it were. Plus, well, you know, I'd rather just have a regular job with a regular payday.'

'Is it hard to manage, then?' Jack asked.

'Not really. It's been pretty easy, actually. I mean, you know how many books I read in a week. I just post reviews, give book recommendations, and share my thoughts on books I'm reading. I do lives every now and then, and reels. Yeah, it's just fun. Simple as that.'

'With that number of people and the number of comments there, people must find it really helpful. Someone must like what you're saying.' Jack winked and chuckled.

Lotta nodded. 'I think so. I get a lot of positive feedback when I post something straight out of my head. It's so not contrived. I think that's the attraction.'

Jack smiled. 'You know what? You should do something with the library room and that.'

Lotta's forehead wrinkled into a frown. 'Like what?'

'I don't know, but even to my non-reading eyes, that place is gold.'

Lotta agreed. 'Thank you, and if it wasn't for your help, it probably wouldn't exist. I really am pleased with how it turned out. I still can't quite believe that I have a library and a place for all my books. It's never something I thought would actually happen to me, you know?' Lotta shook her head in disbelief. 'A bit of a pipe dream.'

The waiter approached their table and asked for their orders before Jack had a chance to reply. Lotta quickly snatched up her menu and decided on the carbonara and Jack ordered lasagne and a bottle of wine. They further discussed the library room, and after a while the waiter returned with two glasses, a bottle of white wine, and a basket loaded full of garlic bread. Chatting over the garlic bread, they further discussed Lotta's social media following and how it had grown. Jack bantered back and forth with questions, and they brainstormed ideas for new posts and how Lotta might be able to turn her hobby into a side income. By the time their food arrived, the discussion had become more serious and animated. Jack leant forward in his chair. 'You know what you should do? Something like a weekend of reading at Pretty Beach to the Breakers.'

'No way! What, have strangers in my house? I'd never do that. That would scare the living daylights out of me! Knowing my luck I'd end up with some sort of literary serial killer.'

'Not in the house. In the guest house,' Jack noted.

Lotta narrowed her eyes. 'What guest house would that be?' Lotta chuckled. 'Last time I checked, I had an old building with a tiny boathouse butted up to it and a double garage full of junk.'

'The old building at the end of the garden next to the

boathouse with its separate entrance onto the road. I had a poke around in there the other day when we were getting rid of the carpet from the bedroom.'

Lotta put down her fork. 'It's a dump.'

'But with a bit of work...'

Lotta nodded slowly. 'You're saying do it up and rent it out, are you?'

'It's crying out for it. You could fill it with books and stuff and share it on your social media account.'

'Nah. That would mean everyone on my account would know where I live. I'm not sure I'd like that.'

'Do it anyway then, but don't connect the two,' Jack said. 'You have somewhere with its own access, at the end of the garden. In a place like Pretty Beach where people come on holiday...' He trailed off and paused for a second. 'You could probably rent it out six times over.'

'You're right. It could work, but it would also take a lot of time and a massive amount of money, and guess what? I don't have a lot of either.'

As they ate, Lotta shared her enthusiasm for her reading account, and they discussed how the building could be used as a part of it. The evening whizzed by, and after finishing with tiramisu and paying the bill, they stepped out into the night where the drizzling rain had stopped and the promise of warmer weather hit their noses.

'That was really nice,' Lotta said as they walked to the car. 'Thank you.'

Jack smiled and nodded. 'I'm glad Holly told you about it.'

Lotta smiled back. 'Me too.'

Jack clicked the remote on the car and winked. 'And we have a plan for your new side income. A reading nook in Pretty Beach.'

'Ahh, I don't know about that.' Lotta chuckled, but she had to agree. The more they'd discussed the building at the bottom of the garden and the more she'd listened to Jack's views, the more it seemed that Pretty Beach to the Breakers could be the answer to all her debt problems. And she very much liked the sound of that.

4

Lotta stood at the window in her newly decorated bedroom and gazed out at the horizon. As she stood there for ages, thinking about her opportunities, she felt something inside her awaken. It was as if a sense of possibility and hope had washed her in a hazy watercolour blur. For so long she had been running on empty, lost in the past, and if she was really honest, she had been sad. But now she was ready to move on. She was oddly settled and ready to create a new life for herself in Pretty Beach. All her thoughts of only temporarily staying until she got back on her feet and had paid off her debts were now gone. She nodded to herself as she gazed out towards the lighthouse; Pretty Beach was going to be her new home.

With a lovely day outside, she pushed up the huge sash window. The air was filled with the scent of the sea and the shrubs in the garden that were beginning to come to life. She did not have much clue about gardening, but maybe there would be honeysuckle and jasmine in the summer? Maybe the garden would be lovely with a bit of love. Perhaps, just like the Sussex cottage she had dreamed about, the old climbing roses on the brick walls would slowly but surely unfurl and surround the place with pretty colours. Feeling the warmth of the sun on her face, she nodded. Yes. This old place was lovely and more; it was her new home.

She turned and looked back at the huge bed with its velvet-covered headboard, the old built-in cupboards beside it now a clean soft white, and the gigantic sisal rug over the wide floor-boards. All of it a far cry from the ludicrously cramped but excruciatingly expensive flat she'd shared with Dan in London. The same place where she'd worked two jobs, as he had supposedly thrown all his energy into his start-up. The same place he'd bored her, and anyone else who would listen, about his attempts at being an entrepreneur. The same place he'd informed her that she'd failed.

She thought about the flat. There was no doubt that it was lovely in its own way – beautiful timber flooring, a Victorian fireplace, a fancy bathroom with a modern standalone bathtub designed for two. But now, as she looked back, she realised how she'd felt trapped by the narrow walls, the dead relationship, and the stale air. She remembered when she was bone-tired from cleaning offices at night, and had crept into bed not wanting to wake up Dan. She shook her head in disgust at the downtrodden person she had been then. She'd been so pathetically worried that if Dan didn't get his precious sleep, it would affect his precious work. She tutted to herself over her scooting around on eggshells around Dan and his app. How she'd worried about money and scrimped and scraped everywhere she could. Dan hadn't even noticed. He hadn't known he'd been born.

She continued to stare out towards the lighthouse and inhaled. Here she could breathe, be free, work hard, read, and stretch her wings. Here, she could start anew. She looked over towards the other window, now clean and sparkling in the sunlight. It reflected the deep blue of the sky on one of the first warm days she'd had in Pretty Beach. It was her kind of day.

Walking out of the bedroom, Lotta crossed the landing and with a more open mind than she'd had when she'd first explored Pretty Beach to the Breakers, she crossed the threshold of the landing and stepped into a world of possibility. She drifted through each of the rooms, wondering at the fact that she could now see the potential of the place. Marvelling at somewhere she would be able to call her own. Somewhere she could just be Lotta and be at home. The house seemed to almost talk to her as she flung open curtains, pulled open doors, and pushed up windows. She touched various things here and there – peeling wallpaper, an abandoned piece of furniture, and little bits and pieces whispering to her and displaying a lifetime of someone's holiday memories. Lotta could almost smell sunscreen and see sun hats as she stepped softly back across the landing and down the stairs.

After making a cup of tea, she ventured out to the garden where the sun had warmed patches on the terrace and was bathing the old ramshackle boathouse in a warm light. Lotta considered what Jack had said when they'd been to the Italian restaurant about it being made to rent out as a little holiday place. Surrounded by weeds and with its peeling paint and rotten gutters, she was yet to be convinced. Even so, she was determined to have a look. Taking the path through the centre of the garden, she gazed up at the structure beside the small boathouse, trying to make sense of its design. The building seemed to be a hotchpotch of ideas, as if bits of it had been added as afterthoughts over the years.

Cautiously, she approached the entrance to the building, cupped her hands over her eyes, and peered in the window. Like the garage, it was filled with what mostly looked like junk. Apprehensive but determined to have a look, she opened the creaking door, stepped inside, and allowed her eyes to adjust to the dim light. The air was stale, musty, and full of stagnated dust, as if it had been locked away for years. All around her,

Lotta could see evidence that Pretty Beach to the Breakers had once been a holiday home – a faded wind-breaker leaning up against the wall, a pile of old fishing nets, a shelf overflowing with long-forgotten books, a collection of picnic baskets.

As her eyes adjusted, she saw the building was bigger than she'd initially thought, though it was still small. It had been divided roughly into a couple of tiny rooms, both piled with old things and needing a lot of love. In the corner of the smallest room vaguely resembling a kitchen, an old sink sat collecting dust in the middle under a French paned window, and a row of cupboards looked as if it had seen better days. Lotta walked around gingerly, her curiosity spurring her on. She tried to imagine the place aired, painted, and clear of its junk. With her eyes squinted, she imagined it full of books, a nice bed, a claw-foot tub. She ran her fingers along the walls, feeling the soft cladding and the dust that seemed to have settled over years of disuse.

She stepped into a tiny hallway and realised, just as Jack had said, that a door led out to a small patch of enclosed grass where there was a gate out to the road. Lotta opened the door and looked at the funny little patch of grass full of weeds. It was just about big enough for an outdoor table and an umbrella. She ran her hands up the outside of the building, smiled at an old gnarly climbing rose, and shook her head at an outdoor copper shower whose head had collapsed and was facing the wall. She wondered who had built the strange small building with the boathouse butted up to the other side. As she looked up and back towards it, she knew there was a tonne of work involved, but that its potential screamed at her from every orifice.

Stepping back inside, she took in the old toilet and shower, shuddered at the vast number of cobwebs overhead, and then, going back into the kitchen, and with a satisfying click, opened a door to a small cupboard. Inside, old recipe books sat along-side vintage maps and all sorts of seaside bits and bobs. Whipping her phone out of her pocket, she called Jack. He answered on the first ring.

'Hey. How are you getting on?'

'Hi, I was calling about the old building here. I'm standing inside it as we speak. I think your idea of a holiday house or a reading thing could work.'

'I'm all for it.'

Lotta looked up at the building. 'I think it could be a great way to bring in some additional income. I was thinking about what you said about my reading thing. I could even use it as a place to host reading, I don't know, evenings or something if I wanted to. I just have to get past the fact that people would be on the property. It wouldn't be as if they were in the actual house. It even has its own entrance.'

'It's a great idea. Let's start looking into it properly and see what the best way to go about it is.'

Lotta felt her heart dance that Jack naturally included himself. 'Sounds like a plan. The first step would be to clear it out. There's a lot of old junk in here.'

'Yeah, I think you're going to need a skip for that. Maybe we can chuck it in the garage with the red carpet, but it's pretty full in there.'

'We'd need to make sure people could stay comfortably,' Lotta mused. 'There'd need to be a bath of some sort. That would cost money.'

'Definitely. No wineglass smashing, though,' Jack joked. 'Did you see the little outdoor bit? That could be outdoor seating and a barbecue area. There's also an old outdoor shower there, did you notice it?'

'Brr! Yes, I did. It's a bit chilly for that. Who would want to do that?'

'I suppose in the summer it's a boon.'

'Yeah, I guess so. Chills me to the bone right now, and it's a beautiful day here,' Lotta noted.

'I reckon it would be lovely on a hot day after the beach.'

'Hmm. Yeah. I'm going to have to think about the decor. I mean, with the setting and all this coastal paraphernalia around, I could make it all beachy and lovely. Imagine it with gorgeous throws and blankets, an old wood burner for the winter, all my books here, there and everywhere. There are loads of things in here I could probably use.'

'Absolutely. I reckon it would look lovely with a load of natural elements…wood, stone, and pebbles and stuff to give it a rustic feel.'

'Ooh, hark at you sounding all interior design-y. That sounds great, though. Yeah, I like it.'

'As the name suggests, I'm a Jack of all trades,' Jack joked.

'Lights and lighting. This place would need to be cosy and twinkly,' Lotta noted. 'Candles, lanterns. Yes, the more I imagine it, the better it seems. Jack, I actually think you were right.'

'Err, is that a compliment, Lotta as in hotter?'

'God, no. You're joking, aren't you?'

'Silly me. How about a pool table, ping-pong table, dartboard, stuff like that?' Jack said seriously.

'Very funny. I know, how about some optics and a bar?' Lotta added sarcastically.

'You should start an Insta account for it. Start building up a bit of interest.'

'That's a great idea. I could do before and afters on my main account, maybe. Everyone could follow along.'

'Yep. All sounds doable. Look, I'm just going into a meeting.'

'No probs, speak to you later.'

As Lotta slipped her phone back in her pocket and looked around her, she smiled. There was something about the funny disjointed building that was telling her her plan for it was going to work out very well. Very well indeed.

5

Lotta was feeling nervous. A mixture of excitement and trepidation swirled around her stomach as she stepped onto the old ferry at Pretty Beach. She was on her way to her new job and filled to the brim with nerves. She was finally arriving at the day when she would start to earn a proper income again. It was a day loaded with feeling; she'd pulled herself out of the doldrums and wanted to feel pride in belonging somewhere, pride in *herself*. It felt nice to be wanted, and not feeling quite as alone or out on the limb of life.

The ferry ride was one of the more pleasurable commutes she'd had in her life. It sure was a bit more pleasant looking out at the sea than it was trying to avert one's gaze away from the nearest man's armpit deep underground on a train. As the ferry's engine started to chug and it pulled away from the wharf, anticipation and anxiousness buzzed up and down her veins. She had high hopes for this new job. Not only that – she *needed* it to work.

As the ferry bumped, she gazed at the coastline, revelling in a gorgeous Pretty Beach day with spring doing all its things. The sun was shining brightly, and the sea sparkled invitingly all the way up the coast ahead of her. Despite the gorgeous day and her lovely surroundings, Lotta couldn't help but feel, along with the nerves, uneasy. She was about to be plunged into a *new* industry with *new* people and *new* things to learn, and this was the first time she'd started a job where she had no experience whatsoever. She swallowed at the thought of the welcome document she'd already immersed herself in and was nervous about how she would get through the day.

She was worried that she would be out of her depth and concerned about how she would be received. But, as she sat at the top of the ferry forcing herself to be confident and positive, she was determined to suck it up and try her best. She'd worked hard to get to this point, dragging herself up out of the bleakness she'd been left in by her ex and his dastardly attempt at designing an app. She took deep breaths as the ferry rocked back and forth, talked herself up, and tried to remember what Liv had told her about just being herself.

At least she was looking good and didn't have to worry about her attire. After her day of planning and preparation, she'd sorted her outfits for the week and what she was wearing was hitting all the right notes – a carefully chosen pair of navy-blue smart trousers, paired with a pale-pink floaty blouse, and a silky dress scarf tied to the side just so. A pair of heels were currently residing in her handbag and a shell-pink polish was on her nails. Lotta's outfit was part of her game plan, one designed to make *her* feel confident and deliver a good impression right from the get-go.

The wind whipped her hair around her face as the ferry made its way up the coast, the faint smell of salt in the air and diesel from the engine in her nose. As the scenery changed and the ferry chugged along, Lotta let her mind wander, and slowly but surely, she began to relax. The steady rocking of the boat rhythmically lulled her into a calmer state, and she soon found herself lost in a world of her own, gazing at the sea and the cliffs around her. The sun glinted off the waves, and she could just make out the disappearing shape of the Pretty Beach lighthouse in the distance.

A while later, the outline of Newport Reef began to come into view and Lotta's nervousness began to return as her mind started to whir. Underneath her determination to be confident, she was marred by a horrible companion, one going by the name of Doubting Thomas, at whether or not she could do the job. However, with not a single other offer on the table, she had little choice but to dive in at the deep end and give it a go. As the ferry got closer and closer to its stop, she couldn't help but feel anxious. Despite a knot of tension in her stomach, she did know one thing, she was prepared and she would give it all she had. If nothing else, Lotta was going to give it her best shot.

As she started to collect her bag and Kindle together, the ferry pulled into the wharf, the sun glinted brighter, and the waves lapped against the old timbers, she smiled to herself. Something was telling her somehow, despite her nerves, that she was going to be okay. Despite old Thomas smirking in the wings, a feeling in her bones was telling her she'd made the right decision, not only to take the job but to make a new start down on the coast. She tried to flick Thomas off and clung to that thought.

As she strolled away from the ferry heading for the arcade, Lotta repeatedly nodded to herself. She would suck in the big girl's pants and would hit any challenges head-on. Yes, she was in control. She'd pulled herself out of the doldrums, she had the support of Jack, Liv, and Timmy, and she was determined to make the most of the opportunity. With a deep breath and a resolute smile, she started to pound along the pavement, ready and willing to take on her new role.

By the time she'd got to the arcade, her resolution had faded and Thomas was flapping his doubt around her head. Lotta had stopped on the corner, changed into her power heels, and then stepped timidly through the black doors of the old arcade, her heart beating nineteen to the dozen with anticipation. As she looked around at the lobby, her nerves were palpable, her palms were clammy and her skin tingling. The thought of being a part of the beautiful, historic building made her almost fizz. She'd come a long, long way. She was far from the interview where the receptionist with the blue streak in her hair had dropped chewing gum wrappers on the floor and snarky interviewers had made her feel about an inch tall.

She looked around as she strolled in, her heels clipping satisfyingly on the floor, and attempted to hide her nerves and appear confident. All around her was breathtaking, with thought put into everything, every which way she looked. The walls were adorned with paintings depicting scenes from Newport Reef's past, a row of huge old pendant lights hung from the ceiling casting a glow over the room, and the same woman who had greeted Lotta when she'd come for an interview appeared and smiled warmly. The woman reiterated her name and held out her hand. Lotta felt a tiny bit of her nerves vanish at the warm smile and nice greeting. She had to stop herself from gushing when the woman remembered her name. Lotta beamed. 'Hi, Marie.'

Marie's heels clipped across the shiny floor as she led Lotta the same way as when she'd been interviewed. 'Righto, Anne's been here a while getting things ready for you. We all share desk space as it were since most of us work from home on and off nowadays. We'll get you settled in.'

'Right, okay, lovely,' Lotta replied as she followed Marie to a black door. Marie keyed in a code, and the door clicked open.

Lotta followed Marie through the inner lobby she'd sat in on her first interview, through a door, and along a corridor until they ended up in an open-plan room more akin to the reception of a nice hotel than an office. Lotta looked at the beautiful timber desks, complete with huge lamps and vases stuffed full of bright flowers. She had to stop herself from blurting out that everything was so nice. Instead, she kept a small smile and bright eyes on her face, as if she totally expected the office to look as it did. She forced herself not to run her finger along the back of a luxurious overstuffed sofa tucked in beside a low coffee table also groaning with flowers. All of it was like something out of a magazine.

Marie smiled and pointed to another door. 'The kitchen is in there. Did Anne tell you about lunch and afternoon tea?'

Lotta shook her head lamely. There was lunch and afternoon tea? Marie continued and flicked her right hand towards her, looking at her watch. 'Sandwiches come in about eleven. They're here for the guests and there's a plate for staff too. Ditto stuff for tea at three.' She rolled her eyes a touch. 'You don't get a chance to even have a wee some days, so yeah, these sandwiches are here for you to grab when you like. You'll be on the run, as it were.'

Lotta thought about the depressing row of brightly lit vending machines in her old job. 'Thanks, that sounds nice.'

Marie waved her hand. 'Trust me, you'll need sustenance when you've been running around here all day. The least they can do is provide a plate of sandwiches.'

Just as Marie was showing Lotta the kitchen, Anne, the woman who recruited her, came bustling in and smiled. 'Hi. You made it. Welcome.'

'I did. Safe and sound,' Lotta replied. 'The ferry was a very nice way to arrive. It was beautiful this morning.'

'Sounds good to me. Marie has shown you around and let you know where the tea is?' Anne asked. 'That's the most important thing in my book; good tea keeps people happy.' She laughed.

'Ha ha. Yes, she's shown me where the tea is and told me about the sandwiches.' Lotta smiled.

'You'll be needing them,' Anne joked.

'Right, Lotta. I'll show you around the whole place,' Marie said.

Marie then gave Lotta a full tour of the building, explaining the various conference rooms and different parts of the arcade. She chatted as they weaved in and out of rooms with huge tables, some smaller areas with sofas and lamps. At the far end of the lobby there was a small bar. After the tour, Marie and Lotta returned to the open-plan office. Lotta chatted to Anne and then sat down with an iPad to look over some training documents. She gulped as she flicked through; she would be required to be on her toes, by the looks of it. Her duties would include planning and organising events, managing the CEOs and their successful arrival, assisting with special events, and helping with day-to-day operations.

Later on that morning, with Anne having gone off for a meeting and Marie not around, Lotta finished reading a document, put her chin on her hand and looked around at her surroundings. She couldn't quite believe it was turning out so well. It was somewhat intimidating and she was nervous, but everyone had been so nice and she was excited to be a part of it all. The gorgeous old building and all the history around her made it probably the best place she'd ever worked. Part of her felt as if the whole thing was just too good to be true.

For the next few hours, Lotta was left to her own devices, with Anne and Marie instructing her to explore the arcade, familiarise herself with its many rooms, and get to know the people who worked there. Lotta did exactly as she was told and quickly found that everyone was friendly and welcoming. As she made her way around the arcade, through corridors and up and down staircases, she marvelled at her luck. She'd not only landed a local job with nice people, but she was in what felt like one of the coast's loveliest buildings. So far so good.

As the day progressed and she settled in, Lotta found herself feeling slightly less anxious and old Thomas was hiding in the corner. If her first day was anything to go by, this new job was going to be one of her best moves in a *very* long time.

~

At the end of her first day, Lotta was exhausted, her brain was mushed, but she was happy. Every part of her was tired, and she felt overloaded, as if her skull couldn't let a single other new thing in. As she was walking back to the ferry, she phoned Liv.

'Hello!' Liv said excitedly.

'Hey. How are you?'

'I'm good. I've been waiting to hear from you! How was your first day?'

'Great! Everyone was so friendly. I felt like I had been there for years instead of just one day. Can you believe it? Oh my gosh, I was so nervous this morning. Pathetic, really!'

'What did you do?'

'Mostly getting to know everyone and going through training things. I learnt about the history of the arcade, all that sort of stuff. Liv, you couldn't make it up. I've *so* landed on my feet. Everyone was nice and showed me the ropes.'

'Sounds great,' Liv said enthusiastically. 'Did you have any problems?'

'Not really. Everyone was lovely. It's a bit full-on. Nothing I can't handle. Hopefully, I'll grasp it all okay.'

'That's good. You'll be fine. Did you get to meet any of the other staff?'

'Yeah, I met a few people. They made me feel right at home.'

'That's so good to hear, Lott. How was the ferry this morning?'

'Too easy. Honestly, what a way to travel to work,' Lotta enthused.

'Fab. So, how did you feel when you left for the day? Happy?'

'Exhausted, but yeah, so happy. I can't believe I've landed on my feet like this. It sort of doesn't feel real.'

'I can,' Liv replied cheerily. 'It was only a matter of time. Onwards and upwards, Lott. You deserve this. This is the start of good things.'

Lotta beamed. She hoped Liv was right. She really, really did.

6

Lotta was sitting on an underground train in London, fiddling with the case on her phone, on her way to meet Timmy for lunch. It felt strange to be back on the same line, deep under the city, she'd been on many times before. As the 'mind the gap' announcement filled her ears and the doors banged shut, the clock in her mind's eye turned back. She suddenly felt a prick of tears at the corner of her eyes as memories flooded through her mind. She'd sat on these train carriages so many times, flitting around London when she'd first started work and raring to get on with her life. Then she'd zipped here and there all dressed up for work, a coffee in her hand, and her head full of the world of books. She was hit with a wave of nostalgia as the rumble of the train, the hiss of the tracks, and the screeching of metal felt as if they'd unlocked a room she'd kept closed at the back of her head. The same room as the one where she kept her ex Dan and his app. Her heart was heavy with sadness as the train made its way around the Circle Line on its way to Chelsea. As the monotonous rumble of the train lulled her, she couldn't help but think about Dan and the memories they had shared in their flat. All of it galloped through her head along with the movement of the train.

Once she'd hopped off at the station, made her way up the stairs, and ambled the familiar streets, a wave of sentimentality washed over her. She couldn't quite shake the feelings of nostalgia for former days when she'd been *so* young and *so* naive and *so* very full of hope. As she passed familiar shops and houses, she realised that there was a tiny part of her who missed the way things used to be with Dan. Not *actual* Dan, but more the idyllic notion of him and their relationship which was never meant to be. Deep down in her bones, she was aware that she'd probably always known that they wouldn't stay the course and be an item, but even now with Jack in her life and her new home, the Dan thing still seemed so very sad. A sad load of wasted time, heartache, and effort.

As she made her way through the backstreets on her way to the pub, she walked down her old road to see the house where their flat had been located. She took a deep breath and steeled herself as she stood looking at the huge entrance steps, the row of names on the intercom plate next to the large, glossy black front door. She stood staring up at the windows for a while, lost in a world of her own. The longer she stood there, the more she realised how things had changed and how she'd now, thankfully, officially closed the door on that chapter of her life.

Standing on the pavement by the railings, looking down into the basement flat and then up at the windows, she thought about the inside of the flat as memories flooded back to her. The kitchen where she'd cooked countless meals for Dan because he'd always been so exhausted with the app. The sitting room where she'd saved up for the sofa but had mostly spent nights on it reading alone. And then the small bedroom where she would creep in after her cleaning shifts, hoping not to wake Dan because he had to get up to work on the app. She felt a prick at the corners of her eyes and tears well up as she realised the memories were not quite tinted with rose. She remembered how beaten she had been at the end when Dan had told her that the app had failed. Standing outside the building, it was all so bittersweet. She knew that her life was all sorts of different now. All sorts of good. She knew she had moved on to pastures new. She had not only started a new chapter in her life, she had improved it vastly, but somewhere deep inside, sadness tinged her edges.

With a lumpy heart, she watched as a woman came out of the shared gardens in the centre of the square and didn't even look up as she walked past Lotta on the way to the front door. The irony of the woman not acknowledging her wasn't lost; in Lotta's new town, people smiled, greeted, and welcomed. Here they very much didn't give you the time of day.

The woman's ignorance seemed to flick some sort of imaginary flick on Lotta's nostalgia for something that perhaps was not actually there. Satisfied that she'd had enough memories for one day, she walked along to the end of the road, took the familiar dog-leg, and then turned right, heading to the pub. It stood magnificently on the corner – a charming old building with a pub sign hanging over the door, a brass door handle that gleamed in the sunlight, and window boxes spilling with colour peering out from little shelves just under the windows.

As she walked in, she was greeted by a hug of reminiscence at the warm pub smell and inviting atmosphere permeating the air. The dark wood bar was polished to a high shine, the walls were adorned with old prints and paintings, and the timber floor creaked and was worn with age. Taking a big breath, she walked up to the bar and was greeted by a jovial barman with a big smile on his face. 'What can I get for you, love?' he asked as he wiped down the bar with a cloth.

Lotta smiled back at him, and after flicking her eyes around

43

and seeing that Timmy hadn't yet arrived, she nodded. 'A glass of white wine, please.'

The barman nodded and set to with a bottle of wine and a glass. As she waited, she slipped out her Kindle and looked around at the quaint and cosy atmosphere of the pub. Apart from the new barman she didn't recognise, everything was exactly the same as when she'd lived in the flat down the road – a pile of board games stacked up on a dresser beside the fire, hanging baskets filled with colourful flowers swaying outside in the wind, and the back door propped ajar to the beer garden out the back. She couldn't help but smile. She might have been filled with an odd sort of melancholic nostalgia earlier, but the pub made her feel at home.

As she sipped her wine and chatted with the barman, Lotta felt her spirits, which had taken a dive since the train, lift. It was strangely nice to be back in the pub. Perhaps, now that she had someone like Jack in her life, she would be able to look back a bit more fondly, or at least be more charitable, about the wasted years with Dan. Perhaps not.

Lotta nodded to herself, did a funny little raise of her glass to the ceiling, and took a sip of her wine. The world turned in mysterious ways, and here she was in her old pub with a completely different set of life circumstances set out right before her eyes. About ten minutes later, her wineglass was mostly still full and sitting on a beer mat, and her Kindle was by her side. Her phone buzzed, and seeing that it was Liv, she smiled and answered the phone. 'Hi. What's up?'

'Nothing. Just checking in to see how you're getting on. Did you end up walking past the flat?' Liv asked, her voice filled with concern.

Lotta sighed and leaned against the bar. 'I did. It was tough seeing it again, but strangely cathartic too, in a weird way. Yeah, I'm fine. I'm in the pub waiting for Timmy. Thanks for checking.'

'I can imagine,' Liv replied sympathetically. 'It must be hard to be up that way again. You know, considering what happened.'

'I know. It's so good though, to finally let go of the past. I mean to properly do it, if you know what I mean. I thought I had before, well, before Jack came along. Now I *really* have. It's strange.'

'You're in such a different place now, and I don't mean location-wise,' Liv stated.

'I know. It's odd, though. I just can't help but feel nostalgic about it all,' Lotta said, her voice tinged with a touch of sadness.

'It's normal to feel that way, I guess. You did a lot of growing up in that flat,' Liv reassured her.

'I did, actually, you're right.' Lotta smiled, feeling a sense of comfort from Liv's words. 'It's a shame a certain person didn't do the same growing up in the flat. I think I did it for both of us. I was just thinking before I got my Kindle out, what a blooming mess I was before I got to Pretty Beach. Thanks for being there for me through it all.'

'Of course, that's what cousins are for,' Liv said with a chuckle. 'I think you may have forgotten a certain grumpy man in the equation. He has helped.'

'I can hardly forget him, Liv.'

'True. He is rather unforgettable.'

'It's strange to feel a bit sad though when I'm, well, I'm ecstatically happy at the same time. Weird.'

'Not weird at all. It's completely understandable. Keep in mind, you deserve to be happy and to move on from the past. Just take it one day at a time,' Liv instructed.

'Are you counselling me, Liv?' Lotta joked.

'Not at all! I've done enough of that, thank you very much.'

'Ha ha! You have. Anyway, I'm fine. More than fine.'

'That's the spirit,' Liv said. 'Right, well, I was just checking up on you.'

'Thanks,' Lotta replied, more grateful than Liv would ever

know. Now that she had come out the other side of the Dan years, she realised how low she'd sunk. 'I really do appreciate you being there for me.'

'Anytime, Lott. Now, get back to your book and give Timmy my love,' Liv said before saying goodbye. 'I know you'll have your nose in a book.'

Lotta said goodbye, put down her phone, picked her Kindle back up, and took a sip of her wine, thinking about her conversation with Liv. Thank goodness Liv had been there for her. From the different place that Lotta now occupied, she realised how much of a support system Liv had been through all of the rubbish things that had happened with Dan and the app. With the benefit of hindsight, she shuddered at the thought of how she might have ended up without Liv at the end of the phone to cheer her on. Just as she was about to flick over to the next chapter in her book, she saw Timmy and Giles walk in.

'Lotta! Darling!' Timmy exclaimed, spotting her at the bar. 'Goodness, you look fabulous! Look at you. Wow, yes, darling, yes.'

Lotta felt herself blush. 'Hey.' Lotta laughed and smiled.

They hugged and air-kissed, and Lotta basked in the positive energy Timmy always brought with him wherever he went. They then ordered drinks, moved away from the bar, and sat down at a table. Chatting and laughing, Lotta looked at the pair of them and thought about the phone call from Liv and realised how grateful she was to have them in her life.

As the evening went on, with lots of chatting and chuckling, and after they'd discussed Lotta's visit to her old flat, Lotta raised her glass in a toast. 'Cheers to new beginnings,' Lotta said, smiling.

'Cheers!' Timmy and Giles echoed, clinking their glasses with hers.

Giles tapped her glass again. 'Cheers to lovelies named Jack.'

Lotta reciprocated and raised her glass up. 'I'll drink to that.'

Lotta felt a little warm spot in her heart as Timmy threw his head back and laughed. Lotta Button was back out to play. She was running around the playground with the wind in her hair. Man, it felt so good to be back.

7

The sun shone down as Lotta stepped off the pavement, crossed over the lights, and headed for the train station. Her drinks and lunch with Timmy and Giles had gone on longer than she'd thought, and the clock was ticking as fast as her brain whirring around about her old flat and how her life had changed. As she hustled along in the busy station, her eyes scanned over the top of the crowds of people and focused on the huge black destination board overhead. She squinted up, looking for the Pretty Beach train, trying to ascertain which platform to head for. Stopping for a second and scanning from left to right, she took a deep breath and looked around her. It was all so frantic and busy, a thrum of energy so thick and frenzied with people rushing, the buzz was almost palpable in the air. She shook her head to herself and wondered why she'd never noticed it before. The air felt thick and dusty, and there was a kaleidoscope of sound and movement fizzing all around her. She couldn't stop herself from gaping at how it was all so very different from Pretty Beach.

All around her was a whirl of activity, and as Lotta pressed forward through the people waiting for their destinations to appear on the board, she was suddenly struck by how much she was ready to get home. As a platform came up for a train to Brighton, she had to duck out of the way as the whole crowd around her seemed to move of its own accord. She sidestepped the throng of hustling travellers making their way past her with their heads bent down to their phones. Finally, she sighed in relief as the Pretty Beach train appeared on the board and she made her way to the platform. Tapping her phone at the gate, she stepped away from the concourse, her eyes scanned along the length of the sleek train, and she felt a little burble of pleasure in the pit of her stomach. With her book bag bouncing against her shoulder, she climbed aboard, found a seat, and, getting her Kindle out, settled in. Lotta was so ready to get back to Pretty Beach.

Fully immersed and totally lost in the pages of her book almost as soon as she'd sat down, Lotta relaxed and got lost in the world of a book as she leaned into the corner of the seat. As the train began to slowly ease out of the station, she flicked her eyes away from her Kindle for a minute and stared out the window, her gaze fixed on the scenery sliding past outside. It was all so familiar, but now, not quite so like home at the same time. The backs of houses and gardens surged past the window in a grey-brown blur as Lotta paused from her reading. A few of the familiar London landmarks went by in the far distance, and she felt as if she was leaving behind her old life as the train pressed on, zipping further and further out of London.

With the methodical movement of the train over the tracks and her Kindle resting on her lap, Lotta found herself going over her day. As she thought about her old flat, she felt a strange tightness wedged at the bottom of her stomach. Visiting her old stomping ground had left her sad and happy at the same time, and she couldn't quite get her head around it. She guessed that at the bottom of it all, she was sad about the old Lotta – sad at what that version of Lotta had lost. But boy, oh boy, oh boy, was she happy at what she'd found. If she hadn't been dumped by Dan, if the app hadn't failed, if she hadn't been given notice on her flat, and if she hadn't missed out on so many jobs, she never would have met Jack. Her world had certainly turned in a mysterious new way.

As slowly but surely the rows of houses and industrial buildings were replaced with the greens of fields and interspersed every now and then with small towns, Lotta's brain began to decompress. As the train continued out of the city, the sun began to set, and Lotta felt more content than she had for a long time. With the sky gradually beginning to be edged with a soft gold-orange hue and her hand resting on her Kindle, she continued to stare out the window, lost in thought. Her mind flitted from her old flat to the dreamy Sussex cottage she'd always thought about, to Pretty Beach to the Breakers. A sense of peace washed over her as she thought about the funny old house that had quickly become her home. Gone were the days of getting home and panicking about money and how she was ever going to make a go of her life and career. Now she could return to Pretty Beach to the Breakers at the end of the day, not care about anything too much, shut the door, kick off her shoes, walk into the library room, and forget about the worries of the world. It was a feeling that was long overdue and deliciously nice.

Half an hour later, the passengers around her had changed and Lotta was well stuck into her book. Its pages had alleviated her brain of the day and soothed her as she got deeper and deeper into the story. She was so lost in the words on her Kindle screen that when her phone vibrated from her lap, she contemplated not bothering to see who it was. Thinking it might be Jack, she opened the cover and then frowned when she saw it was her mum calling. Lotta's mum rarely called, if ever. If she did bother to communicate with Lotta, she nearly always sent a message and considering the time in Singapore where her mum lived, it was an odd time of day. Lotta felt immediate concern and grabbed her phone with a crease between her brows, stabbing at the button. She spoke cautiously, with a very strange feeling that something was wrong. 'Hi, Mum. How are you?'

'Hello, Lotta,' her mum said, her voice sounding oddly coherent and calm. All Lotta's initial thoughts that something was wrong intensified at the sound of her mum's voice. 'I'm sorry I haven't spoken to you for a while,' Lotta's mum stated slowly. Lotta was now very alarmed. Firstly, the calm, and then the apology. It did not bode well. There was *definitely* something wrong. Her heart thudded in her chest. It was bad news. She was certain of it. On top of both of those things, Lotta's mum appeared to be sober, which never ended well. Lotta felt her heart sink. 'No worries. I presumed you were busy the last few times I called. Are you okay?'

Her mother hesitated. 'I'm fine.'

'You don't sound it,' Lotta replied, picking her words very carefully. One wrong word and her mum would go off. Her mum was like a firework waiting to explode, and it could happen at any time. 'Are you sure you're okay?'

'I'm, yeah, I'm doing okay.'

Lotta could tell there was a 'but' coming. She waited for her mum to ask her for money.

'I've not been feeling well. I've been for some tests. Dave asked me to call you, but I don't want any of your drama,' her mum said.

Lotta ignored the drama comment and felt a lump in her throat. 'What's wrong?' she asked, her voice trembling.

Her mother sighed. 'I don't know for sure. I've been to the doctor and then the hospital. They said it's hard to know until I have more tests. They're not sure what it is. As I said, I wouldn't have bothered to call you, but Dave felt it was the right thing to do.'

Lotta drew her hands to her mouth. She tried to ignore the fact that her mum had to be told by her partner, Dave, to call her. 'Sorry, you need to rewind a bit. What happened?'

'I had a bit of a funny turn.'

Lotta nodded. She had seen many of her mum's 'funny turns' over the years. All of them fuelled by marijuana or alcohol. Often a combination of both. There was no way Lotta was going to mention that, though. Everyone had to pretend around Lotta's mum that she was as sober as a judge. 'So, what, did Dave put you to bed?' Lotta asked. Lotta had been the one putting her mum to bed for many years.

'Well, no, I went to hospital.'

'What, you went to hospital?' Lotta asked.

'Yes. They think I had a mini heart attack,' Lotta's mum replied, her voice low and tight. 'That's it, really.'

Lotta's mum's words hung in the air. The train carriage had suddenly gone very still. Lotta gripped her phone, and her chest felt tight. A heavy silence followed her mum's announcement. Lotta squeezed her eyes together, her body frozen and unable to speak or move. She didn't know what to say. Her relationship with her mum was tough at the best of times, and it always had been, but this had come like a bolt out of the blue. 'What? No!'

Her mum's voice was strangely, uncharacteristically weak and quiet. There was a distinct lack of its usual inebriated slurring. 'I'll be okay.'

'I don't know what to say,' Lotta said as she felt the train start to slow down and the people around her gather their things. The signs for Pretty Beach were coming up. She was almost home. Her mum's voice seemed to fill the air around her as she told her more about what had been said at the hospital, and her mum went on to explain that it wasn't life-threatening. 'I just have to, well, to change my lifestyle a bit,' she heard her mum say.

Lotta's voice was just above a whisper as she dared to

mention her mother's alcoholism. 'What, like you have to stop drinking?' she said, unsure as to how mentioning alcohol would go down. Lotta's mum had never admitted she was an alcoholic. It was a shrouded secret, hidden by the power of parenting and eyes looking the other way.

'Don't start with the drama, Lotta. I knew you'd have to start. I hardly drink anything these days.' Lotta's mum's voice was sharp and loaded.

Lotta's hand shook as she held the phone to her ear, her heart racing. Her mum was going to do her usual denial routine. Why change what she'd always done now? 'A mini heart attack,' Lotta repeated. 'Do you need me to come there?'

Her mother's voice on the other end of the line was calm, but Lotta could hear the underlying agitation in her tone. 'I'm fine,' she said. 'The doctor says it was just a warning. I need to make some lifestyle changes, eat healthier, and exercise more. Stuff like that. No, you do not need to come here. See, this is why I said to Dave not to call you.'

Lotta took a deep breath, trying to steady herself. She felt a mixture of emotions. Mostly, there was the unspoken thing in the air about Lotta's mum's problem with drugs and alcohol. 'I'm just getting home. I'll call you in a bit,' she promised.

'You don't need to. I wasn't even going to bother to call. I was just going to text you, but Dave said I had to.'

Lotta's mum's words stung. She wasn't going to bother. Nice. Lotta had heard that and been on the end of it so many times in her life, right from when she was a little girl, but it still hurt.

Her mother assured her that there was no need to call back and abruptly ended the call.

As the train came to the end of its journey and rolled to a stop at Pretty Beach, Lotta closed her eyes and sighed. Everything had been going so well, too. She shouldn't have let herself be happy. She mindlessly walked over the footbridge at the station, her world spinning slowly, her mind caught in a spiral of her own thoughts. All she could see was her mother's face and the words she had said.

I had a mini heart attack. I wasn't going to bother to call.

Lotta tried not to let tears prick at the corners of her eyes, even as her throat constricted and her heart raced. Deep down she had known this was coming. She'd even discussed it briefly with Liv. Her mum had been drinking her whole life. It had only been a matter of time. But something about the way her mother had said she wasn't going to bother to tell her made Lotta feel, as she often had, alone in the world.

Arriving back at Pretty Beach to the Breakers, Lotta had also had a quick call from her mum's partner, Dave. Lotta felt a sting of tears in her eyes as she opened the front door. What was going to happen next? She thought about all the things her mother had done and not done because of drink and drugs. All the things she'd missed. She let out a deep sigh as she slid off her shoes and hooked her book bag over the bannister. Heading straight for the kitchen, she flicked on the kettle, slammed it onto its base, and then went into the library and curled up in the corner of the blue velvet sofa. Thoughts of the past rushed into her head. All the drink-fuelled Mum moments that had ruined her life. All the times her mum hadn't turned up. How her mum had never been to see her play netball, never arrived for a school open evening to hear about how well Lotta had done in class. When Lotta got her exam results and her mother barely looked up from her joint. When she'd got into university and her mum had sniggered in a haze of vodka. All the secrets Lotta had kept from various people when she was young about what was really going on at home.

As she went back into the kitchen to make the tea, Lotta had never felt more alone. She closed her eyes and let a tear slip down her cheek, then wiped it away with her cuff. She was not going to cry. Taking her tea back to the library, she texted both

Liv and Jack, and after messaging back and forth with Jack and finishing her tea, her phone buzzed. She put her phone to her ear, happy to hear Liv's voice.

'Hey. What awful news. How are you doing?'

'I'm just trying to take it all in. I mean, I knew it was coming. We all did. I can't believe it, though, you know. I knew this was going to happen at some point. Why did it have to be now? I was just thinking about how happy I was and how my luck seemed to have turned a corner, and then boom, I get bad news.'

'I know. I said the same to James,' Liv said with a sigh.

'I'd only say that to you. You're the only one who understands. That sounds nasty, do you think? I mean, I don't want to make it all about me...' Lotta trailed off. 'Mum said I would cause drama.'

Liv picked up on Lotta's words straight away. 'Don't be silly! It makes sense, and I do understand, at least as much as I can. It's normal to feel this after what she's put you through in the past.'

'I still feel bad even thinking about it, though.' Lotta sighed.

'How is she doing?'

'She's *saying* she's fine.'

'And Dave?'

'His usual detached self, from what I can gather.'

'It must be really tough for you,' Liv noted.

'Yeah, whatever. I'm a big girl. I wonder if I should tell anyone in the family.'

There was a big sigh from Liv. 'She's done so many bad things over the years. Not a single person talks to her, Lott. I don't really know what else to say.'

'I know. I don't know what to do. Everyone has washed their hands of her. We knew this was going to happen at some point.'

'Yup. I'm here for you, is all I can really say,' Liv stated resignedly.

'Yeah, thanks. It's a lot to take in. I've been waiting for this call for years, if I'm honest. It's still a shock, though.'

The concern in Liv's voice was unmistakable. 'It's awful. Is there anything you need? I can come over with a curry?'

'No, I'm fine. Jack's coming.'

'Oh, okay, good.'

'I was thinking about going to see her, but when I spoke to Dave afterwards, he said he'd rather I didn't for now in case I upset her.'

'Cheek! In case you upset her!' Liv exclaimed. 'Blimey, Lott. She really does take the biscuit.'

'I know, right? The irony of that statement alone.'

'I'm not sure if it's a good idea for you to go, anyway. We all know what happened last time when she had one of her fits and exploded. Has she stopped drinking?'

'It's hard to know. I would say she was sober when she called, but who knows how long that will last.'

'Yeah, I bet. Dave didn't say, then?'

'No. It was sort of skirted around, as usual. We all have to pretend we don't know about her drinking. I don't need to tell you that.'

'Probably a good idea to keep away for now. It's a long way to go not to be wanted.'

'I guess so. I just don't want to add any more stress to her life right now. I hate that I even say that, but we all know it's true. Bottom line is I've always rubbed her up the wrong way.'

'I'm sorry, that's true. It is what it is, though,' Liv replied resignedly. 'You just have to try and stay strong, Lott.'

'Yeah, I'll try. I just hope she heeds the warning.'

Liv sighed. 'I'm not sure she will. You need to be ready for that. By past experience, nothing will stop her from drinking.'

'You're right. Look, thanks for calling.'

'Anytime. I'm here for you if you need anything - you know that.'

'I do.'

'What are you going to do now? Start a new book or something?'

Lotta looked around at her books. 'I'm going to have a shower, put my pyjamas on, make a hot chocolate, and wait for Jack.'

'Good. Get an early night in.'

'Yeah.'

'Hopefully, I'll drop off to sleep later. It's been a really long day.'

'Just message me if you need me.'

'Thanks. Will do.'

8

A few days later, Lotta was sitting at the kitchen table after a restless night. Her head had buzzed with thoughts about her mum all night, and in the end, she'd had to call an end to the tossing and turning by making herself a cup of tea and tucking herself into the conservatory with a book. She'd flicked from reading to watching the early morning light in the garden change.

Now, the shadows from the wisteria climbing over the back of the house swept across the floor as the sun shone through clouds with what looked as if it was going to be a nice day. Lotta could feel warmer weather in the air and see a shimmer coming off the sea in the far distance. She didn't really care about the weather though and couldn't really focus on much of anything. The news from her mum and the way it had been delivered had been horrible, and she was in free fall from the aftermath. Her mum's phone call had seriously upset the equilibrium of Lotta's world and left her wondering what to do. It was as if it had picked up her life, thrown in memories of her childhood, given it a good shake and left her to pick up the pieces. Lotta couldn't get over the call and her mum's attitude.

Once she'd had a shower, washed and dried her hair, and put on her softest, comfy clothes, she was mooching around the kitchen making breakfast. Having found out that one of Jack's favourite breakfast things was soft-boiled eggs, she'd obliged and was slicing buttered bread into soldiers. She smiled to herself at the soldiers, remembering how they'd enjoyed them at the country house hotel he'd taken her for a surprise. Jack had recalled childhood days when eggs and soldiers had been on many a menu in his house. Lotta had been sad then that she didn't have a single similar memory, but now her sadness was tenfold.

As she pottered around the kitchen, she thought about her childhood. Her mum had definitely not made her boiled eggs. Her mum had either been absent or passed out most of the time, and Lotta had lived off basic brand cornflakes and home brand baked beans. She tried to shake the memory of her mum blacking out on the sofa and having to feed herself with tins of beans. She shook her head wryly at it all. She still couldn't look at a cornflake without feeling all a jumble. Lotta's mum, of course, had no idea. She'd always either been high or drunk or both.

When she heard Jack's key in the door, she felt her heart jump. At least she had Jack in her life now. He walked in, came straight across the breakfast room and around into the kitchen, and hugged her hard. She forced herself not to get emotional and slathered on a smile.

'How are you feeling?' Jack asked, his concern evident all over his face.

Her face went blank for a few seconds as she thought about how to answer him. 'I'm fine.'

'How was the night after you texted me goodnight?'

Frowning, Lotta looked out at the conservatory. 'Yeah, not great, to be honest,' she said, her voice almost a whisper. 'I was tossing and turning all night again. Worse than the night when I got the call.'

Jack nodded, reached down, and grabbed Lotta's hand. 'I don't know what to say,' he said quietly.

Lotta gave him a small smile and squeezed his hand tightly. 'Thanks for coming over.'

They stood in silence for a few seconds until Lotta spoke again. 'It's just hard sometimes where mum is concerned.' Her voice wavered. 'As I explained – it's complicated.'

Jack nodded. 'I can do complicated.'

Lotta smiled a weak smile and narrowed her eyes. 'Can you?'

Jack smiled. 'For you, yeah. For anyone else on the planet, that would be a no.'

'I'm so glad you're here.'

Jack looked over at the breakfast table and winked. 'Is that why I have soldiers?'

'Yep. Your favourite. And if I remember rightly, you told me you don't have a favourite food. So clearly then you weren't telling the truth,' Lotta joked.

Jack rolled his eyes. 'Oh no, the question list of fake dating doom. Don't mention that. Did I say I didn't have a favourite food? I can't even remember!'

'You did. You also said you don't like vegetarians.'

Jack grinned. 'I did indeed. The vegetarian bit was obviously a joke.' He leaned over and kissed her cheek lightly, his hand still holding hers. 'Thanks for this.'

'You're welcome,' Lotta said with a smile.

Jack smiled back, then looked at the plate of food. 'So... egg and soldiers.'

Lotta nodded. 'To say thanks for, I don't know, being here,' she said softly. 'I'm grateful that I can talk to you about the stuff with my mum.'

Jack smiled, his eyes serious. 'You don't need to feed me or say thank you.'

Lotta nodded as she took the bubbling coffee machine from the stove. 'I wanted to. Coffee?'

'Love one.'

Jack pointed at the Baccarat coffee maker. 'It smells amazing.'

Lotta smiled as she poured two cups of steaming coffee and then took a plate of cinnamon buns out of the oven. 'It's been a while since I had a proper breakfast like this,' she said as they sat down to eat, again reminded of the bowl upon bowl of corn-flakes she'd had when she was growing up. She shuddered at the thought of the kitchen cupboards, where row upon row of the bland basic brand boxes had been lined up.

'So, you need to tell me more about your mum. You said you needed to explain a few things,' Jack said as he looked up and sliced the top off an egg. 'Only if you want to.'

Lotta took a deep breath and tried to keep her emotions in check. 'It's all a bit tricky and embarrassing.'

'Embarrassing?'

As she always did, Lotta felt awkward and ashamed in one. It was hard explaining her mum to anyone. She found it a challenge to even bring it up and the only person who really understood it was Liv, and even she didn't know the full story of some of the things that had gone on. 'Yeah, you know, it's embarrassing to admit to someone what she's like. They usually want to distance themselves from you, or they become uncomfortable or something.'

Jack didn't seem perturbed. 'Right. You don't have to tell me.'

Lotta shook her head slowly and bit her lip nervously. 'I need to tell you. There's no way we can have, well, a relationship without me telling you. I have to be honest with you about who my mum is and what she has done in the past... and still does now sometimes. It's not pretty, though I suppose it could have been worse in a way. There are some things that are difficult to talk about, but I'm going to need to let you in on it for whatever we're calling this thing between us right now.'

'I'm all ears.' Jack looked into her eyes, his gaze intense as he listened carefully. 'Anything you want or need to say is fine by me.'

Lotta hesitated, her eyes cast downward, and then she nodded slowly before taking a deep breath. 'She spent most of my childhood, no scrub that, all of it, high and drunk.'

'I see, well, I don't actually see. That must have been awful.'

Lotta nodded slowly before taking a deep breath and exhaling sharply, as if trying to expel the memories from her mind. 'On top of that, when she was with it enough to say things, she would be... really, *really* horrible.'

Jack squeezed her hand reassuringly. 'It sounds terrible.'

Lotta shook her head. 'Yeah, it wasn't nice.'

Jack sighed heavily, pushed out his chair, and came around the table. He sat down and put his arm around Lotta's shoulders and pulled her close to him. 'I'm here for you, Lott.'

Lotta looked up at Jack and smiled before burrowing herself into the crook of his neck and letting out a sigh of relief. She then flicked her head and pulled away slightly so she could look into his eyes. 'Okay, so I'm not really wanting to dwell on it too much,' she said, feeling a wave of emotion wash over her. 'Look, maybe I shouldn't have gotten into it. I don't know...' She let her voice trail off and picked up her coffee.

Jack took the cue and went back around to the other side of the table. 'It's good to talk about stuff like that. Especially when someone has a heart attack and doesn't tell you about it at first in case you cause drama. I mean, you couldn't make it up.' He paused and took a deep breath before continuing. 'From where I'm standing, that's not very nice.'

'I know. Right?'

'Probably not a good idea to have to deal with it on your own,' Jack acknowledged.

'I think I might leave it there.' Lotta's eyes closed as she took in a shaky breath. 'I don't want to get upset.' Her words hung heavily in the air.

'You don't want to talk about it any further?'

'Nah, it's alright, I'll be fine. It's good to have that bit off my chest.'

'Let's just go with the flow,' Jack said earnestly.

'Thank you. That means a lot.' Lotta fiddled with the bottom of the coffee pot. 'So, this has been a bit of a weird one, hasn't it?'

'What do you mean?'

'I suppose, I mean, that, well, we're only just going out, and I've dumped a load of emotional baggage on you. I wasn't expecting or wanting that to happen.'

Jack mulled over what she had said for a second, his face serious. 'I wouldn't say we're *just* going out or that you've dropped emotional baggage on me.'

Lotta felt her heart do somersaults. 'You wouldn't?'

'No, not at all. You get a horrible call with news like that, and we're not *just* going out. I love you, Lott. It's that simple. If you hadn't told me, I'd be more concerned.'

Lotta swallowed. 'Right. Yes, thanks. Yes, okay, umm.' She waved her hands around in front of her. 'Look, I don't want to talk about it anymore.'

'Fair enough. Just say the word.'

'I will.' Lotta smiled. Jack was pushing all the right buttons and saying all the right things. As he smiled, there seemed to be a strange unspoken thing between them. Lotta felt odd even thinking it, but just having him there, she felt comfortable and, in some way, protected all at once; something which she had been missing in her life pretty much since the day she was born. Suddenly, Lotta just didn't feel *quite* as alone.

9

After a long week at work, Lotta walked towards The Rose and Anchor pub that clung to a sloping hillside just on the outskirts of Newport Reef, tucked away from the noise of the town. As she strolled along, decompressing from her day at work, the setting sun bounced off the pub's white walls. She smiled as she got closer. Overflowing hanging baskets were jammed with colourful blooms, and a pub sign hanging from a bracket above the door swung back and forth in the coastal breeze.

As she approached the quaint old pub where ivy covered most of its facing side, she cupped her hands over her eyes and peered through the windows. She loved a good old-fashioned pub, and this was ticking all her boxes. Yanking open the heavy oak door, its hinges creaked, and as her eyes adjusted to the dim light, she revelled in the lovely cosy old pub smell. It welcomed her with its happy mix of freshly pulled pints, polished wood, and dried hops. The Rose and Anchor was dimly lit, with a low beamed ceiling and huge white pillar candles in lanterns flickering from the windowsills and shelves. Old wooden floorboards covered with faded rugs creaked beneath her feet, and a thick, cosy layer of comfort seemed to almost settle on top of her as she peered around looking for Jack.

A long bar topped with polished wood sat on her left, backed with a haphazard row of bottles and glasses. A group of pensioners were gathered around a set of stools, chatting in low voices, and a woman behind the bar with a beaming smile raised her eyebrows in greeting. Lotta strolled past an inglenook fireplace, with logs set ready to be lit, and smiled as a group of women huddled together on armchairs and sofas, cradled glasses of wine, and laughed. She couldn't help but smile at the loveliness of the pub as her eyes scanned the room for Jack until she saw him sitting at a table on the far side near another fireplace. He got up, waved her over, and when she got to the table, he kissed her on the cheek as she took in the walls lined with old scenes and pictures from Newport behind him. Lotta smiled brightly, warmly greeting him with a hug. 'Hey, how are you?' She looked around at the pub and swept her hand around. 'This is lovely!' She peered out the window at the view of the coast outside. 'And the view. Wow!'

'I thought you might like it.'

'Like it? I love it,' Lotta said as she pulled off her jacket and sat down.

'Wine?' Jack asked.

'Yes, please. I'd love one.'

Jack went to the bar and was back in a jiffy, placing a glass of wine on the table. He inclined his head to the window and the view. 'What an evening,' Jack said, looking out at the sea.

'I can't believe I actually work down the road.' Lotta sighed, looking out the window at the sea in the distance. 'Not a bad place to work with that as your backdrop. On top of that, the people are actually nice and really friendly. I mean, what more can anyone ask for?'

Jack nodded in agreement, and they continued to chat. As Lotta sipped her wine, she revelled in Jack, the conversation, and the golden hour taking place outside the window as the sun slowly travelled down the sky and dipped below the horizon.

'Phew, I'm shattered,' Lotta said as she leaned back in her chair.

'Busy day?'

'Manic. Talk about jumping in at the deep end with that place.'

'The only way in my experience.'

Lotta nodded in agreement. 'Yeah, there's only so much a training manual can tell you.'

Jack motioned to the menu on the table. 'Hungry?'

'Yep, I wolfed down a sandwich with Marie at lunch, and that was it. So much for afternoon tea. Honestly, the job is much more full-on than I anticipated.'

'Good job you spent all those hours preparing then,' Jack deadpanned.

'Yeah, but now I realise how simple the training documents made it look!'

After fish and chips, another glass of wine, and a lot of discussion about the situation with both Lotta's new job and her mum, Lotta and Jack left the pub. The warm evening air wrapped around them as they strolled towards the ferry. Lotta felt her phone buzz in her pocket, pulled it out, and then frowned as she looked at her messages. 'Err, why are you texting me when I'm standing right beside you?'

'Open it.'

Lotta stopped and opened the message which contained an email address, a password, and a link. 'What? What's this?'

'If you need to book a flight to Singapore, you can do it there.' He then told her an additional passcode number.

'What? I don't understand.'

'Just in case you need to. I know you said you weren't going to go yet, but you know, you might change your mind. I don't want you to have to worry about...' Jack paused for a second, searching for the right words. 'I don't want you to have to worry about anything.'

'No, no. You don't need to do that.'

'I know I don't *need* to. I want to,' Jack stated. 'You can be there in a working day. Twelve hours. Or thirteen actually, I think.'

'I know,' Lotta answered, remembering the times she'd taken the long journey to Singapore to see her mum. Most of the times she'd visited had ended up in Lotta being upset.

'I thought it might just take one step out of the equation for you.'

'Right, okay, wow. Thanks.'

'As I said before, I'll come with you if you want me to.'

'What about work?'

'I can work from my phone,' Jack stated sombrely. 'Are you thinking more about going over then? I know you said Dave and your mum said not to.'

'I don't know. I'm not wanted. I really don't know what to do. I've spent way too long on Google looking at the consequences of mini heart attacks. A heart attack is a heart attack at the end of the day.'

'True. Well, as I said, the offer is there if you need it.'

'Thanks, but I couldn't…'

'Oh yes, you could.'

'Thank you.' Lotta's voice was barely a whisper.

Jack's face broke into a smile. 'And just so we're clear, you won't be at the back of the plane.'

Lotta frowned, not having a clue what he was talking about. 'Sorry. What do you mean?'

'I mean, book yourself a business class ticket. It's stressful enough as it is. Trust me.' He squeezed her hand.

Lotta swallowed a lump and felt tears at the corners of her eyes. 'That's so kind of you.'

'I'm full of kindness, me,' Jack bantered. 'Brimming with it.'

Lotta thought about how grumpy Jack had been on various occasions when she had first met him. 'Lol.'

'I am to you, anyway. Kind, that is. I hope you appreciate I do not behave like this with any old Tom,' Jack joked with raised eyebrows.

'Oh, yeah? Why's that then?'

'Obvious, at least to me. I love you, Lott. It's really as simple and straightforward as that.'

Lotta's heart did a double back and smiled. From her end, it was just as simple too.

10

The following week on her way to work, Lotta had hopped on a ferry much earlier than she'd needed to and had arrived in Newport Reef with time on her hands. Her intention was to walk the twenty or so minute stroll to the arcade to get a takeaway coffee and to read a few pages of her new book whilst sitting in the bandstand looking out to sea. She strolled up to a tiny kiosk tucked in next to a row of shops and smiled as she got to the front of the queue. A woman in a white apron with bright red hair and a grin looked out at her. 'Morning, love. Lovely day for it. We have sunny days ahead all week. At last!'

Lotta smiled and followed the woman's gaze. 'Yep. I've just got off the ferry, and it was lovely coming up the coast.'

'What can I get you? Tea?'

'Can I have a large coffee, please?' Lotta nodded over towards the bandstand. 'I'm early for work, and I'm going to sit over there and have a read of my book before the day starts.'

'Ooh, I like how you roll,' the woman said. 'It'll be cosy in the bandstand on a morning like this. You'll be right as rain there out of the wind.'

'I will. Not a bad way to start the day.'

The woman handed over a coffee with a little biscotti tucked on top of the lid. 'Ahh, I wouldn't change it for all the tea in China. Though there are some chilly days down here sometimes, that I can tell you for free.'

'I bet! Well, have a lovely day.' Lotta smiled as she took the coffee, then turned around and as she popped the biscotti into her mouth, she headed towards the beach and made her way to the old ornate Victorian bandstand standing proudly in the sunshine. As she stood in its warmth, she looked up at the octagonal bandstand roof with its filigree scrollwork and marvelled at its details. Taking a seat, she couldn't help but feel happy at the place she now called work. The waves crashed down onto the beach not far from the bandstand where a little bed of flowers and a tiny green lawn sat in front – the perfect spot for a combination of reading and coffee. Just out of the wind, the salty sea air filled her lungs. She took a deep breath in and then let it out slowly, feeling everything but her book, the view, and her coffee slipping away.

Lotta looked out over the sea, brimming with shimmers, and the waves crashing against the sand, wondering what the day would bring. As she sipped on her coffee, she could see the odd boat in the distance, and a few seagulls gliding above. As she sat and watched the waves, she thought about the future. She wondered what it would be like to have a successful career, dare she even call it a career. She mused what it might be like to not be constantly threatened with redundancy and money worries.

Once she'd finished her coffee, after stuffing her trainers and her Kindle in her bag, she slipped on a pair of heels and clipped over towards the traffic lights. She looked up at the domed green roof of the arcade, her eyes drawn to its glinting in the sunlight. The building was nothing short of fantastic. It sure beat some of the holes she'd ended up working in. It was definitely better than the horrible uniforms and cleaning office block toilets she'd endured so that Dan could be free to work on his app.

Pushing open the arcade's double, shiny black doors, she zipped across the lobby, saying hello to the man watering the plants and nodding to the receptionist. When she got to the offices, Marie was sitting on the sofa with a coffee on the table and an iPad in her hand.

'Morning!' Marie looked up from the iPad. 'How are you?'

'I'm good,' Lotta replied.

'How's your mum?' Marie asked in a concerned tone.

Lotta felt too ashamed to say that her mum hadn't wanted to talk to her since the initial call when she'd been on the train and that she hadn't really heard from her much. 'She's good, thanks,' she said.

'No other problems?' Marie asked.

'No, touch wood,' Lotta said, reaching down and touching the coffee table. Lotta didn't add that she wasn't too sure. She'd spoken and messaged with Dave, but she hadn't heard much from her mum at all, despite constantly calling her.

'Good, coffee's just brewed if you want one.'

'I just had one from the kiosk, actually.'

'Ooh, I love that place.'

'Yeah, same. I got an early ferry this morning and thought I'd make the most of it.'

'Good one. It's a gorgeous day out there. Shame we're going to be so busy today.'

'Yeah.'

'Not a problem. I like it when the day's full and before you know it, it's time to go home again. Nothing worse than a slow, boring day, in my humble opinion.'

Lotta nodded. She was in total agreement.

'Are you good with everything for today? We've got a lot on what with all these different groups coming through. It's been all go since you first started. I did try to warn you.' Marie chuckled.

'I think so.'

'Any questions?'

Lotta considered for a quick second. 'The only thing is one of the CEOs wanted special milk. Plant-based something or other.'

Marie wrinkled up her nose. 'Sorry. What, like what? What sort of milk?'

'Good question. We didn't have any, and they didn't have it in Sainsbury's. I had a look on my way home last night.'

'Ahh, that's good of you to go out of your way like that.'

Lotta waved her hand in dismissal. 'Ahh, it's nothing at all.'

Marie nodded. 'Yes, it is. That's *precisely* why we wanted you on board.'

'What do you mean?'

'This job – it needs people who go above and beyond. Someone who stops at Sainsbury's. Not everyone would do that, you know,' Marie noted with a little shrug.

'No, right, I see,' Lotta replied. 'I just thought it would be easier to do it that way.'

'It is, but a lot of people don't think the same way as you. Ask me how I know that.' Marie chuckled and drained her coffee.

'I suppose not.'

'We need more Lottas in the world, I guess,' Marie joked.

'Oh goodness, I don't think we do,' Lotta bantered. 'I think we'd be in trouble.'

'We certainly do,' Marie said with a smile.

'Well, thank you,' Lotta replied.

Marie smiled back. 'You're welcome. I'm just glad we got somebody like you on board.'

Lotta felt a warm feeling go through her veins. She hadn't seen that coming. It felt good to be part of something, and it felt *so* good to be liked. She beamed as she stood in front of Marie. It felt fabulous to be at the end of such a nice compliment. 'Thank you, Marie. That's such a nice thing to say. I'm really grateful. I'm loving it here.'

'Same from my end,' Marie replied. 'I like having you around.'

'Thank you!'

'Ha,' Marie said, pushing herself up off the sofa. 'Rightio, I have a group of highly skilled software engineers and their needs for morning tea to sort out.'

'Good luck with that.' Lotta chuckled. 'At least you don't have to worry about plant-based milk. I'm off to find that now.'

'And what about the delicious fake dating boyfriend?' Marie asked. 'How's it going with him?'

Lotta chuckled. Even though she and Marie hadn't known each other for that long, they had immediately hit it off and were quite friendly. Lotta had ended up telling Marie about how her relationship with Jack had started off as a fake date. 'It's going really well.'

'Good,' Marie replied. 'I cannot wait to hear some more of your escapades. If only I got to dress up in a ball gown and go to a palace!' She sighed. 'One day I'll come into work with tales...'

Lotta laughed in response. 'I'm not sure anyone would want to do anything similar,' she said.

'Sounds a whole lot more exciting than my life sitting on the sofa watching telly.' Marie laughed as she rinsed out her coffee cup with water and turned it upside down to drain.

'Ahh, I can assure you that my life is not that exciting,' Lotta said.

'It sounds exciting to me.' Marie patted the back of her head to check her hair and readjusted her blouse. 'Okay. See you in here for sandwiches later?'

Lotta widened her eyes and nodded. 'If all goes to plan, yes. See you at lunch.'

'You can tell me how the CEO with his plant-based milk is getting on.'

'I can indeed.'

~

Lotta's morning had been full. There had been an issue with someone getting stuck on the motorway, a cab hadn't turned up at Newport Reef train station, and one of the CEOs had the signs of a virus and had wanted the live stream set up so that he could participate in the session from home. It had been all go since Lotta had left the office, and she'd been on her feet the whole time, not even having time to go to the loo.

Her supposed lunch with Marie had been a very quick egg and cress sandwich and Marie had relayed similar problems with her morning, including an engineer who had vomited and ended up being sent home. Lotta shuddered at the vomiting and sick bag story, thinking about when she was at the ball with Jack. Images of the big American woman in the red dress and her head in a bucket flashed into Lotta's brain.

As she plonked on the sofa next to Marie, both of them with their shoes off and feet up, she'd shuddered at what had happened on the night of the ball and started to relay the story to Marie. 'I was sitting next to this American woman at the fake dating thing, listening to her go on and on about her meat allergy.'

Marie wrinkled up her nose. 'I didn't know there was such a thing.'

'Hers was to do with a tick bite.'

'Ooh, err, sounds not very nice. You see, that is why I love good old Blighty. Know what I mean? No worries about stuff like that. What even is a tick?'

Lotta wrinkled up her nose. 'It's a tiny little insect thing. It bites you, I think, and then leaves these wiggly bits in you.'

Marie grimaced. 'Yuck! Vile. That sounds revolting.'

'I know,' Lotta agreed.

'So, hang on, how does that make you allergic to meat?'

'No idea. I do know though that it left this Brandy covered in hives.'

'What, she accidentally ate meat at the ball, did she?'

'Nope, not at the ball, she didn't. She did, like me though, have a shed load of prawn vol-au-vents.'

'And then what happened?' Marie asked with wide eyes.

'She projectile vomited into a wine bucket.' Lotta chuckled.

'What in the name of goodness?'

'Yeah, she suddenly gripped the edge of the tablecloth, and I could see she was going to be sick so I got the champagne bucket.'

'Could put you off prawns for life.'

'Tell me about it.' Lotta nodded.

'So what, did she reckon it was the prawns?'

'Yeah. They got me too. I ended up vomiting into a black bin liner at the bar right in front of Jack.'

'Ahh! You didn't tell me that part of the story before!' Marie exclaimed.

Lotta chuckled. 'I think I tried to erase it from my memory.'

'I'm not surprised. It sounds hideous.'

'It was not pleasant. Funny thing was, you know when you're sick, and then you feel so much better right away? It was just like that.'

'Yeah, it's funny how it works like that.'

'So the moral of the story is be very careful of a prawn vol-au-vent, even if you are in a palace with a lot of posh people in fancy frocks.'

'Lol, you're funny.' Marie laughed.

Lotta shuddered at the memory of the smell from the inside of the black bin liner and the contents of her stomach. 'I certainly didn't think it was funny at the time.'

'I bet.'

'I thought it was awful,' Lotta said, recalling that she'd also mistakenly thought that Jack liked someone else.

'Oh well, you live and learn.' Marie got up to make a cup of tea. 'You just never know what is around the corner. I mean, look at that situation. You were on a fake date and now, well, now you're in a thing with Jack. I need that to happen in my life.'

Lotta did not need to be told how life could change in a split second. It had most certainly happened to her, and she was enjoying the ride. 'You don't know what's around the corner, for sure.'

'I wonder what's to come,' Marie pondered.

'Who knows?' Lotta shuddered a little bit. She was quite happy with how it was in her life now. She'd be quite happy if there was nothing around the corner for a very long time to come. The trouble was, as she knew only too well, life never really worked like that.

11

A week or so later, Lotta sat at her little desk in the corner of the library room in Pretty Beach to the Breakers and sent her last email regarding a conference she was organising at the end of the year. She then finished off the last of her paperwork, which in fact was not paperwork at all, but fully digitalised admin via a very nice work tablet sitting beside her. She sighed and felt her shoulders drop, extremely pleased with herself that she'd powered through her work. Her motivation had been the promise of an early evening tucked up in the library room, loading her latest book review online, and doing a live of her going through the book chapter by chapter. Lotta checked the time on her phone. She had time to work for a bit on her book account, phone Liv to check how she was, and then she'd earmarked a couple of hours to work on the boathouse building before she could settle down to read for the night.

Since she'd moved into Pretty Beach to the Breakers, she sometimes felt as if she was on a roundabout of things to do, not leaving her anywhere near enough time to read. Her TBR pile was growing by the day. Every day, she would get on the roundabout of her new life and then do the very same thing the next day – a conveyor belt of work, housework, and doing little things here and there to improve the house. She was so very far from complaining, her life was not bad. She was a trillion times better off than where she'd been at the beginning of the year, but she had to admit she was a tad on the tired side. Getting one's life together wasn't easy, nor was transforming oneself and heaving oneself up from the bottom of a horrible heap. There just weren't enough hours in the day.

Pleased that she'd cracked on with her work, she walked out of the library room to the kitchen, made herself a cup of tea, took a crumpet out of the bread bin, popped it in the toaster, and waited for it to jump back out. Once she had a cup of tea in hand and a buttered crumpet, she ambled back to the library room and sat back down at her desk. Tapping her social media reading account, she smiled and clicked on her DMs. She had lots of messages from followers about her latest book review and loads of comments. She spent a bit of time answering questions and then frowned at a message about halfway down her DMs where she came across a more formal message. She screwed up her nose and analysed it; it was from someone at one of the big five publishing houses. Lotta blinked slowly and reread what she'd initially quickly scanned. It was unbelievable. Astonishing. She swore and shook her head over and over again.

**** *my life.*

Someone, and not just any old random bod with a Gmail account, was interested in working with her online. Could she please provide further details of her rates for her book reviews? They were particularly interested in her live broadcasts from the library room. Pah! Pah, ha, ha ha! Preposterous.

Lotta blinked furiously and swore to herself repeatedly. It had to be a scammer. She wasn't even going to let herself get her hopes anywhere near up. She went to the profile and then typed the name into her laptop; she nearly dropped her phone in surprise as she stared at the profile picture on LinkedIn. Unbelievable but true. It seemed as if this was not a wind-up, nor indeed was it some sort of a scam. This person was, by the looks of it, for real. For *real* real. *Oh. My. Goodness.*

Lotta stared at the message for a long, long, *long* time. The irony of the situation was not lost on her at all as she shook her head and blew breath out of her mouth. She'd spent years and years trying to get onto the publishing career ladder, and had sadly mostly stayed right on the bottom rung of the entry-level jobs no one really wanted to stay in for too long. Dan and his app hadn't helped rung-climbing career progression matters at all, and she'd slid further down the ladder until she'd been so low she'd fallen off. Now it seemed that not only was she being asked to climb back onto the ladder, she was, in fact, being asked to jump back on on her terms. It was flabbergasting, and all around, quite preposterous in light of what had happened to her over the preceding years. The message was so unexpected that she didn't know what to do or what to think. She pressed to phone Jack and he answered on the first ring.

He sounded happy to hear from her. 'Just who I wanted to speak to. The lovely Lotta as in hotter. How are you?'

Lotta felt her heart do the gymnastics tumble it always did when Jack spoke. It then did a quick salto on the balance beam as she started to answer. 'Umm, I'm good, *so* good, really, really good. You're not going to believe this! I'm gobsmacked. I had to tell someone.'

'What? Try me,' Jack replied mock-seriously.

'I've only gone and received a DM from one of the big five,' Lotta said, adding a little squeal at the end.

'Sorry, a DM and the big five? I don't know what either of those means.'

Lotta laughed. 'One of the big five publishing houses and a direct message on my socials. They want to work with me!'

'Oh yeah, really! Wow. What does the message say?'

'Only asking me what my rates are. Do I have a rate card? Ha ha,' Lotta chortled. 'I mean, that in itself is pretty hilarious! Does little old bookworm Lotta, who couldn't keep a job in publishing, have a rate card? You couldn't make it up.'

'Do you? Do you have a rate card?'

'Well, sort of. I mean, my old blog indicates that I have one. But no, not at all.'

Jack's tone turned serious and more business-like. 'Okay, well, whatever it is, you need to triple it and send it to them. Then work from there.'

Lotta's voice was confused. 'Triple it? Why would I do that? I don't get you.'

'Because they came to you. The simple and first rule of business. If you're in demand, you can command what you want. That's about the bottom line of it.'

'I can? I can command what I want?' Lotta asked unbelievably. 'But I'm not in demand. I've had one solitary direct message.'

'Doesn't matter. They don't know that. I did try to tell you this. Hundreds of thousands of followers is not a small thing, Lott. These days that is something one cannot buy. Not genuine followers anyway. Digital media makes the world go around.'

'I know you did tell me. I didn't really think much of it before. I always just thought it was a little game.'

'Yeah, you said. It's not. It's so not. You're a commodity.'

Lotta took a moment to digest what Jack was saying. 'I was so deep down a hole wanting to get into what I thought was real publishing that I thought this wasn't a thing.'

'The world has changed,' Jack stated.

'I know you said that.'

'But you didn't believe me for publishing.'

'Not fully. I mean, obviously, I'm aware of the digital side, but well, I just thought...'

'The irony is, Lott, that you've garnered a massive following for the stuff that sits in your brain before, during, and after you've read a book. That is clearly gold.'

'I have,' Lotta swore. 'Gosh, I actually think you're right. Wow. Go little old me, eh?'

'You are a commodity,' Jack deadpanned. 'I'm going to trade you.'

Lotta burst out laughing. 'Too funny.' Lotta scanned the message again. 'By the looks of this, I am.'

'Do you need an agent? I know a man who might be able to help.'

'Yes, do you know of any who are good-looking and a bit of a dab hand at DIY as well? I need that in my life,' Lotta fired back.

'Hmm, I might know a bloke. He charges a lot, though.'

'Ha!' Lotta giggled.

'As an aside, how long exactly have you been collecting books and stuff? We didn't cover that in the fake dating questions,' Jack asked.

Lotta considered for a second. She'd more or less had a nose in her book her whole life. Reading had been a much-needed escape from what was going on at home. When her mum had been drinking all day, Lotta would sit in her bedroom with piles and piles of books from the library and try to lose herself. She'd used books to distract her from the hell that was going on in her *actual* life. 'Forever,' she replied simply. 'It grew from there, really. My real collecting side of it started in my teens, though, once I had a bit of my own money and I didn't have to rely on the library. I didn't think people would actually like my thoughts on it all, though.'

'Well, they clearly do.'

'I know. Listen to this.' Lotta put Jack on speaker and read through one of her posts, and scanned the comments below. The post showcased her current TBR pile taken in the library room. It was almost as if the post had a life of its own. With so many likes and comments, Lotta had hardly been able to keep up. She looked down at the post and then around at the room. 'I suppose it does look quite nice here if you're a bit of a bookworm. There is that. This room is pretty spesh. That's helping with it too. Maybe that's why I got the message.'

'From a non-bookworm, I'd confirm that,' Jack replied. 'The desk is the pièce de la résistance.'

'And I have you to thank for that,' Lotta said gratefully.

'I'm a man of many talents.'

'Right, so getting back to the publisher. What do you think I should reply?'

'I think you should reply as if you get asked this all the time and that you might be able to fit them in next month unless you get an opening,' Jack replied with his voice again returning to its business-like tone.

'Really. Why would I do that? Gosh, I have no clue about this stuff!'

'Yep, make yourself seem even more in demand than you actually are. Tried and tested.'

'Oh no, I've just thought, what if I don't like the actual book they want me to review? That wouldn't be good.'

'You'll need to put that in your terms and conditions. That's the whole point of it, isn't it?'

'Yeah, I think that's why I've amassed so many followers – I say what I think. A vast majority of book reviewers who get the book for free don't tell the truth. Because if they get it for free, it's obviously not what they really think. Whereas I say what I really think.'

'Yeah, you can't do that. You'll lose followers in seconds. People aren't stupid.'

'No, I know. It's something to consider,' Lotta mused.

'Just say that in your terms and continue as you were. You'll kill it. You really will. I thought that the first time you showed me your account.'

'Right, okay,'

'And didn't I tell you people would adore that library room?'

'You did,' Lotta admitted.

'Right, well, imagine giving them a slice of that in the garden and include somewhere they can actually stay in. Lott, it's a no-brainer.'

'Hmm. I don't know.'

'Trust me, you need to run with it,' Jack advised. 'Strike while the iron's hot.'

'It would be nice if I could do it like this room.'

'We're getting it sorted.'

'Right, thanks.'

'I need to shoot. I'll speak to you later. Well done you. Get those terms done, and the rate card, and get back to them.'

'Will do. Thank you.'

'Love you, Lott.'

'Love you more, Just Jack.'

Lotta put the phone down and pondered it all. Jack really did have a point. Perhaps her reading was going to take her somewhere after all. She rolled it around deliciously in her head. Lotta Button in publishing. It felt so very good to be back.

12

Lotta was sitting at a little table tucked up in the corner of Maisy's café in Pretty Beach, the sound of chattering and the hum of people bustling in and out around her. The café was busy with locals, and Lotta had popped in for a cup of tea and a read of her book. Lost in a world of her own, she was suddenly brought back to life by tapping on the back of the chair opposite her. She looked up to see Holly and Xian from the bakery with big expectant smiles on their faces. She beamed back. 'Hi, ladies, how are you both? You're looking well.'

Holly took her bag off her shoulder and rested it on the chair in front of Lotta. 'I'm good, thank you. What are you up to? No sickness from prawn vol-au-vents?' Holly asked with a chortle.

'Ha! No, thank goodness. I've been busy, actually,' Lotta replied as she put her Kindle down.

'Same here. I've been up to my eyes in it,' Holly replied and flicked her hand out towards the road. 'We've just bought another bakery. I must be losing the plot. So busy!'

'Oh, wow, that does sound busy,' Lotta acknowledged.

'Yep. Anyway, what have you been doing? How is the house?'

'Slow is what it is. It's going very slowly,' Lotta said. 'What with my new job, and trying to get on my feet, I haven't had a moment to think. It's good, though. I love it down here. It's getting better and better as the weather is warming up.'

'It sounds like you're just as busy as us. No rest for the wicked, as they say. The thing is, would you want to be sitting around doing nothing?' Holly asked, the diamonds in her ears catching in the light.

Lotta considered whether she would like to be sitting around reading for a lot of the day, she had to admit that it sounded quite attractive to her with the size of her current TBR pile. 'Probably not. Right now, I'm more concerned with getting my house shipshape and getting my debt back on the straight and narrow. Actually, talking about that, I was going to mention something to you.'

Holly inched closer. 'Yep.'

'I bumped into Suntanned Pete, and he was telling me all about his holiday cottages and how he could rent them four times over at certain times of the year.'

'Yeah, the same as us. We've got some holiday properties too,' Xian said.

Lotta shook her head. These women were powerhouses. It seemed they had their fingers in many pies. 'Right. Well, yes. There's a building next to the boathouse with its own entrance there. A personal gate.'

'Yup. I know it.' Holly nodded.

'I'm thinking about using it for a new business. It would really help me over the next few years.'

Holly's eyes narrowed. 'What sort of business are we talking?'

Lotta clicked her tongue and wrinkled up her face. 'I'm not really sure yet, but I have a social media account for reading and… yeah, so I'm thinking about doing something in combination with that.'

'Sorry, I'm confused. What you read online or something? Is that it?' Xian queried, her nose wrinkled up in confusion. She swigged from a little silver flask and then narrowed her eyes further.

Lotta shook her head and clarified. 'No, no, like reviews and stuff, and reading and talking about books I read. All in all, a lot about books. It's grown quite big over the years.'

'Oh, right! I see. What's that got to do with the boathouse there?'

'I don't know yet, but Jack reckoned it could be a bit of a side income to get me out of my debt. Well, my ex-partner's debt on my credit card. It is what it is,' Lotta explained.

There was another swig of the flask, and then Xian asked another question for clarification. 'Sorry, so people would go there to read, would they? To your house, as it were? Am I understanding that correctly?'

'Yes and no. I don't know yet. They could come and stay if I went down that road. Or maybe workshops or something. Not sure yet.'

'Yeah, it would do well. Loads of people have places on Airbnb now down here. You'd need it to be super nice. There's a lot of competition around for holiday lets. Ask me how I know.' Holly cackled.

'I was thinking of a similar look to what I've done in the library room,' Lotta said. 'I've got enough books to fill it, that I know for a fact.'

'Oh yes! You did a fantastic job there in the library. Right, yeah, I'm getting you now. It could be a sort of reading retreat by the sea. Not that I know what one of those is,' Holly said.

'Yep. A reading retreat by the sea,' Lotta reiterated.

'The perfect spot for one of those,' Xian murmured. 'I need a share dealing retreat.' She cackled.

Holly looked over towards the counter as someone waved to her. 'Anyway, got to go. Pop into the bakery if you want to chat about it a bit more. You might need to talk to the council about things or maybe not, depending on what you want to do. I have contacts in the council.'

Lotta's eyes widened. She'd no doubt that Holly and Xian had contacts just about everywhere. She smiled widely. No doubt to survive in Pretty Beach you needed to keep these two on side.

~

A couple of days later, Lotta clicked the button on a video call, and a few seconds later, Liv appeared on the screen, her hair scrunched into a huge floppy bun perched precariously on the top of her head. Liv was in her bedroom surrounded by piles of clothes and had a roll of white bin bags in her right hand.

'What are you doing?' Lotta enquired, looking at the screen on her phone with a frown.

'Decluttering,' Liv deadpanned as she waved the bin bags around before setting them down and nodding. 'I'm deep into this. Deep. There's no going back now.'

James appeared behind Liv and rolled his eyes. 'I've had enough. I'm going down the pub.'

'I think that might be one of your better ideas in life.' Lotta chuckled. 'Get out while you can, or you might be put in a bag for the charity shop.'

Liv had been on the phone the day before telling Lotta that she was going to be having a huge clear out, and she certainly was.

'I've spent all day doing it! How did I manage to accumulate so much junk so quickly?'

'I know, tell me about it,' Lotta agreed. 'It's like it has a life of its own.'

'What are you up to?' Liv asked.

'I've just finished that rate card thing I was telling you about,' Lotta replied.

'Oh, well done.'

'Yeah. Who knows if they'll bite?'

'I hope so, and I think so,' Liv stated.

Lotta continued, 'I went with what Jack said. It seems way too expensive to my mind, but he told me he knows what he's doing, so who am I to argue?'

'I make him right, Lott. Also, you need to back yourself more.'

'I suppose so.'

'How funny that you're going to end up making money out of your reading. I did say this to you ages ago. Please let that be noted when you make your millions.'

'I know. I should have listened to you. I should always listen to my much-more-clever-than-me-cousin, Liv.' Lotta laughed.

Liv nodded and smiled. 'Yep, you should. All that time you were trying to get a job at one of the big five, and now they're contacting you. It's gold.'

'The irony is not lost on me. Not in the slightest,' Lotta agreed. 'It is almost unbelievable, though.'

'It's not lost on me, either. You're talking to the person who had to see you get turned down from interview after interview.' Liv waved her hand. 'You were too good for them anyway, and now they're knocking at your door. Got to love that, right?'

'Yeah, thanks. Anyway, what else have you been up to?'

'Nothing but working and decluttering. Oh, we did go to that restaurant you went to with Jack. Goodness, no wonder you liked it! The food was outstanding.'

'I know.'

'What about you? What else have you got on the agenda?'

'I'm going to get stuck into the building out the back and start working on a way to get a second – or should I say third, if the book thing happens – income into my life.'

'Hard work. I'll come and help once I get all this sorted.'

'I bumped into Holly, you know, from the bakery, and she said that she reckoned it would be too easy to rent it out. In fact, she had an idea – a reading retreat. Jack had similar thoughts. What do you think of that?'

'What do I think? I think that, my friend, sounds right up your alley.'

'You think so?'

'I do. And those followers on your account? They'll eat that up for breakfast, from what I've seen.'

Lotta nodded, agreeing that Liv had a point. All she had to do was sort it out.

13

A few days later, Lotta was at work and was winding up a very busy day. She said goodbye to the last of her CEOs, finished her log of how the day had gone, and closed everything down on her desk. She picked up her bag, grabbed a bottle of water from the fridge, and walked out to the lobby. With her heels clipping on the polished floor of the arcade, she stood craning her neck through the huge arched windows to the promenade to see if she could see Jack's car. Most days she took the ferry to work, but that morning Jack had dropped her right at the door, and he was back to pick her up. It felt so very nice to be loved.

Seeing his car parked on the far side of the road near the bandstand, she walked over past the lobby sofas, waved goodbye to the receptionist on the desk, and headed towards the entrance. She pushed open one of the huge old shiny black doors and took a deep breath in as fresh sea air hit her squarely in the face. Lotta's day had been full-on since the moment she'd stepped in, and it had been a long and tiring week. She inhaled and let the work day slip away as the sea breeze flipped her hair around and she waited at the pedestrian crossing. Walking up to

Jack's car, she got in and beamed. He kissed her on the cheek, then tapped her on her leg. 'How are you? How was your day?'

'Good! Long, but good. I like being busy, though. That place always throws up things I don't see coming. I'm really enjoying it. You?'

'I've had quite a cruisy day, so I'm winning,' Jack said as he turned on the ignition, checked his wing mirror and waited for a van to go past.

'I have so not had a cruisy day! I can't wait to get home and put my feet up. I don't think I've sat down all day. I need to elevate my legs. Legs-up-the-wall pose I believe it's named in yoga. All I can say is my feet know about spending the day in heels.'

'I'm with you on relaxing on the sofa,' Jack replied as he reversed out onto the road.

'Yeah, I need a calm evening with my books. I have to crack on with my TBR pile, and I need to get that book report done.'

'I was going to stay over,' Jack replied. 'You'd rather be on your own?'

Lotta chuckled to herself. It wasn't even a question. She loved reading, but having Jack for the evening was always going to be a better offer. Every single time.

'Are you hungry?' Jack asked.

'I am. That's sorted, though,' Lotta replied, waving her hand in front of her. 'I put a piece of pork in the slow cooker this morning before I left for work.'

'Right. That's organised.'

'Spicy pork which, by now, will be falling apart,' Lotta noted.

'Very domestic and sorted of you,' Jack deadpanned. 'You can stay.'

Lotta chuckled, but inside she thought about why she was organised on the meal front. It came from years of having to, and the latter app years whereby she'd had little option but to cook every night. There had been no money for much else, and she'd managed on a tiny budget. Sometimes she'd felt as if Rubber Chicken was her middle name. She shuddered at the thought of cooking and dinner and Dan, who'd always made sure he'd reiterated how important his diet was so that he could perform optimally in his entrepreneurial world. It's just that he didn't actually do any of the cooking or the shopping for said diet. It wasn't quite important enough for him to sort it out for himself.

Jack picked up the change in Lotta's body language as she thought about Dan. 'You alright?'

'Yeah, yeah. I was just reminded of Dan when I thought about the slow cooker.'

'Right, what? Why would that remind you of him? He liked spicy pork, did he?' Jack chuckled.

Lotta flicked her hand this way at that and mimicked Dan's voice, 'He had to make sure that his nutrition was finely tuned so that he could perform at his best.' Lotta put her fingers up to sign speech marks around 'finely tuned,' she then stuck the same fingers down her throat.

Jack didn't miss a beat. 'Sounds like a right idiot.'

'Tell me about it. One of the many red flags I should have taken heed of.'

'Hindsight is a wonderful thing,' Jack joked. 'So, would our Dan and his app approve of your spicy pork? Would that be good enough for his emo needs?'

Lotta burst out laughing. 'At the time, it was. I can't remember the name of the diet thing he was doing. Bio something or other. Biohacking or something. No doubt now he's plant-based. He did like to jump on a bandwagon or six.'

'Too funny. Well, I'll like your pork anyway.' Jack winked.

'Thank you.'

'So what's in this amazing gadget that's been cooking away all day, sorting out your nutritional needs?'

Lotta giggled. 'Lots of garlic, onions, chilli, a shed-tonne of wine, chipotle.'

'My mouth is watering, even though I have no idea what that last word you said was.'

Even though she was joking along with Jack, Lotta couldn't stop thinking about her life in the flat with Dan when they were in the thick of the app. An image of herself scheming how to make dinners stretch to her lunches and other meals so Dan didn't have to spend any app money on food zoomed into her mind. She stole a glance at Jack and thought about how different it was with him. It was nothing to do with money, just more that Jack was the opposite, so much so that it was as if he was a different species altogether. She pushed her thoughts to the side. 'Chipotle. You don't need to know what it is. All you need to know is that it's really nice.'

'Just like the person who cooked it.'

Lotta felt her heart do a tumble towards the vault. 'Thanks.'

'I think I might need a beer. It is, after all, Friday night. I'll stop at the off-licence.'

'Yep, sorry, there's only wine in the fridge.'

'You don't have to say sorry. I'm a big boy, Lott. I can manage to buy some beer.'

Lotta smiled. 'Yeah, sorry, old habits die hard and all that.'

Jack screwed up his face. 'Was he really that bad? Did he need to be babysat? Did you do all the cooking and everything? Like all the time?'

Lotta felt embarrassed. She'd more or less wiped up after Dan's every move. If he'd asked her to jump, she would have said how high. 'He didn't do anything other than work on the app. I did everything at home. On top of that, I was also working on the app and at one point, I had two other jobs.'

'It doesn't sound like you were having too much fun with old Danny boy,' Jack replied and patted Lotta on her leg. 'Lott, he sounds like an idiot.' Jack then repeated what he'd said, adding a swear word.

Lotta sighed and squeezed her lips with her hand. 'I think the main idiot was me. I shouldn't have put up with it. Why would he have behaved any differently when he had someone tending to his every need? You live and learn.'

'You do,' Jack said, touching Lotta gently on the arm. 'You're well rid of anyone like that in your life. Now you have moi. I am here to serve you,' Jack jested.

Half an hour or so later, they'd stopped at the off-licence and had arrived at Pretty Beach to the Breakers to the smell of the spicy pork wafting out onto the driveway.

Once they were inside, Lotta had showered, put her comfy clothes on, and poured herself a white wine spritzer. She'd walked down the path through the overgrown garden, past the boathouse and all the way to a little suntrap at the end. Surrounded by climbing roses going up and over the old side wall, she plonked herself down on an old timber outdoor chair and sighed. Holding her head up to the sky, she took in long breaths in and out, felt the sea air on her face, and then let her eyes drift up to the back of the house. Pretty Beach to the Breakers somehow didn't seem to look as sad and unloved as it had done when she'd first arrived. The chimneys were still wonky, and the garden was still mostly overgrown and needing work, but her effort here and there was beginning to show. The windows were clean and sparkly, the abandoned gardening tools and water barrels had been cleared away, and the hanging baskets full of dead plants and weeds now swayed back and forth happily full of actual live plants. She wasn't sure how she'd kept them alive, but they weren't dead, so it worked for her.

Jack came out of the French conservatory doors with a beer in his hand. He strolled down the path in a t-shirt and low-waisted grey tracksuit bottoms. Not that Lotta noticed, of course, how low the bottoms were slung or that a very taut set of abs was on show. There was no way she was interested in that. Jack sat down beside her and followed her gaze, which she had quickly averted from the lowness of his trackies back to the chimneys.

'Penny for them,' Jack asked as he took a swig of his beer.

Lotta shook her head. *Abs. Things near abs.* 'Nothing really. I was just thinking something a bit ridiculous.' She nodded towards the house. 'It's like me. It seems happier now. Maybe it's just me being weird. When I arrived here it was so, well, I don't know, so uncared for and unloved.'

'It was. Remember that red carpet?'

Lotta chuckled. 'Who could forget that beauty? Crikey, that thing was hideous.'

'It was that. Weighed a tonne too.'

'It's lovely being here. I'm so pleased I took the leap.'

'Not as much as I am.'

Lotta chuckled as she felt a whoosh of something delicious rush through her veins. 'You're full of all the nice words today.'

'Ha! Do you want me to be horrible to you? Do you want Grumpy Jack?'

'I *did* quite like him.'

Jack rubbed Lotta on the leg and turned to look at her. 'I'll bring him back just for this evening.'

Lotta chuckled. 'I've never had a better offer.'

'It seems like the bar was set quite low by the one named Dan.'

'Yeah, the only way is up.'

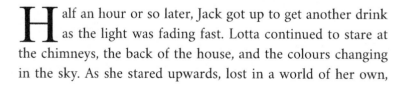

Half an hour or so later, Jack got up to get another drink as the light was fading fast. Lotta continued to stare at the chimneys, the back of the house, and the colours changing in the sky. As she stared upwards, lost in a world of her own,

Jack's phone, which was on the arm of his chair, flashed with a notification.

Out of interest, she glanced over and then squinted. She could see a few words and someone named Sam. As she read the first line of the text without thinking, she frowned. Jack hadn't mentioned anyone named Sam, and what she could see of the message made her blood run cold. Sam apparently really missed Jack. There was also a kiss. As Jack walked back down the path and then sat down, Lotta nodded towards his phone. 'There was a notification on your phone. It lit up.'

'Oh, was there?' Jack said, picking up his phone. He glanced at it and then hastily put it into his pocket.

'Who's that messaging you on a Friday night?' Lotta asked, keeping her voice as nonchalant and casual as she could muster.

'Oh, it's nothing,' Jack said quickly with a dismissive tone to his voice.

Lotta didn't say anything. Now she was really wondering who the message was from. Sam and a kiss? What was going on with that?

14

The next day, Lotta had not thought too much about the message she had seen on Jack's phone and had spent most of the morning in the library room reading and doing reading-related posts for her social media account. It was a beautiful day with all the windows and doors open, and a lovely fresh breeze rushing through the old house.

After seeing a post for the Farmers Market on the Pretty Beach community page, Lotta had messaged Liv to see if she wanted to go. Liv had replied with a thumbs up and Lotta was looking forward to getting some sea air, having a stroll around Pretty Beach, and an amble through the stalls. Before that, she'd calculated that with Liv's estimated time of arrival, she just had time for a read in the bath.

Whilst she unloaded the dishwasher and sprayed the sides in the kitchen, Lotta turned on the taps on the bathtub in the wonky bathroom just off the utility room. Pouring in a huge handful of magnesium as the water gushed into the tub, she sighed at her lovely easy day. Pottering around whilst the bath ran, she fetched a book from the library room and made a milky coffee. She may have sloshed in a tiny plop of Xian's Special

Drink which Xian had secretly slipped her – it was a weekend day, after all. With her coffee in hand, she then stood by the side of the bath, waiting for it to slowly fill up and then stepped in, sinking down into the soft hot water.

As she let it wash over, she let out a long, deep, contented exhale. Closing her eyes and leaning her head back, she thought about her mum in Singapore. She'd called much earlier that morning, but Dave had answered and told her that her mum was in bed. Lotta's mum had always spent a lot of time in bed or comatose on the sofa. Or lying on the kitchen floor. Lotta had taken Dave's resigned and loaded words that Lotta's mum being in bed meant that she had been drinking, but neither of them had mentioned that. She sighed. Not even a heart attack would stop her mum from continuing down the same road. Why was Lotta even surprised? She'd been here in some form or another many times before.

Sinking down further, she sloshed water over the back of her neck, reached forward for her book, and with her right hand held it out in front of her. There was not a whole lot she could do if her mum didn't want to talk to her and wouldn't accept anyone's help. As had been the case her whole life, her mum was concerned with one thing and one thing only; herself and the bottom of a bottle of vodka. It had never occurred to Lotta's mum in the slightest that Lotta might be concerned, or that Lotta might also need a bit of support. Mostly, what Lotta's mum was preoccupied with was where she was going to get her next drink. It was why she'd fallen out with the whole of her family and why no one any longer had anything to do with her. Lotta, and very rarely sometimes Liv, were the only two left.

Trying not to think about it, Lotta forced her brain to get lost in the words of her book. Once she'd read for a while and just in time not to be late for Liv, she pulled the plug, watched the side of the bath as the water went down, got out, and got dried. Pulling her hair up into a knot on the top of her head, she sprayed the whole lot with hairspray and chuckled as she put on earrings with tiny little gold books dangling on the ends. With a quick layer of foundation, a touch of mascara, and a fluff of blusher, she looked at herself in the mirror. What had happened to the tired Lotta who had arrived in Pretty Beach so very jaded from an entrepreneur and his ridiculous app? That Lotta was gone. This Lotta was taking care of herself. She was so much brighter, despite the situation and worry about her mum. This Lotta had been transformed.

With a little bit of a buzz from her lovely morning and trying to convince herself that her mum would be okay, she stepped into turned-up jeans, a ruffle front blouse and white trainers. Putting her Kindle in a French market basket that had been hanging from the end of the bannister in the hallway, she opened the huge old front door and studied the sky. A beautiful blue Pretty Beach day without even a hint of a cloud. She'd had worse weekends in her life. As she stood on the front step looking at the weather, Liv arrived on the driveway.

'Perfect timing!' Lotta said as Liv got out of her car. 'How are you? Lovely day for it.'

'I am feeling full of the joys,' Liv said with a beam. 'What a gorgeous day to go to a market. The sun is shining for us, Lott.' Liv pointed to Lotta's French basket. 'I see you're well-equipped. No book bag?'

'Don't worry, I have my Kindle in here.' Lotta chuckled, tapping the basket.

Liv squinted and looked Lotta up and down. 'Blimey, Lott. What's happened to you? You're looking more and more like the old you every time I see you!'

'It's the glow-up,' Lotta said with a small smile. 'I'm still working on it. It's the financial stuff, I think. It's taken such a load off my mind. I finally feel as if I might be able to climb my way out of the Dan and his app years.'

'Yeah, it must be a nice feeling,' Liv noted. 'You really do look and seem so much better.'

'I *feel* better. For the first time in a very long time, I feel in control and I feel worthy. I feel like I'm doing something that matters, even if it's just to me.'

'Yep. I never doubted you, but those dead-end jobs were awful.'

'Yeah. My new career path is a breath of fresh air,' Lotta agreed.

'You're doing grand, Lott. You should be very proud of yourself and don't let yourself forget it.'

'Thank you. You've helped me so much, don't you forget that either.' Lotta chuckled.

'Ha. Right, enough of this soppiness. Let's go market strolling, shall we? Could there be anything much better than ambling around Pretty Beach on a beautiful day in the sunshine and sea air?'

'Not much,' Lotta agreed.

'Cinnamon buns and a coffee on the way there?' Liv asked.

'Sounds like a plan.'

Strolling along chatting, they stopped at the bakery in the laneway, waited in the queue snaking out the door, and left with takeaway coffees and a bag of LO cinnamon buns. Heading to the Farmers Market, they chatted and Lotta let out a long, deep exhale as she took in the bustling market filled with Pretty Beach locals.

Liv's eyes widened as they arrived at the first of the stalls. 'Ooh, this looks like my kind of market. Everything is so pretty.'

Lotta squinted down a long aisle of matching stalls, their white awnings edged with pastel pink and blue scalloped bunting rustling in the sea breeze. Each stall, beautifully set up and adhering to the Pretty Beach bylaw colours Lotta had read about, made for an amazing sight. They started to mooch down the aisle and began to weave in and out of people, strolled along stopping here and there to look at stalls, and said hello to the odd person as they passed by.

Ambling along in companionable silence, they happily mooched through the market. As with everything in Pretty Beach, the market surpassed their expectations; a dodgy market with stolen goods and old blue awnings it was not. Beautiful stalls, each identical apart from their differing pastel livery, snaked away into the distance and pastel bunting was strung between anything that didn't move. Lotta wide-eyed to Liv as they came upon Pretty Beach Herbs, where stacks of huge white pots held bunches of greenery which scented the surroundings. Lotta stood sipping on her coffee, just gazing at pots over-spilling with parsley, rosemary, and thyme. She touched the edge of a white flour sack lining the table and smiled at a woman in a butcher's apron who was busily wrapping a huge pot of greenery in white paper.

She had to pinch herself as she strolled around in the sunshine with her coffee and chatted with Liv. The market and the strolling reminded her somehow of happier days when she'd been carefree and had first arrived to work in London. Then she had zipped around with a buzz and a feeling of excitement about her life. All those dreams and naive hopes had been zapped by Dan and his app, but now it seemed she was on a different path. A path where she was in control of her own destiny, and it all felt rather deliciously nice.

Just as they were walking away from the herb stall and Lotta was in possession of two pots of rosemary tucked into her basket, they bumped straight into Xian from the bakery. Xian was shuffling along with a pair of gigantic headphones lodged around her neck, electric pink sliders with socks, and a super-market carrier bag hooked over her arm. She wore a pair of reading glasses hanging around her neck and had a massive pot plant in her hands.

Xian's eyes lit up and her face broke into a smile as she saw Lotta. 'Hello! How are you?'

'Very well,' Lotta replied and turned to Liv. 'This is my cousin, Liv, I was telling you about. Liv, this is Xian.'

Xian struggled with the pot plant, juggling it into the crook of her arm and held out her hand. 'So nice to meet you.'

'Xian is Holly's mum. The one who loaned me the jewellery for the ball,' Lotta explained.

'Ahh right! I see. Nice to meet you.' Liv beamed.

Lotta could feel Liv's body language change as Xian, in one swift move, whilst balancing the pot plant in her arm, slipped a small silver flask from her pocket, put it to her lips and swigged. Not missing a beat, she continued, 'Yes, likewise. Popped down for the weekend, have you?' Xian's eyes flicked up towards the sky. 'Lovely weather for it.'

'It is!' Liv replied. 'I've just popped down for the morning, actually. I live in Newport.'

Xian smiled. 'Nice part of the world.'

'Yes.' Liv gesticulated around at the market. 'I don't think much beats this, though. Pretty Beach takes markets up a notch in my book. Everything is just so lovely.'

Xian swigged the flask again and cackled. 'Well, we do everything well here, especially if my daughter is in charge. Which she is. Woe betide you if you even think about bringing a dodgy old tarpaulin into this market. Your life wouldn't be worth living.'

Inside, Lotta was mildly alarmed at the look on Xian's face. She was still getting used to and learning the intricacies of this funny little town by the sea. 'I don't think I'll be getting a stall anytime soon, so I'm safe.'

Xian looked around. 'Oh, I don't know. We could do with a little bookstall, don't you think?'

Liv chuckled. 'Oh, don't encourage her to buy any more

books, Xian! She already has loads of them, and she thinks we don't know about her secret storage unit full of them.'

'I don't know what you're talking about,' Lotta said, giggling.

Xian cackled. 'Are you still thinking about doing something with that old building down the back of your place?' Xian asked, her eyebrows raised in question.

'Hmm. Yes, I've decided to take my social media account about reading a bit more professionally and then go from there with the building. We'll see what happens.'

'Sounds good to me.' Xian nodded. 'It's the way of the world these days. I love my Facebook groups. They have told me a lot about dealing.'

'I can imagine.'

'Oh yes, indeed.' Xian nodded.

Lotta continued, 'It'll be quite a lot of work, and I'll have to spend a bit of money on it. We'll see what happens, though. I'm a bit nervous about it, but if you don't try you don't know, do you?'

'Let us know if we can help at all. Holly knows just about every tradesperson known to man around here.'

'Oh, right, thanks,' Lotta replied, beaming. 'Will do.'

There was a loud buzzing from a ringtone coming out of Xian's pocket. She fumbled quickly to get her phone out and held up her phone and waved it. 'See you. I need to get this. I'm doing a deal at the moment. Duty calls.'

'See you, Xian,' Lotta said, and they watched as she shuffled off past them.

Liv shook her head. 'Blimey. What in the world?'

'I know.'

'Sorry, but what was she swigging from that flask?' Liv giggled.

'Good question. I'm not sure anyone knows. She left me some of it when they came with the jewellery. I may have had some in my coffee this morning. It really wasn't very nice. It nearly blew my socks off.'

'She's legit walking along drinking.' Liv laughed. 'In the middle of the day.'

'Yup. She lives on the stuff, apparently.'

'We need to get hold of it and sell it. It clearly hits the mark.'

'Lol. You'll be lucky. Word on the street is that the recipe is held under lock and key.'

'Too funny.' Liv took a sip of her coffee. 'Gosh, this place is lovely.'

'Tell me about it.'

'I bet you're so pleased you moved here,' Liv stated.

Lotta nodded. Never had a truer word been said.

15

It was the day after Lotta had worked three full and long days in the arcade in Newport. She'd set her alarm to get up at the crack of dawn, had worked for a good few hours and had planned the rest of her day to get on with her other jobs; growing her reading account and working on the reading retreat. After tidying the kitchen and making a cup of tea, she picked up her mug, walked through the conservatory, and stepped out into the garden. The garden glistened from an overnight downpour, and a tree branch from the cherry tree by the back door dripped water onto the terrace. The old twisted wisteria climbing up the wall at the back of the house rustled in the sea breeze, and the rain smell seemed to seep into Lotta's bones as she walked through the middle of the garden, past the old clinker boats to the personal entrance gate tucked into the wall at the side.

Yanking the bolt across the top of the gate to the narrow lane at the back, she stepped outside with her mug of tea in her hand. Standing with her eyes squinted towards Pretty Beach to the Breakers and the old building by the boathouse, she tried to imagine what it would be like to have people stopping there for a reading retreat. Would it be weird to have part of the garden rented out? Would she feel uncomfortable? As she stood musing, a dog barked in the distance, and a sweet little cat gingerly tiptoed along the neighbour's wall and then sat perfectly upright, everything tucked in, eyeing Lotta with a look of half amusement, half disdain.

Lotta gazed up at the house and wondered if it would be her forever home. Would she settle here for a long time? Would she start to forget about ideas of a life in publishing and the zippy bookworm Lotta who flitted around in London all tickety-boo? Would, dare she even think it, there be a future here for not only her but for her *and* Jack? It all seemed both huge and not at the same time.

With her mind decompressing, she perched on the corner of the wall with her hands cupped around her mug and sat thinking about everything that had happened to her. In a mere few months, her life had gone from having no hope and only just keeping her head above water, to her feeling as if she was in control. The most important change had been her new job. The steadiness of the income had made her feel more comfortable than she had been in a long time.

Until she'd seen the money come in with her first salary payment, she'd not realised how emotionally tied up she'd been in debt. Pretty Beach to the Breakers and her new job had released a valve and given her a breather, and it felt all sorts of good. She realised as she sat gazing at the house, that before she'd moved to the coast, every waking moment had involved thinking about or worrying about money. Previous to that, it had been about sinking money into Dan's app.

She couldn't stop her mind from straying into Dan territory; oh, how he had promised her all sorts. They would be rich. So rich. She wouldn't only have a country house in Sussex, she'd be able to have a house pretty much anywhere she fancied. There would be a yacht. She'd be able to buy books galore as he had promised. Heck, he'd buy her a book-shop if she'd been so inclined. In the future, he'd said, of course. If only she didn't mind cleaning a few office blocks at night, just until he was up and running. If only she could ensure his emotional needs were met. Could she just make sure he had a selection of fresh vegetables with his dinner so his nutrition was fine-tuned like a machine? *Pah. What an absolute idiot,* she thought, and not only about Dan, but also about herself. How had she been so blinkered? How had she stayed so long?

She looked at the boathouse building, flicked on her phone, and examined both her bank account and the amount on her credit card. It made her shudder. She opened her notes and looked at her workings regarding her finances; there was no complicated spreadsheet or app, it was a quite simple equation of credits and debits. Looking down at her phone and then up at the outbuilding, she knew an extra income, just like it had with the app, would be a game-changer. If she could find a way to make the building and her reading account give her a second income, the credit side of the equation would look a whole lot on the healthier side. She nodded to herself and picked up her mug. She was going to give it a go, or at least try to.

Once back inside, she was determined to crack on with her day and get started on the next part of her transformation plan to get the library room shipshape and ready for her first paid influencer work. After she had sent her rate card to the publisher she'd had an online meeting with them, and her first paid book review was lined up and she needed the library room to be swoon-worthy for her live broadcast.

First housework, then bookworm work. After vacuuming the whole house, mopping the kitchen floor, and cleaning the bathroom, she stood in the library room with her umpteenth mug of tea of the day contemplating. It was very tempting to collapse on the velvet sofa with a book and let money take care of itself, but she was not going to give in. It was time to take the library room up a notch. Time to get to work.

Putting her cup of tea on the mantelpiece, she stood back, held up her phone and checked how the library room looked through a lens and how it appeared to her followers. She adjusted a vase on the windowsill a millimetre to the left, stood back, and then with her head cocked to the side, mused what to do to cosy the room up even further. It was lovely, but she wanted it to be Pinterest-level wow.

Ten minutes later, she was standing in the garage, surrounded by piles of junk and old furniture, hoping for inspiration. She didn't know where to look first as she stood in the dust. Everything seemed old and daunting. Piles of chairs slotted upside down on top of each other and an old mirror leant precariously by the back wall. Three rows of cardboard boxes were stacked up to the roof. Right at the back she spied two armchairs, their cushions piled up beside them. Gingerly picking her way over all sorts of paraphernalia, clouds of dust billowed up into the air. Finally reaching the old chairs perched between a bedhead and a dusty stack of puzzles, Lotta peered at two once-white slipcovered armchairs. They were most definitely no longer white. She touched the piped edges on one of the arms and sighed at the brown debris that had dropped from the roof down onto the seat. Crouching down, she sniffed the seat pad. Not too bad. Most definitely needing a clean and an air, but miraculously no damp or mould smell. The chairs could work in the library room.

Lotta turned around and looked towards the door. She was completely surrounded by junk and wondered how she was ever going to get the chair from the garage to the house on her own. Taking her phone out of her pocket, she thought about calling Jack, thought better of it, and decided to have a go at it herself. She didn't need anyone to help her. She wanted to do it herself. She mused how she was going to make a path to the door and how she was going to get the chairs in the house. Half an hour later, she had cleared a pathway to the door and, covered in dust, old cobwebs, and dirt, she'd dragged, pushed, heaved, and pulled one of the chairs until it was out of the garage and on the terrace. Covered in grime, sweating, and pledging to start going to a gym, she continued to push and shove for all she was worth.

Once the chair was in the hallway with more huffing and puffing, she changed her plan. There was no way she was going through that scenario with the other chair. She'd leave that for another day.

With the chair sitting in the hallway, she knelt down and examined the stains on the cover and slowly began to ease the thick white fabric from the frame. Underneath, she was pleasantly surprised. Though the cover would need its fair share of stain removal, the seat pad and chair itself were in surprisingly good condition.

Virtually skipping back out to the garage, she shimmied in and out through the piles of old furniture and junk, pulled the cover from the other chair, went into the house, and took both covers into the utility room. Filling the old sink with hot water, she poured in detergent, plonked in the slipcovers, and as the hot water bubbled up, she pushed the fabric down into the water with a wooden spoon. A few hours or so later, the slipcovers had been soaked twice, had been through a hot wash, and were flying high up above the garden on the old pulley washing line.

Sitting underneath them, perched on the edge of the terrace with a sandwich and a glass of orange juice and her Kindle held out in front of her, Lotta took her eyes away from her book for a second and looked up towards the washing line. A blue sky peppered with clouds looked back at her as she watched the white slipcovers blowing back and forth in the wind. Not a bad few hours' work. She smiled to herself as she heard the ferry horn go off in the distance. Part of her had to pinch herself that this was her life now.

In an instant, she was suddenly flashed back to the grotty hotel she'd lived in for a few weeks when she'd not been able to find a job. She remembered the television bolted to the cabinetry and the industrial-sized plastic body wash container screwed to the wall. She shuddered at the memory of the grey-white threadbare towels and the revolting terracotta-red runner on the end of the bed. She shivered, so pleased she wasn't there now. She might have a while to go until she was out of the woods on the debt front, but she was a very long way from the day when she'd had to wash her dress in the hotel sink. It felt good to be in this new place, pushing old chairs up overgrown paths.

After getting lost in her book whilst she finished her lunch, she wound the rope on the pulley washing line and nodded to herself as she unpegged the slipcovers from the line. She'd come a long way from the hotel and the days when her brain had been suffocated by memories of entrepreneurs with ridiculous apps.

The slipcovers had still been damp when she'd brought them in, so she'd hung one of them up in the airing cupboard and, not wanting to hang around any further, had hoped that ironing dry the other one would work. It had just about done the trick, and once she'd pulled and pushed the slipcover back into place, she dragged the chair into the library room and pushed it over into the corner not far from her desk.

She then spent a bit of time poring over Pinterest, looking at pictures of libraries and studies. By the time she'd recovered from falling down a vortex of house lusting, she didn't know where to start first. The library was already lovely; her books surrounded her, the old velvet sofa was doing its thing, the floorboards gave the place a soft muted feel, and the fireplace was amazing. However, Pinterest was telling her she needed next-level decor; she needed fairy lights by the dozen, jugs, flowers, jars, and candlesticks. All the things to up the ante and push her reading from the library and her book reviews to a whole new level.

Five minutes later, she found herself back in the garage. Ten minutes after that, she was carrying an old standard lamp with a pleated silk lampshade, a vintage fruit crate, a huge rush fisherman's basket, and a terracotta plant pot, and was on her way back to the library room.

By the end of the afternoon, Lotta had been out to relieve herself of money to buy fairy lights and was standing on top of a ladder, wobbling precariously. She'd seen a picture of fairy lights strung across the entire top of library shelving and had loved how it had looked. Actually, making it happen had been another matter altogether.

Lotta pottered around adding bits and pieces. By its nature, the room was always going to be a work in progress, but it felt a whole lot cosier than when she'd first moved in when she'd been despondent about just about everything in her life. She shook her head as she looked around at the transformation. The once-empty bookshelves she'd inherited lined the walls and were now filled with a wild array of titles and her most treasured possessions. She ran her fingers along the shelves and touched a few spines; a kaleidoscope of colours and textures. Old and worn, some new and vibrant, and everything else in between. As she surveyed her handiwork, she almost purred in pleasure. It was as if behind the books, the entire room was alive with stories and book friends, new places to go and adventures to begin. A whole mix of reading waiting to be discovered.

She patted the back of the white linen-covered chair, which was now sitting in a grouping by the window. A little round table with a pile of books sat to its side and the standard lamp with the pleated shade was tucked up next to it. On the blue velvet sofa, a plump line of mismatched cushions welcomed a sit-down and an invitation to stay a while. The floor-to-ceiling windows let in the soft coastal light of early evening, and the seaside air filled the room. Lotta sighed contentedly and stepped back to take in the full effect of what she'd created from more or less a cobbled-together collection of things from the garage and bits and bobs from her life. It all somehow just slotted in and worked. It felt like a haven; a soft, cushioned safe place, somewhere to take refuge from the real world outside.

She shook her head, almost in disbelief. Right there in front of her eyes was the Sussex cottage of her dreams transplanted to the library room of Pretty Beach to the Breakers. It was not just exactly how she had envisioned it; it was much, much better. Mostly it was better because her old dream had included Dan, but this dream she had obtained by herself. She was independent, happy, and in control. And goodness did that feel good.

She was humming happily to herself, moving books around on the coffee table when her phone rang. She pulled it out of her pocket and saw Jack's name on the screen. She smiled, felt her heart jump, and answered the call, her voice bright and cheerful. 'Hello, how are you?'

'Hi, sweetheart,' Jack replied. 'How are you getting on with the library room?'

Lotta chuckled at him calling her sweetheart. It had become a bit of a running joke between them when she'd told him she'd abhorred Dan calling her 'love', but she'd never been brave enough to tell him. Jack had started calling her sweetheart as a joke and it had stuck. 'You're funny. It's going *very* well. I've been on the go all day, but I'm almost finished. It's looking great. I wanted to take it up a level in the library for the book review, and well, I think I've only gone and done it. My back may regret it, but go me.'

Jack laughed. 'I can't wait to see it in the flesh. Not that I'll be reading a book in there. More like watching the football.'

Lotta laughed back. 'You can do whatever you like in here as far as I'm concerned. It can be a room of many things.'

'What about the building renovation? Any further thoughts on that?' Jack asked. 'You said you might go and have a bit of an investigation out there today.'

'Yeah, I went out there earlier with a cup of tea. I did a few numbers and figures. The extra income would really accelerate paying off the credit card. I need to stop talking about it and make it happen. I wanted to get the library room done first.'

'Have you thought about a name for it? Something along Xian's idea for a reading retreat.'

Lotta paused. She hadn't thought any further about what she was going to do in the building or what she was going to call it. She had been so focused on how much work was involved that a name hadn't even properly crossed her mind.

'No, not yet,' she replied. 'I'm sure I'll come up with something eventually. What do you think? Any ideas?'

Jack thought for a moment. 'I don't know. Book Lovers Retreat? Err, yeah, names and creative things are not my strong point. It'll probably come to us once it's done up and ready.'

Lotta smiled. 'I hope so. The more I think about it, the more I just want to sort of recreate this out there.' She waved her hand and gesticulated around the room even though Jack couldn't see what she was doing.

'Yeah. Pretty Beach Book Retreat.'

Lotta repeated softly what Jack had said back to him. 'Hmm. Not sure.'

'Need to keep working and thinking on that one.'

'Yep,' Lotta agreed. 'I really do want to do something with this place. I want to make it magical.' Her voice was filled with hope.

Jack was silent for a moment. 'It won't take long if we knuckle down.'

Lotta was filled with all sorts of fuzzies as she listened to Jack discussing what they would do first. She loved how he just naturally included himself in her plan to get a second income so she could pay off her debt. She felt so lucky to have someone like Jack; it almost made her feel sick. It *did* make her feel sick. Not prawn vol-au-vent sick, lovesick.

'Thank you for, you know, being in all this with me,' she said. 'I'm so glad you're helping me. It really means a lot.'

'I'll want payment,' Jack deadpanned.

'Happy to oblige,' Lotta bantered.

'Rightio. I'll see you later then. If we're going to be working, I'll bring something easy for dinner, shall I? I can cook, up to you.'

Lotta was very used to being asked what was for dinner. She wasn't used at all to being offered help. 'Already sorted,' she stated.

'What? I like you as a boss,' Jack joked. 'You are a star, you know that, Lott? I don't mind working with you when you feed me as you do.'

Lotta also wasn't used to someone being nice. It almost felt too good to be true. It was as if she was waiting for Jack to announce that he was going to do a start-up and start designing an app just to bring her back to earth with a bump.

'As I said, I want payment for my DIY grafting with very nice things,' Jack bantered. 'Right, I need to get back to my *actual* work. It's like a zoo in here today and loads of things have gone wrong. Anyway, see you this evening. Be ready. We have a retreat to create.'

16

The following week, the smell of a chicken roasting surrounded by slices of lemon and cloves of garlic wafted around Pretty Beach to the Breakers. As Lotta walked out of the library room and into the kitchen, she inhaled its cosy, comforting smell. Opening the oven, she gave the chicken's crispy skin a satisfying poke and pulled out a pan lined with roast potatoes. The potatoes had been cooked in dripping she'd saved from the week before and a healthy dose of sea salt from Essex. Low calorie they were not. Everything about the aromas emanating from the oven made her feel good. Cooking something nice in Pretty Beach to the Breakers made her feel like she was home. Mostly, it made her feel safe. Was there anything better than a cheeky mid-week roast? She thought not. It wasn't a proper roast as such, more like what she called in her head a cheat's roast. It involved little more than putting a lemon in a chicken, throwing a few herbs around with abandon, and parboiling a few potatoes.

Truth be known, her cheat's roast had come to be in a fit of invention one night in the Dan and the app days. The same days when Dan had assumed, as he sat with a pre-dinner drink, that

115

his supper just appeared on the table as if by magic. As she shook the potatoes around the tray, she remembered the day when she'd arrived back to their London flat exhausted from a day's cleaning and Dan, and his inherited misogyny, had raised his eyebrows in expectation at what was for dinner. She'd dutifully panicked, flung open the fridge, and scrambled her brain on what she was going to cook. She'd shoved a whole chicken in the oven and quickly chopped some potatoes and slung them in beside it. The potatoes in that cheat's roast had involved a quick chopping and the skin was most definitely on.

She thought about how different it was with Jack. Jack was so far removed from Dan, it was like chalk and cheese. She chuckled to herself. Jack, therefore, had parboiled, skinless roasties lovingly cooked in pork fat. Once she'd got her act together and her finances improved, the pork would be changing to duck. Life goals.

Shooing thoughts of Dan, who was of no interest to her whatsoever, out of her head, she inhaled the garlic-y, lemon-y, chicken-y smell and sighed. She loved that smell. The sweet scent of comfort, of home, and security. A simple chicken in the oven, coupled with potatoes roasting away and filling the place with a happy fog, was doing something to make Lotta feel all the feels.

The ringtone for Liv started buzzing in her pocket as she continued pottering around the kitchen. She settled herself down at the breakfast room table, pressed to accept the video call, and waited for Liv's face to appear on her screen.

'Hey! How are you?' Liv asked. 'You look good. Really well.'

'Thank you. So do you.' Lotta squinted into the screen. 'You're glowing, Liv. What have you been doing?'

Liv looked a bit shifty and screwed up her face. 'Nothing. Just working.'

Lotta laughed, holding her phone closer. 'Are you sure? What are you up to?'

'No, no, nothing at all.' Liv smiled and turned her phone around. 'I just got home from work and I thought I would have a quick check in with you and see how you got on with the library before the big day of the influencer work tomorrow.'

'Very well. I am now endowed with fairy lights and I have another chair in there. I found it in the garage. Do not ask me how I got it out of there on my own, but somehow I managed it,' Lotta said. 'There was a lot of huffing and puffing involved.'

'Blimey. What else are you going to find in that garage? It's a goldmine.'

'Dunno, but right now it's working for me. There's a hundred years' worth of old furniture in there, and I don't have much else at my disposal if I'm going to get this credit card balance cleared at some point or another.'

'Hmm. Just be careful lugging around stuff. You don't want to do your back in. That's the last thing you need at the moment, what with the job and everything,' Liv advised, her voice brimming with concern.

'No, all good. I only moved one because I thought the same. Anyway, yes, so I'm all set. A bit nervous, but I'll be fine once I get going on it.'

'You don't need to be nervous. Trust me, they will lap it up.'

'I hope so.'

'It's not like you've got a lot to lose,' Liv said, chuckling. 'You did nothing with that account before anyway.'

'Yeah, good point.'

'Have you heard anything more from your mum or Dave?'

'No, have you?'

'Nope. She's not replied to my message. I didn't think she would.'

'I've phoned three times over the past few days and had no answer. I've messaged every day and had one-word answers back. There's not a lot more I can do.'

'No. It is what it is.' Liv sighed resignedly. 'We've been here before.'

'Yup. Many times.'

Liv changed the subject. 'What else is going on? How's lovely Jack?'

'Lovely Jack is more lovely than ever. He's been over to help out with the back, and he's coming over tonight to do a bit more.'

'I bet that's not the only reason he's coming over,' Liv joked.

'Of course not.'

'I also bet you're cooking something nice.'

'I am.'

'Is it a cosy roast moment? Or a cheat's roast? Are the potatoes parboiled?' Liv clarified with a chuckle.

'The very one.'

Liv laughed, and then her face turned more serious. 'All joking aside. How is it with Jack? It's all moving very fast.'

Lotta squeezed her nose for a second and flicked her eyes up in contemplation. 'Honestly, it's better than I could ever have hoped.' She hid a little shudder from Liv as she thought about the text she'd seen on Jack's phone from someone going by the name of Sam. She'd done the best she could to forget that. It was better than she'd hoped, apart from that. She'd decided, though, to put the message totally to the back of her mind. He wouldn't be around her and seeing her as often as he was and agreeing to help with things if he was being dishonest, would he? She felt a horrible tenseness in her stomach as she tried to convince herself that the text was nothing. She proceeded to reiterate that everything with Jack was great, dug a hole, popped the text in and buried it deep. She'd not even think about it. It would be fine.

17

Lotta moved a huge jug of roses an inch on the shelf behind her in the library room and then picked the whole thing up and popped it on the coffee table. She then straightened a pile of books and turned a candle around so its label didn't show. Looking at the book in front of her with anticipation, she shuddered at the thought of going onto her account and doing the live review for the publishing house. She felt so nervous and so anxious that her stomach was churning, and her palms were sweaty. It wasn't as if she'd never done a live review before, in fact, she'd done loads. It was more that she was being paid for this one. She shivered at the premise that her followers wouldn't like it and bristled at the thought of getting tongue-tied. The concept of saying something wrong or making a mistake made her fidget on the sofa.

Taking a deep breath to try to calm her nerves, she tipped her head back and closed her eyes. There were a lot worse things and jobs she had done than sitting surrounded by books, reviewing a book she loved. She knew that she could do the review, it wasn't that; over the years, she'd done dozens of the things and had been doing similar things for years. It's just that none of them had been paid and all of them had been a hobby.

She thought about her account's following – it had started in the early days when, on a whim, she'd published a book blog. On the blog, she'd documented her views on the books she'd read and her TBR piles for all the world to see. It had taken off from day one, and Lotta had never really considered much about it all other than people loved her reviews and always commented on her posts. If there was one thing Lotta had learnt over the years from her blog days, it was that where reading was concerned, boy did she know her stuff. She knew that her followers knew that too, and now they were following this part in her journey where she had a library room to read her TBR pile, and according to her direct messages, they were loving it almost as much as she was. She talked herself up silently in her head. All she needed to do was just relax and let her love of books do the talking.

She looked around her at the library room. The spines of her books alone told her the stories inside. They stood colour coded and in sections, and she knew exactly where everything was. In between her books, she'd propped little things here and there that made her feel happy; a picture of her and Liv on Liv's wedding day, an old lamp she'd found in a charity shop nestled between her favourite cookery books, a little jug filled with things from the garden. As she looked around at her books, she started to feel her shoulders loosen just a tiny bit. Her books were like her friends, all of them special to her in some way. They were the stories that had helped her through tough times, taken her to other places, and softened her fall in lots of areas of her life. Some had inspired her, some had made her laugh, and some had made her blub for days. Some, she was well aware, had saved her from dropping down into a place no one wanted to be. Most of all, she loved delving into her books and landing in a place where she felt alive.

As she looked along the shelves, she realised that she didn't really need to be worried. She was among her book friends anyway, just as she always was. She turned over the book she was about to review – a contemporary romance book she'd absolutely ploughed through in less than a day. She didn't really need more than that to tell her that the book and the writer were on form. When that happened, she knew she liked a book.

She pressed the button on her phone to start the live, and saw the shelves and the fairy lights behind her looking back at her from the screen. Taking a deep breath, she peered into the little circle at the top of the screen, smiled, picked up the book, made one of her usual jokes and she was off. As the comments and hearts started to come in, she felt herself relax. So far, so good.

Lotta opened the book and began to read some of the things she'd highlighted. She talked about the themes and characters in the story and heard herself veering off here and there into things the book had made her feel and think. How she'd loved it on her first speed read, and how it had accompanied her for its second read on her lunch at work and on an afternoon at the beach. As she continued to talk into the camera, all her nerves were gone, and she felt as if it was just her and the book and her followers discussing what they loved. On her account, not just when she was actually reading the book, she was lost in a world garnered by someone's words.

Simultaneously reading and answering comments as the review came to an end, she heard herself speaking, 'I really hope you've all enjoyed my review this evening. If you haven't read the book yet, I highly recommend it.' She paused for a second as she read some of the comments. There were lots of requests for more lives in the library room and questions about the makeover. People also wanted to see more of what she'd done. She moved out of the way of the screen, let the camera focus on the shelves, and smiled as more comments came flooding in.

Then she flipped the camera and panned around the room. What looked back at her made her feel warm and cosy; the fireplace dressed in a big vase of flowers and the Fortnum and Mason basket she'd found in the house when she'd first moved in was propped to the side. Strings of fairy lights lit up the bookshelves, and a huge glass vase was filled with pebbles and things she'd found on her morning strolls by the sea. Everything was just right.

After lots of compliments on the library room and finishing the tour of the room, Lotta ended the session and put her phone on the table. She was mentally spent and totally exhausted. She was also over the moon.

Opening the library door and heading to the kitchen, she couldn't quite believe it. Not only had she done the sponsored post, but it had gone well. She had just been paid to review a book, and what's more, it was what she *really* thought about the book and not some publishing house's PR spiel.

As she opened the fridge and poured herself a white wine spritzer, she smiled. Another big step forward in her journey. Another part of her transformation. She was buzzing, it felt so good.

She looked around the breakfast room and then out towards the conservatory, taking it all in. She had come a long way. She'd picked herself up, dusted herself off, and made good of the cards she had been dealt in life. She could barely take the smile off her face as she sipped on the wine and pottered around the kitchen. She was feeling grateful for everything; for her new job, for Pretty Beach to the Breakers, for Jack, for the silly green fascinator she'd worn when she'd first met him, and for the fact that she ended up in Pretty Beach. But more than that she was grateful for her books. From the moment she'd learnt to read, they had brought so much into her life. And here she was, working them into a way to include them in her work. Just as she'd always wanted to. As Lotta sat down at the breakfast room table with her wineglass and a little bowl of olives, life had really never felt as good. Despite the niggling voices in the back of her head about the text she'd seen on Jack's phone and her worries about her mum, her world was looking up. Long may it last.

18

A week or so later, Lotta stared out the window at the city skyline as the fast train slowed down as it got closer to London. Lost in the moment, she remembered when she'd been driving the other way out of London to Pretty Beach, and how she'd felt her life would never recover. Now she was in a different relationship altogether.

She remembered the day when she'd begun to lose hope of ever getting a job in publishing when a taxi had sloshed dirty London water over her feet, and she'd been temporarily living in a hotel. In those grim, depressing days, she had never imagined that she might bump into Jack in a bookshop. Nor had it even entered her wildest imagination that she would go on a fake date with someone. Or that he would surprise her, and they would actually get together and be in a relationship.

Putting her Kindle down and leaning her head against the glass, Lotta felt the train tracks underneath, and warmth from the sun streaming through the window, and thought about her life. In her head, before she'd gotten the job in Newport Reef, she had imagined herself commuting from Pretty Beach up to London to a job in publishing. Today, here she was in a completely different industry and job altogether, learning new things, meeting new people, going to a meeting and going to visit Jack's offices for the first time. She was so very far from publishing but was loving it every step of the way.

She took a deep breath and closed her eyes at the day ahead. There was no denying how nervous she was; part of her threatened to be overwhelmed by a serious case of feeling inferior and nowhere near good enough. She was meeting Anne Fisher, her boss, and members of the wider team who did the same job as Lotta, but in other venues around the country. On top of that, all of them were going to lunch with the big bosses, who had flown in from overseas.

Lotta had a lot riding on the job and the day. She had taken to it from day one and was proving herself as good, if not better, than anyone else, but there was still a tiny part of her with imposter syndrome. Plus, there was another part of her who thought that it was all too good to be true. At the thought of sitting in a big fancy pants meeting, she felt her heart beat a little faster and her palms getting sweaty. She had no idea what her day was going to entail. Was she going to be able to perform, to say the right things, to look as if she had a clue what she was doing? She hoped so, she really did.

Ten minutes later, she was sitting on an underground train stuck in a tunnel. She tried to take her mind off her nerves and studied the other passengers as the train hummed and the lights flickered. She stared at the swaying hands and arms of commuters above her and then looked across to the seats opposite; a tall man was slouched in his seat, his oversized feet splayed out in front of him. The man beside him shifted in his seat, and then a stubby hand wandered to his mouth and scratched. On the end seat, a woman looked as if she had got dressed whilst half asleep and in a hurry; her suit jacket was rumpled, her skirt creased, and she had missed a button on her shirt so that an expanse of skin poked out from underneath.

Lotta felt mildly uncomfortable on the overfull, very hot, dirty train. When she'd zipped here and there all over London, she'd loved the tube. She'd relished going up and down the elevators, whizzing here and there on the train. Now with new eyes, it all seemed so very busy and full, and everything was washed in the grey tones of London grime.

Eventually, the train started to move again, pulled into the station, and she followed the instructions to the Corchrane offices. Once she'd got to the building and gone up in the lifts, she stepped out of the doors and had to steady herself. Just like the arcade, everything was styled and thought about to within an inch of its life. The reception was nothing short of breathtaking. This was not the office for people with imposter syndrome. She squelched the urge to run and checked herself in. The receptionist smiled warmly and welcomed Lotta, asking her to sit down while she let Anne know that she had arrived. Lotta sat down, looking around in awe at the beautiful old building. It was bigger than she had imagined, better than she imagined, and she realised with a gulp that she was sitting with successful people. Just like the tables she'd sat at many times at weddings with the successful people, it appeared that she was now not only amongst them but one of them. It seemed Lotta Button had jumped up a rung of the ladder of life. The rung felt both exciting and daunting at the same time. It was most definitely wobbling.

Hoping she looked the part, she sat with her feet tightly together and clutched the side of her Kindle through her bag. She suddenly remembered a reception she'd been sitting in at the beginning of the year. Then she'd watched in disgust as a woman with a blue streak in the front of her dark hair had dropped a chewing gum wrapper on the floor and totally disregarded Lotta entirely. Lotta had spent the interview and the rest of the day thinking that her life had reached a new low. Now she was again sitting in a reception. This time, though, things were immeasurably different; the air was scented with something she couldn't put her finger on, the tall, handsome male receptionist had a distinct lack of electric blue in his hair, there was no dodgy water machine in the corner, and as far as the eye could see, there wasn't a single piece of smoked glass – always a plus in Lotta's book. Lotta had arrived at the success ladder, and boy, did it warm her to her bones.

After what felt like an eternity of meetings where Lotta had kept a smile plastered on her face and had met lots of new people, she finally walked out of the conference room, letting out a breath it felt as if she had been holding since she'd been sitting in the reception. She had been nervous all day, her stomach in knots over the possibility of things not panning out well. She'd veered wildly from one thing to the next, constantly thinking that someone would work out that she was an imposter. But it was over now, and everything had gone surprisingly well, and with the benefit of hindsight, she realised that she shouldn't have worried about the meetings in the slightest. All of it had been fine. Jack had told her it would be and so had Liv and Timmy, but she'd been nervous and worried nonetheless.

She'd got her knickers in such a knot over the day that she'd even practised in the mirror on the back of the door of the under-stairs cupboard. She'd stood there, talking to her reflection, practising responses to imaginary questions aloud into the mirror. She'd remained there for ages, trying to anticipate any possible curveball that might be thrown at her and rehearsed her responses. Now, as she made her way across the lobby and out of the building, all her silly talking to herself in the mirror and hustle had paid off; she'd more than held her own.

Lotta felt an immense weight lift off of her shoulders as

she walked along in the sunshine. A strange sense of relief mixed with a subtle buzz of excitement over the knowledge that the meetings had gone well, washed over her. She thought about how much she'd planned for the meetings and how much it had been stressing her out. But it had all gone swimmingly, and she'd ended up at all the meetings and the following lunch surprisingly capable. She'd been worried and fussed that *she* would be a disaster, that she'd say something wrong and that she'd be found out for being in the wrong job. Now that it was all over and she was surrounded by the lovely old familiar London buildings, she felt her worries dissipate and a tonne of bricks float off from her shoulders down the road.

As she made her way to Jack's office, the street was bustling with people going about their business; an old man walked with a walking stick just in front of her, a food delivery guy on a moped whizzed by, and a woman in a floaty dress on a Pashley bike swerved to miss a pothole. She observed as they and their London lives weaved in and out in front of her, their paths merging and diverging with hers. She smiled. She used to be so *in* it all too, so desperate to get on in publishing, so desperate for success. Now she was back in the thick of it, but with different eyes and a new perspective, her view had changed.

She looked up at the sky and took a few deep breaths of the heavy city air. The smell of London streets and sunshine amalgamated in her nose. Passing a flower stall jumbled with flowers of every colour and size, she was lost in a world of her own as she walked along the street, almost as if she was in one of her books. Glancing into shop windows as she passed, she dodged in and out of busy, important people with heads bent to their phones. Continuing on, she turned down a side street and passed a pub she'd been to with Timmy many times. She remembered many occasions when they'd laughed and chatted and had way too many drinks. Next, she came across an old bookshop she'd always loved, and checking her watch, kicked herself for not having time to stop for a mooch.

Lotta thought about Jack as she walked. She was buzzing to be going to meet him at his office for the first time. Who even was this person walking along the pavement after a successful day? Who was this happy, thriving person strolling along in the London sunshine, on her way to someone who actually cared about her? It felt all sorts of good. Who was this person who had been a part of meetings, performed well, and whose opinion actually seemed to matter?

Lotta nodded, buoyed by feeling a success. She knew one thing – her day had felt a whole lot more prosperous and fulfilling than it had when she'd been working two jobs and had spent the vast majority of her time pandering to the needs of an overinflated ego and its sidekick app. Lotta smiled, feeling calmer and more confident than she ever had. She was on her way to meet Jack and bask in the successes of the day. She was no longer a nobody with a dead-end job. She was someone with a life.

Once she was at the door to Jack's offices, she side-eyed at what greeted her. Another thing in her life that was a very nice surprise. This was certainly no grotty eighties building with rusty stainless steel numbers and plastic-backed doormats with curled-up edges. Oh no, this was a whole other playing field altogether. A brass plate informed her she'd arrived at Jack's business, and on either side of the door, bay trees in huge pots swayed in the breeze. Lotta took a deep breath before she walked up the stairs. The day was getting better by the minute.

By the time she had been shown where to go, she was having a hard time keeping her chin from the floor. The offices were gorgeous – elegant, classic and expensive. She remembered Dan and his stupid app when he'd ploughed all the money into trendy offices and ergonomic chairs. This was the other end of the scale in terms of classiness, and it pushed all of Lotta's feel-good buttons six times over. Finally arriving at Jack's small office, she smiled as she saw him standing in front of his desk. He smiled broadly as Lotta appeared.

'Lotta as in hotter. Just the person I wanted to see.'

'Hey, Just Jack. How are we?'

'How are you, more like? Well, you look okay so it must have gone without any major hitches. You didn't stuff anything up?' Jack asked as he put his arm around her waist and kissed her in greeting.

Lotta took an intake of breath at business-like Jack. He was smartly dressed in a nice collared shirt which didn't make him look ugly. The shirt, the trousers and the Chelsea boots, plus his cologne and the small elegant office, lent him a confidence and authority she liked very much. This Jack was very, very nice. Lotta smiled back at him, trying to hide the fact that she thought he was gorgeous. She pretended her heart hadn't just done a flip on a balance beam and stepped closer to him, putting her hand on his back and hugging him.

'It went so well,' she said, her voice shaking a little.

'I knew it would,' Jack replied.

Lotta put her bag on a chair and looked around as Jack gesticulated to the window and then led her over, and they both looked out over black railings to a patch of green surrounded by trees in the middle of the square. He pointed out the BT Tower and a few landmarks, and Lotta didn't quite know what to think of it all. He'd clearly underplayed his business, his office, and then some. 'So, yeah, umm, this is different from what I expect-ed,' she said, struggling to find the right words.

'Is it?'

'You didn't say where it was or that it was like this,' Lotta said, waving her hand around.

'It's a co-sharing place. I run everything on a skeletal basis. It's less impressive than it looks.'

Lotta was again reminded of when Dan had ploughed her

money into renting a trendy warehouse with oversized industrial pendants and ping-pong tables where twenty-something
techies had sailed around on scooters.

'Right. I see,' Lotta replied. Despite what Jack said, it *was*
impressive. It was so very impressive; its location, its decor, its
whole feel. Lotta felt a little bit as she had when she'd attended
the ball with Jack when they'd been fake dating. Then she'd
arrived at the hotel none the wiser and had suddenly felt all
sorts of small in her charity shop blouse with her secondhand
dress in tow. Now she felt along the same lines.

Jack frowned at her. 'You okay? You've gone a bit quiet.'

'No, no, I'm fine.'

'I'll go and get us a cup of tea. You look like you're in need of
one.'

Lotta looked around the quietly opulent, quietly luxurious
office. There were pictures of old London in black frames
perfectly aligned on the walls. There was a view of a square.
There was a lush, healthy potted palm in the corner, and
through the open door, she could see the corner of a large
glossy black desk on the other side of the corridor. There were
matching wicker storage containers seemingly on every surface
hiding business things and making everything just look *so* nice.
She got up and ran her finger along the desk, touched the top of
an old-fashioned reading lamp and looked underneath the desk.
Even the flipping wicker bin was stylish. She looked behind the
desk out the huge sash windows over towards the park. Her life
sure had stepped up a few rungs on the ladder if this was the
sort of place she was going to be meeting her partner after
work.

She stared back at the desk, lost in a world of her own and
randomly pulled out a drawer. That too was perfectly organised
with a wicker storage tray, a pen pot and a little jar full of mints.
She suddenly stopped as she gazed in. There in the tray was a
pale pink leather keyring that clearly wasn't Jack's. He must

share the desk with someone who knew nice accessories. She opened the lower drawer and saw a bottle of high-end perfume wedged next to a pile of papers. It suddenly didn't feel right. There were a few personal things that clearly weren't his. She squinted her eyes, shook her head and just after she'd quickly shut the drawer, Jack returned with two mugs clutched in his hands, and he kicked the office door shut with his foot. As the door swung shut, Lotta's gaze flicked to the hooks on the back of the door where she could see Jack's leather bag, the same one he'd been using when she'd met him for the fake date at the hotel. His jacket was alongside it and something else caught her eye; tucked behind Jack's jacket, she could see a pink Chanel-style bouclé jacket swinging gently on a hook. Lotta went cold and felt as if the office, and the world, started to spin.

She tried to hide a frown as her mind went over the keyring, the jacket and the bottle of perfume. She sat down and took the mug, and Jack perched on the edge of the desk. 'Okay, I just have to send a quick email and then we'll be off. Are you hungry?'

Lotta had barely eaten all day, even at lunch she'd been more worried about making mistakes than eating and had hardly touched her food. Suddenly though, she didn't have much of an appetite. 'I am. I've not had much all day,' she lied.

'Good. I thought we'd get dinner before we head to the train. Fancy that?'

Lotta stared at him but could not stop thinking about the text she'd seen on his phone and now the pink jacket behind the door and the bottle of perfume wedged in the drawer. Her stomach turned over, and her mind raced back to their fake date when the American woman Brandy had led her to believe he liked someone else. Then it had made her feel sick to her core, and she was feeling along similar lines now. She gripped her mug tightly, not knowing what to do. She felt far from comfortable, but she didn't know what to say. Her mouth seemed unable to work as the perfume was front and centre of her mind. She felt ridiculously pathetic and desperate to even mention the perfume. It was all probably nothing. The person Jack shared the desk with was obviously a woman. There was absolutely nothing wrong with that. But as she sat there, listening to him chatting as he tapped away at the screen, she was in a daze, her heart thumping and not in a happy way. Her hands were suddenly damp and clammy as she pretended to be really interested in what Jack was telling her about a man he'd bumped into that morning who had just come back from a holiday in Spain.

Staring at his mouth moving but not really hearing what he was saying, she sat there feeling sick inside as something dawned on her. She realised that Jack was everything in her world and if anything went wrong, it was a much bigger deal than she had ever imagined it might be. And she did not like the way it made her feel. At all.

19

The day after the pink jacket in the office, Lotta was getting ready for Liv to come over for dinner. She dumped a butter lettuce into a salad spinner, ran the tap, and then whizzed it until there wasn't even a hint of water left. As she turned the plastic top around furiously, she felt as if her brain was the salad spinner and the pink jacket was the lettuce. Around and around it went in her mind. Lugging wine from a bottle into a chilled wineglass, she took a swig, grabbed a jug, poured in olive oil and then added a couple of dollops of Dijon mustard. Dumping the butter lettuce leaves into a gigantic mango wood salad bowl, she then pottered around making her way to the conservatory.

The conservatory's resident stain that had come with the place when she'd first arrived was still evident but only just. The huge old vine which had looked dead to her on first inspection was now full of leaves and positively alive and lush as it snaked up the side of the house and over the door. Lotta flicked a long, cotton tablecloth with a just visible pale stripe over the table, and added wicker placemats and water glasses. Filling a jug with water, she mooched around the garden, snipping bits here and there, placed it on the centre of the table and then lit so many tealights in tiny little votive holders that the whole of the conservatory seemed to dance in the light. The dancing light and pretty room didn't do much to improve her mood.

She heard Liv letting herself in the front door and strolled across the breakfast room with her glass in hand, meeting her in the entrance hall.

'Hiya!' Liv breezed happily and looked at Lotta's wineglass pointedly. 'Starting early?'

'I am. I hope you're hungry.'

'Always. What have we got?'

'Pasta.'

Liv trailed into the breakfast room behind Lotta. 'What sort of pasta?'

'Fettuccine,' Lotta answered with a strained attempt at casualness to her voice.

Liv's head snapped up from rummaging in her bag for her phone. 'Alfredo?'

'Yes.'

Liv swore. 'I knew something was wrong as soon as I saw you and when I spoke to you earlier. You're doing that overly casual airy thing you always do when something is wrong.'

'Nothing's wrong,' Lotta insisted. 'I just fancied fettuccine. Everything's just peachy.'

Everything is not peachy. There's a horrible pink jacket and a bottle of perfume. Everything's dreadful. Peachy things are not.

'Nothing's wrong? I don't think so,' Liv repeated. 'Trust me, if we have fettuccine alfredo, something is wrong. Plus, you're doing that casual thing with your voice.'

'Nope. Not at all. I just fancied carbs,' Lotta urged. 'Nice, comforting, calorie-filled carbs.'

'Yeah, of course you did. Sorry, not working, Lott. Not buying it. What's wrong?'

Lotta waved her hand in dismissal as she poured Liv a glass of wine. 'I just fancied pasta. That's it. End of story.'

'How long have I been your cousin?' Liv asked with her hands on her hips and her eyebrows raised.

Lotta pretended to muse Liv's question, putting her head to the side. 'I'd make it my whole life.'

'Exactly. Meaning I know when you're like this.'

'Like what?'

'All breezy and weird.'

'Not at all,' Lotta replied, shaking her head and attempting to ignore Liv's concern. She took two blue and white striped linen napkins out of a drawer and turned on the hob. She continued pretending to be fine as she poured fettuccine into a large pan of heavily salted water.

Liv put her wine down when she saw the pasta. 'And we've got the posh pasta! What in the name of goodness is going on? Do I need to call Timmy?'

Lotta turned the top over on the pasta bag and tutted. 'I got it yesterday at that fancy deli I used to lust over. Now I can just about afford to go in the door. It was an arm and a leg, but it's so nice.'

'Yeah, I still don't believe you. We only ever have the posh pasta on high days and holidays and not when I'm just popping over for a glass of wine. Something is up.'

'I know we do. But I was up there yesterday and I thought why not treat ourselves? All is fine.'

Half an hour later, Lotta had poured thick cream into the pasta, followed it with copious amounts of Parmesan and butter, and spooned it into a serving dish. They'd sat down in the candlelit conservatory, both of them laughing as Lotta sprinkled a load more cheese on the pasta for good measure. With the wooden bowl full of salad and the pasta between them, she passed over two salad servers and topped up Liv's glass. Liv looked at the glass pointedly. 'I take it I'm staying over. Lott, I can barely keep up with you. You're knocking it back like it's going out of fashion.'

Lotta frowned and looked at her glass. 'Am I?'

'You are, and you're acting *very* weird. Casual and not caring and weird. Plus, you brought your Kindle in and put it on the chair over there. Don't think I didn't notice. You do that when you're stressed and like to keep it in sight at all times.'

Lotta laughed and took a gulp of her wine. 'I'm fine.'

Liv started to pour the salad dressing on the leaves and then used the salad servers to put some on both of their plates. 'You've said you're fine about fifty times. You might as well just tell me now.'

'For the last time, I'm fine!'

Liv didn't push it and changed the subject. 'So, how was town?'

'Yeah, good.'

'Did you feel like you missed it?'

'Do you know what? I did, and I didn't. I realised that it's not all it's cracked up to be. It seemed so frantic and busy. Maybe I've just forgotten that side of it. And the trains were filthy.'

Liv smiled and shrugged. 'Agree. It's nice to be able to dip in and out, though. When you live down here, you sort of have the best of both worlds.'

Lotta nodded. 'So true. I never thought I'd hear myself say that.'

Liv took a forkful of pasta and popped it into her mouth. 'I know, I'm the same. I didn't either. So much for the world of publishing, eh?'

Lotta nodded and rolled her eyes. 'Yeah, I'm over that complete waste of time.'

'Now you have them contacting you for your book reviews and eating out of your hand,' Liv said, taking a bite of her pasta. 'Love it, Lott. Love it. Way to go.'

'Too funny,' Lotta replied, smiling. 'It's still a long way off before reviews pay the bills, but it will help with the blooming great credit card debt.'

'Yeah, good riddance to that as soon as possible.'

They continued to talk, laugh, and chat. Enjoying their pasta, the conversation moved from Lotta's day in London to a woman at Liv's work who was annoying her. They laughed and chuckled and reminisced about a similar woman Lotta had worked with.

Two hours later, they were still sitting in the conservatory with the candles flickering around them. Liv had relayed a long and complicated story about James's cousin who she didn't like, who had been larging it that she was commuting between Dubai and London with her very important job as a drama teacher. 'I mean really! Really! The only reason she's in Dubai is because no one else wants to live there. It's so hot you can't even go out! Drama teacher, my bottom. And the only reason she has that house is because her ex-husband, who may I add was twenty-five years older than her, was loaded. Am I right?'

Lotta chuckled. She loved Liv when she'd had a drink. She got on her high horse and rode around on it, dishing out her advice on anything and everything to all and sundry. 'You're funny.'

'You are.' Liv giggled.

'I am not anywhere near as funny as you when you've had half a bottle of wine. How is it up there on your high horse?'

Liv fired back a question, quickly returning the conversation to Lotta. 'Come on, tell me why we're having the posh pasta.'

Lotta was a bit less uptight than she had been when Liv had first arrived. She decided to tell Liv about the text she'd seen on Jack's phone and the pink jacket. 'I found something on Jack's phone that I'm not sure about,' Lotta blurted out and then squeezed her eyes shut together for a second.

'I knew something was wrong! What do you mean?' Liv said, her forehead creasing into a big, thick frown.

'I found a text message from what I'm assuming is a woman.'

'What? Are you sure?'

'I am,' Lotta stated solemnly. 'It's not good. I knew I shouldn't have let myself fall for him.'

'Well, who is it?'

'I wish I knew. I don't know who she is or why Jack would be exchanging texts with her,' Lotta said, exhaling dramatically at the end. 'I can't stop thinking about it.'

Liv scrunched up her nose and fiddled with the edge of her wineglass. 'Well, that doesn't sound right. What did the message say?'

'I couldn't see it all. It was just what flashed up on the front. You know, in the notification window.'

'It could be anything. Possibly a bit suspicious, but not really. Have you asked Jack about it?'

'Not yet. I'm afraid of what he might say about me snooping.'

'Hmm, yeah. I suppose it could seem like that, especially if it's nothing which it will be.'

'I don't know what to do,' Lotta said.

'It's probably best to confront him about it if you're having doubts,' Liv reasoned.

'Yeah, but I can't bring myself to ask him. I feel pathetic and desperate.'

'Has there been anything out of the ordinary with him?'

Lotta shook her head. 'Nothing. He's been working a lot, but other than that, everything has been fabulous. In fact, he's been so nice I've thought it's too good to be true. Now, I'm wondering if that's correct.'

'This is the man who arrived at the wedding in a suit and swept you off your feet.'

'I know.'

'You have literally no reason to doubt him other than a glimpse at one single text. Is that correct?'

Lotta swallowed and then coughed. 'There was a bottle of

perfume in his drawer and a pink jacket underneath his on the back of his office door.'

'I knew it! I knew something was really wrong when you got that pasta and the cream out.'

'You know me too well.'

'Hang on, so there was a bottle of perfume in his drawer?' Liv looked confused. 'What?'

'Yeah.'

Liv swore. 'Were you snooping?'

'No, that's the thing. I just sort of opened it out of interest and then went cold.'

'Didn't you say, though, that it's a shared office?'

'Yep.'

'That's it then. You're overthinking it.'

'Yeah, I know. It's just all playing on my mind.'

'You're going to just have to bring it up without making it seem like you're accusing him of something.' Liv chuckled. 'Just do that casual not caring thing you do when you really care. He won't have had the years of experience that I've had, and he won't pick up on it and what it really means.'

Lotta sighed. 'I just don't know.'

'You could just ask him in a non-confrontational way. Explain that you found this text message and you're just worried that it might be from someone else. Ask him if he can explain it to you.'

'That's the thing, I did casually do that, and he was uppity.'

'Oh.'

'Yep.'

'When you say uppity, what was he like?' Liv questioned with her lips wrinkled up and her forehead frowning.

'Dismissive.'

'Hmm. That's not so good,' Liv replied, sounding legitimately worried.

'And you see, the thing is…'

'Yep.'

Lotta squeezed her eyes shut for a second and winced. 'I have this bad, Liv. Like so bad. Like much, much worse than Dan.'

'How can it be worse than Despicable Dan? You had it bad then.'

'No, that's precisely what I mean. That's my point! I thought I had it bad then. Now I *know* that, actually, I did not. This is... Well, this is the real deal.'

'Yikes. Right, I see. Hmm.'

'Why did I have to be so stupid and go and fall for him?' Lotta asked as she scratched the back of her neck in frustration and then jerked her thumb upwards. 'I really must have irritated a god or six for this to be happening to me again. I thought I'd had my fair share of dickheads with Dan.'

'Hey,' Liv said consolingly, putting her hand across the table and giving Lotta's arm a tiny squeeze. 'It's not happening again. At least not yet, anyway. There's probably a perfectly reasonable explanation for this.'

'I'm furious with myself for letting this happen. Why does he have to be so... I don't know, just Jack. You know?'

'Hmm. He is very nice, Lott.'

'He is *very* nice, and I have it *very* bad. This is a catastrophe of cataclysmic proportions. I loved him from that bookshop meeting. Crikey, Liv, what *am* I going to do?'

20

The following week, Lotta was having a hectic day at work. It had all started well enough with what was becoming for her quite a regular routine; an early ferry ride up the coast, a stroll to work, and then a coffee in the bandstand with her Kindle. She'd had worse working environments surrounding her working day, that she knew for a fact.

From the bandstand that morning though it had slowly but surely gone downhill. Firstly, her computer had not wanted to turn on, then she'd spilt orange juice down her white blouse, and now her phone was buzzing with an unknown mobile number which she felt was ominous. The small, exclusive conference she'd organised was due to start in less than an hour and a half, and the keynote speaker hadn't yet turned up. Lotta had built in plenty of time for the speaker to be late, but even so. She had a feeling it was going to be a long day.

'Hello. Lotta?'

Lotta felt her heart sink. It was the professor she'd spoken to on the phone just the day before to confirm. 'Listen. I've had a few logistical problems this morning. I'm afraid I'm not going to be able to make it.'

'Sorry. What do you mean? It's scheduled to be taking place soon!' Lotta exclaimed, her voice echoing around the walls of the inner office where she was sitting at her desk.

'Yes, you see, as I told you, I'm working on a huge research project at the moment. Something has come up.'

Lotta shook her head rapidly, she'd thought this professor was in a world of her own when she'd spoken to her, now she was sure of it. She needed to get her off the phone quickly and work out what in the world she was going to do. A few minutes later, after quickly ascertaining the professor really couldn't care less, she put her phone face down next to her, sighed heavily and stared at her computer screen. Her brain scrambled and as she pushed out her chair and got up, wondering how she was going to save the day, Marie, her colleague, walked into the room with a cup of tea in a takeaway cup in her hand.

'Morning!' Marie said breezily. 'How's everything? Ooh, blimey, by the looks on your face, everything is not good. What's up?'

'Professor Brownman has decided she's not coming.'

'What? No! At this late hour! Not good. Not good at all.'

'Tell me about it! I knew it too. I just had a funny feeling about her. Ahh. I don't know what to do…'

The room fell silent, and Lotta felt a chill run down her spine. This was her first major hiccup at her job, and she didn't like how it made her feel in the slightest. She needed this job and didn't want to do anything to jeopardise it. Marie put her bag on Lotta's desk. 'Are any of the backups we have local? You have a look at the spreadsheet. I'll make us a coffee. Don't worry, I've been here before. We'll sort it out. We've just about got time.'

Ten minutes later, Lotta had already called two people but to no avail. With two mugs of coffee on the desk, Marie was sitting beside her, squinting at Lotta's computer screen. Marie pointed to a name on the spreadsheet. 'She's really good. Give her a go.'

Lotta started punching the number into her phone. It went to voicemail, and she shook her head. 'This is a nightmare. I suppose I'm just going to have to shift everything around and let the attendees know.'

Marie nodded. 'Yep, you do that. I'll keep trying down the list. Hopefully, we can get someone in this afternoon.'

'I'll quickly change the run sheet and update the document so they won't be much the wiser once they sit down. Hopefully,' Lotta said.

Marie sounded a lot more confident than Lotta felt. 'Yep. Right, you go and supervise the arrivals, and I'll continue with this. Don't worry, it will be fine.'

Lotta tried not to panic. She knew how much these CEOs of financial organisations had paid to come to the exclusive event. She didn't need it to be going wrong. Inwardly, she cursed the professor who'd let her down. The woman had doctorates in all sorts of things, most of which weren't based in the real world. Lotta wanted to kick herself for not going with her gut instinct from the get-go. She'd known from the offset that the professor had been sketchy. She cursed herself for not going with her gut, but she tried to remain calm as she walked through to the reception area. Marie had seemed okay about it all, as if it had happened to her before. At least there was that. Lotta felt sick though. To her, it was a big, *massive* deal, and to make matters worse, it seemed like she was beginning to run out of options and had exhausted all possible solutions.

She gulped as she took in the gorgeous old lobby. It was abuzz with chatter and arrivals as attendees came through the main entrance door and were greeted by one of the reception-ists. Lotta tried not to think about the professor and the missing slot, and strolled around saying hello with a big smile on her face. She then checked the welcome area. At least, that was as it should be. After making sure everything was in place and taking a deep breath, Lotta's mind went at nineteen to the dozen, trying to think how she could fill the empty slot of the speaker. The professor had been the main drawcard for many of the CEOs, and they had been keen to hear this expert in her field exclusively address them. Now there was not only no expert, but an hour of nothing.

She scoured her mind for a solution, but nothing came to her. As her stress level kept increasing, she tried to focus on the task at hand, making sure the attendees were happy, but all she could think about was the fact that this was her first main fully solo event and it had gone wrong. There was one good thing to come out of it all; at least she wasn't thinking about the pink jacket, the text, or Jack.

As she directed one of the CEOs to the toilets, she felt her phone buzz in her pocket. A text from Marie told her one of the backups was desperately trying to juggle her afternoon around so that she could get to the event. Lotta crossed her fingers, and as she tried to hide her anxiety, she plastered a happy smile on her face as she continued to work her way around the room, checking in with everyone and making sure they were okay. Her stomach churned with worry as she waited with anticipation to hear back from Marie.

Ten minutes later, as most of the attendees had arrived and were standing around chatting and drinking coffee, a text from Marie told her that the backup speaker was able to make it. Lotta sighed in relief, feeling the tense knot in her stomach release a little bit. She'd thought it was going to be a very different outcome and had spiralled; she'd envisaged people complaining, failing, and her getting the sack.

Her mind had whirled in the background into thinking that she would lose her job and be doomed. But it seemed that her life was no longer a disaster, and teamwork had saved the conference. As she whizzed around, she let out a gigantic inner sigh of relief and looked around at the CEOs, all of whom seemed happy enough. They were none the wiser about her disastrous morning, and hopefully, they would be happy with the replacement speaker. It seemed Lotta had not failed. She'd actually worked out a solution to save the day. After all that had gone on with the app and her previous dead-end jobs, it felt nice for something to actually go her way. Lotta Button's world, even when it went wrong, had changed immeasurably.

The hours flew by as Lotta flitted around, making sure the rest of the day went smoothly. She'd ordered an Uber for the backup speaker to get to the fast train and a pick up at the other end, and she'd done a quick bit of research on the new speaker and changed the blurb in the document on the tablets in front of the CEOs. She'd worked diligently and quickly for the rest of the day, ensuring it was a success and had not had time for lunch and barely time for a wee.

The day, though, had continued to throw up all sorts of surprises, and Lotta lurched from one thing to the next, making sure everything was okay. She'd worked hard to smooth out any further hitches, fuelled by some sort of innate adrenaline and a frantic need and determination to prove she was good. She'd learnt one thing; she was most definitely earning her keep.

As the hours passed, she couldn't help but reflect on how she'd worked through it all. Being good at something and part of a team hit her between the eyes; it felt fabulous to be *someone*. Not the partner to an entrepreneur, not working a second job cleaning toilets to keep said entrepreneur in nice shirts, but her doing all the things. In terms of her job, Lotta felt more in control, more independent and more sorted than she had in a very long time.

As the conference came to a conclusion and was finally winding down, Lotta was exhausted. She sighed with relief as the last person left the conference room. Her head pounded from all the talking, the balls of her feet were on fire, her lower back was aching from the hours of standing, and she was exhausted from scooting about here, there, and everywhere.

Once everyone had left, and she'd helped clear up, she'd collapsed on one of the sofas in the office and was having a much-needed cup of tea when her phone pinged. She glanced at it and a smile spread across her face; Jack.

I hope it went well today. Love you.

Lotta felt her heart tumble, and then she shook her head as it swirled in confusion. He was messaging her that he loved her. Was this the sort of message from someone who had a secret? Did you tell someone you loved them when you were keeping something from them? She didn't really know what to think and was torn. Frowning, she dropped her phone in her lap and rested her head back against the sofa. She simply had no idea whatsoever what to do.

Sipping on her tea, she listened to a couple of little voices in her head. One was on the left, telling her to just ask him about the text, the jacket and the perfume. The other one on the right was saying to just bury it and not worry about it. As she finished her cup of tea and flicked from one solution to the other, she decided, for the moment, she'd bury it. If it was something horrible, for now, she really didn't want to know the truth. She'd had enough of that in her life already.

21

A week passed by and Lotta had continued burying her thoughts about the perfume, the jacket and the text and on the surface at least, life had rumbled along quite nicely. In ripped jeans, an old white polo shirt and her hair in a messy bun, she stood beside Jack, looking into the building beside the boathouse. They were starting on the plan to turn the place into a reading retreat and get it working to give her a second income. From where they were standing, the road was looking long. The place was old and forgotten, a relic from a time gone by. Everything was veiled in a thick layer of dust, zigzagged layers of cobwebs laced across the ceiling, and the windows were so grimy it was hard to see out. There were piles of old furniture here, there and everywhere, and the floor was littered with forgotten items as far as the eye could see. Lotta looked on with her face creased into a wince at the sight of old wellies, discarded toys and an array of gardening tools and things that had been left for dead many years before.

Jack bent down and picked up an old pair of secateurs with timber handles and wiggled them in front of her. 'We'll be needing these for that wisteria going up the side of the wall.'

'Yep. I think that's your job.' Lotta laughed.

'What, while you get on with lugging all this furniture into the already full garage?' Jack deadpanned.

Lotta sucked air in through her teeth. 'Sheesh. There is so much to do. What were we even thinking?'

'Nah,' Jack said, swatting the air in front of him. 'This will be done in no time.'

Once they'd cooked up a plan and were into it, they marvelled at all the old junk and the things from another life-time, another era, that had been left behind. An old striped blue and white canvas rain cover for a boat was neatly folded on a dusty old shelf, a collection of antique and very much forgotten fishing rods were stacked in a corner, timber reels of fraying twine sat in a jumble, and an old tackle box brimming with all sorts of rusty hooks and old lures had seen better days. Standing by the window in the corner, a stack of timber oars and paddles, chipped and cracked with age, threatened to topple on the floor and dusty, dirty life jackets looked as if they had just stepped out from another century.

Lotta hadn't known where to start, but once she'd got going and some of the junk was in the garage, she stared at the piles of old furniture, wondering how she could repurpose them for the retreat. An old Adirondack chair really only needed a lick of paint, a side table was crying out for a clean, and three vintage parasols covered in cobwebs were just waiting for summer days and jugs of ice-cold drinks.

Whilst Jack started pulling out chairs and furniture, Lotta got to work on what was piled haphazardly on the shelves. She worked swiftly, neatly placing all sorts into baskets – old jam jars full of nails and screws, a faded, tarnished compass from a bygone age, piles of leather-bound fishing books, and note-books with yellowed pages filled with handwritten notes, tables, and drawings. As Lotta cleared off the shelves, she found more and more things that would work for the reading retreat; an old tin full of antique stamps, a small piece of parchment paper with a watercolour painting of the sea, a plethora of old timber photo frames displaying all sorts of pictures from the past. The further she sorted and cleared whilst musing the reading retreat in her head, the more she thought the whole idea could work.

After a couple of hours of Jack working hard lugging around furniture, they were beginning to see some leeway. Lotta had spent the whole time having to stop herself from poring over the fascinating old things she'd found, but as the building became clearer, she was beginning to see that it could possibly be the way out of her debt.

On a bit of a break, they stood outside the building in the afternoon sunshine and analysed their work. Now that the building was clear of junk, it was a shell. A shell shouting two things; a lot of potential and most certainly, a lot of work.

The outside was asking for help too; exterior paint had weathered and faded and was peeling off in flakes here and there, giving the entire place a look of neglect. The old wisteria that climbed over the door needed a good prune, and the climbing English roses had seen better days.

'It's better and worse than I thought it was going to be,' Jack said, looking up towards the roof as he sipped from a mug of tea.

Lotta nodded in agreement. 'In what way is it better? Personally, I'm faced with potential and then a lot of work,' she said and shook her head. 'Is anyone really going to want to stay here? I'm having quite a hard time imagining this place as a retreat. Earlier when I was clearing the shelves I thought it would work, but now, hmm, I don't know. It seems as if it's going to be an uphill struggle to get this place shipshape.'

Jack ran his hand along the cladding butting up to the windows. The whole place had been neglected – the wood damaged by years of sun and rain, and the entire place wore the effects of life by the sea. He pointed to one of the window panes which was wearing a crack straight down the middle and the side door hanging off its hinges at the top. 'We have our work cut out for us, there's no question about that. It's crying out for it, though,' Jack said, his voice full of determination.

Lotta nodded in agreement. 'I don't even know where to start. If it wasn't for you being here, there's no way I would have been able to do this,' she said, her voice far from full of enthusiasm. As she looked at him, her mind also flitted to the perfume bottle and the pink jacket suddenly appeared in front of her eyes as if it was a movie playing on a screen. She flicked her eyes over Jack standing in old jeans, his face squinting in thought at the broken glass pane. Surely this wasn't the face of a person who was lying and seeing someone else? She tried to bury her thoughts as she collected the mugs and Jack started to hack at the wisteria strangling the architrave going around the window.

The next few hours continued with the prep work; Lotta vacuumed for a solid two hours, Jack filled holes and rubbed down skirting boards and assessed the damage. Then they sat on the step outside the door, brainstorming repairs and painting plans. Lotta forced herself not to think about the text message or the pink jacket and busied herself with the walls so that they were ready for painting. She didn't really have a clue what she was doing, but she'd had worse people showing her what to do. The biceps working beside her were one of the better colleagues she'd had in life.

As they worked with a radio playing beside them, Lotta found herself lost in thought. She was in her mind's eye back in her old flat that she'd shared with Dan. Dan had barely lifted a finger and felt it was too much for him to even put his dishes in the dishwasher. He'd left everything to her and had little interest in where they lived at all. She stole a look at Jack and the contrasting scene going on around her. Strong and full of energy, Jack was going at everything hard. As Lotta pushed the vacuum arm back and forth over and over again, she couldn't stop thinking about how different Jack was from Dan. She tutted to herself at what an idiot she'd been with Dan. He'd blindsided her into being his little lapdog, tending to his every need. Here beside her, this man Jack, got on with the job at hand.

Once the whole place was empty and prepared, they started working on the woodwork. Lotta didn't have much of a clue about what she was doing and had listened to Jack's plan. Once she'd been instructed, she'd started rubbing a sanding block over the skirting boards. As she pushed it back and forth over the timber, it was as if she was sanding off years of not only the building's neglect and giving the wood a new lease of life, but hers too. This new place and new start were going to give her the freedom to finally get rid of Dan and his ridiculous app.

They worked in mostly silence for hours as the sun moved around the building, landing in puddles on the old floorboards, and a breeze came in from the sea. When Lotta was so tired and aching all over from crawling around the floor with a sanding block, Jack rallied her for one more push. He poured paint into a tray, handed Lotta a roller, and she began to plaster bright white primer on the old walls. And as she slowly made her way around with each roll up and down as the white paint covered years of grime and life, everything began to change – the light, the smell, and the whole aura of the place. Right there in front of Lotta's eyes, it was as if, as the coat of white primer went on, the old building sighed out in relief and sat back smiling to itself.

With Lotta feeling as if she never wanted to do a day's work again, and once the primer was done, she stood back with her hands on her hips and shook her head, trying to visualise the place as a retreat. She squinted and tried to imagine the shelves full of books, maybe a linen-covered sofa tucked up by the window, lots of little tables here and there with frames and flowers. She tried to imagine the windows sparkling, the roses winding their way and blooming around the windows, and the old stable door opening to a breeze coming in off the sea. She smiled and nodded repeatedly, as the more she stared, the more she realised the dream could become a reality.

'Thanks,' she said.

Jack put the roller he'd been using down, squeezed Lotta's hand, and with his other hand gesticulated around the room. 'Looking good, right?'

Lotta nodded in agreement. 'So much better than I thought. It's really nice!'

'Yep. I knew it. Okay, let's get this show on the road and clean up. I need a drink.'

'You and me both,' Lotta replied as she watched him scooting around, tidying up. Was this a man who was lying to her? If he was, he was a master of deception. For the millionth time, she dug a hole and chucked her doubting thoughts into it. No, everything was fine.

'I think a trip to the pub is in order, if you've got the energy to walk down there. What do you reckon?' Jack asked as he rammed a lid back on a tin of paint.

'I don't think I've ever had a better offer. There's no way I have the energy to cook something,' Lotta replied with a chuckle. 'In fact, you might have to push me down the pub in that old wheelbarrow we found.'

After a final half hour clearing up and prepping for the next day, as Lotta sorted out the paint pots and Jack fixed the hinges on the doors, they were both shattered. Jack flicked on the light as they stood by the door and looked back at their progress. All the junk had gone, the old sash windows were fixed, the floor was clean, and the walls were bright white. Jack shook his head. 'Not a bad job, Lotta as in hotter.'

'Thanks.' Lotta chuckled. 'It's come up a dream. I can actually envisage it now, even though there's still a long way to go.'

'Yes, loads more work on the horizon. Right, shower and then the pub,' Jack said, a grin spreading across his face.

Lotta smiled in agreement, and the pink jacket didn't even enter her mind. It was buried along with the perfume and the text until the next time she dissected it and its meaning, anyway. 'Show me the way.'

22

Halfway through the next week, Lotta strolled along the shoreline and looked out to sea. Pretty Beach was looking good. She could feel the warm sun on her bare arms, and her feet squelched into the cool sand by the water's edge as she ambled along with her head full of thoughts. A cool coastal breeze whipped her hair around her head, and the sound of the waves crashing beside filled her ears.

She was lost in a world of her own as she strolled along, grateful for the moment of peace and the chance to embrace the fresh air. Her mind went over the situation with her mum and how her mum was barely bothering to answer texts. It did not bode well. Lotta had been in a similar situation with her mum on multiple occasions. The difference in those times being her mother's mental health and alcoholic state – both of which had never been good. This time there was a heart attack thrown in for good measure.

Her mind then flitted to thinking about her job and how much she was enjoying it. She hadn't thought it at the time, but the catastrophe with the speaker had, in actual fact, turned out to be a great thing. The aftermath of the professor not turning up and how Lotta had handled it had resulted in her boss Anne being more than pleased, so much so that the next day Lotta arrived to a box of chocolates on her desk. She'd chuckled to herself as she read the thank you note that had accompanied the chocolates. This was her kind of job, and then some.

Still with the sea air in her hair and her feet in the sand, she then thought about Pretty Beach to the Breakers. It was coming along nicely. She pondered the contrast between the house she now called home and the tiny flats she'd lived in London. Before her move to the coast, she'd believed she still wanted a slice of that London life, but now she wasn't so sure. In her days in various little London flats, she'd always dreamed of a busy, successful fancy existence in London and a weekend place in the country. That dream had involved a Sussex cottage, but it had always been just that; a dream. Now it seemed as if a version of that dream was part of her *actual* life. She'd never thought in her wildest dreams that she'd live in a gorgeous house with a spiral staircase, a little boathouse, and a real-life conservatory complete with a vine. And there were chimneys and chimney pots in the vicinity. You knew you'd made it when you had a chimney pot in your life.

Not only that, Pretty Beach to the Breakers was so much more than the Sussex cottage she'd lusted after in her head as she'd cleaned office block toilets and hoped Dan's app would be a success. Pretty Beach to the Breakers was somehow better – a part of her now. Old, a bit tumbledown, classic, and most of all, it was as if it had somehow become like a friend. With the completion of the library and her slow but sure doing up of the rest of the house, Pretty Beach to the Breakers appeared to have taken her under its wing; a place to come home to at the end of the day.

She followed the waves back and forth with her eyes and mulled over everything – her mum, the house, and her new job. As she continued along, with the lighthouse in the distance and the sand dunes as her destination, her phone buzzed. She pulled it out of her book bag and saw that it was a text from Jack. She felt her heart flip, as it still had a habit of doing when Jack was anywhere near her, as she opened the message.

Yep. Can't wait to see you later.

Lotta frowned, she went cold, and then she stopped with her feet in the water, the waves sloshing in and out as she reread the text. She wasn't seeing Jack later. She started texting him back, and then she shook her head and deleted what she'd written. Who was he seeing later, then? He'd told her after they'd spent the weekend working on the reading retreat that he had a really full week and was getting some early nights in because his days were starting at the crack of dawn. Clearly, he had time for someone else.

Feeling pathetically paranoid and putting her phone in her pocket, she continued along until she was through the sand dunes and walking up and away from the beach, her worry growing with every step. She tried not to overthink the text and failed massively. She tried to tell herself it could be anything. She tried to push it out of her mind. She attempted to focus on the nature all around her, the sound of the waves, and the warmth of the sun on her skin. But despite her surroundings, the thought of Jack texting someone else about seeing them later kept creeping back in.

As she got to the road, and after brushing her feet of sand and lacing her trainers back on, she took her phone out and sent back three question marks. She wasn't going to spend the whole day stewing. It was time to ask him what was what. A message came back almost instantly.

Oops. Meant for someone else. Sorry. Xxx

Lotta was stumped. Jack's response didn't make her feel any better in the slightest. Her heart sank as she read the words. He didn't seem concerned at all. If he was cheating, he was very brazen about it. She screwed her face up. Now what? The perfume, the jacket, and the message she'd seen on his phone and now this rattled her cage further. She held onto the sides of the cage as it shook like crazy. She'd jumped in with six feet and let herself be swept up in everything Jack. She felt doom wash over her. Maybe Jack wasn't quite as nice, or quite as in love, as she thought.

**** *my life.*

Trying to control her galloping brain full of emotions, she put her phone back in her pocket and turned from the pavement so that she was looking directly out to sea. Gazing at the horizon, as the wind whipped through her hair, she sighed in frustration, and for the first time in a long time, she felt awful and most spectacularly alone.

Taking a deep breath, she tried to remind herself that at the end of the day, even if things didn't quite work out with Jack, it didn't matter. She was on her way up the mountain, with or without him. She'd found herself a little niche where she had a house and a job. Did she need a perfect relationship to keep her head above water and make her feel good about herself? Did she heck.

23

Lotta had been tossing and turning for hours. Nothing seemed to get her mind to stop whirring. She'd been awake in her bed, unable to sleep since 3 a.m., the witching hour when insomnia liked to sometimes whack her over her head and reiterate to her who exactly was in charge. She'd had insomnia as a best friend often in the days when she'd wondered how she was ever going to turn her life around. It had taken her fears, given them a good squeeze, and amplified them in the early hours by a trillion per cent. It had been gone for a while. Now it was back, lying beside her on the bed.

She had been there for ages, staring up at the ceiling rose above, her mind racing with thoughts about Jack's text. It had all been very strange and when she'd messaged Jack back, she'd been expecting something different, something more... but what? She couldn't work it out. What had she expected? Something more meaningful, something cold or impersonal? He'd just simply sent back an oops, sorry, wrong person. A perfectly reasonable response, wasn't it? Whatever it was, his message and seemingly nonchalant attitude had left her feeling even worse and so very uneasy. Now her mind was going around like a washing machine as she willed herself to drop back off to sleep.

No matter how much she tried to distract herself, her mind kept drifting back to the text. She tried counting sheep and had even had a go with cows. She'd pretended she was the heroine in one of her romcoms and walked herself through scenes in books, but that only made her more frustrated. She'd tossed and turned, trying desperately to get some kind of rest, but to no avail. Just Jack, the pink jacket, and the text were front and centre of her mind.

After a while, she finally sat bolt upright and switched on the bedside light. She reached over to her phone and stared at the screen. The little machine that had sent her into a tailspin, set her world turning. Sighing heavily, she leant down with her right hand to look for her slippers, and once they were on, she heaved herself out of bed. Grabbing her dressing gown from its hook behind the door, she pulled it around her, the fluffy pink fabric soft against her skin, as she padded across the room and opened the curtains. Maybe a gaze outside would calm her racing mind. As she pulled back the curtain, a full moon shone down over the sea and moonlight washed into the room, landing on the old hardwood floor. With her arms folded, Lotta just stared out of the window, gazing out to sea as it seemed to stretch away for miles. She could hear the sound of the waves lapping against the shore. As she listened to its rhythm, it didn't do much for the pounding thoughts about Jack that were going on in her head. She watched the horizon for a few minutes, contemplating going down to make a cup of hot chocolate and attempting to make her thoughts drift away and think about anything but Jack.

Five or so minutes went by, and she found herself standing in the kitchen, opening the fridge and yanking out a pint of milk. She heard the old vine in the conservatory rustle and the floorboards in the breakfast room creak. As she put a mug down on the worktop, she reached up for a tub of hot chocolate, spooned it into the bottom, and poured on milk. She watched as the chocolate powder dispersed through the milk, and as she stirred the mixture with a spoon, she tried to stop her brain from swishing around and around like the powder. When all the powder had dissolved, she placed the mug in the microwave, pressed the button, and watched in the dark as the mug circled the inside.

The tiny kitchen was quiet apart from the hum of the microwave, and as she glanced over at the clock on the oven, she realised she'd been awake for a long time and it was not getting any better. Her head was full of anxious thoughts that had been racing through her mind since more or less the first time she'd seen the notification on Jack's phone from someone going by the name of Sam.

She went over and over the text from Jack and analysed it for the millionth time. It had been innocent enough, and she was just about still able to rationalise that it was probably nothing. The other part of her brain, though, was anything but rational and imagined all sorts. The other part of her brain was having a lot of fun making her paranoid.

Lotta tried to work out two things; why it was making her feel so bad and why the heck she didn't just come out and say something to him about it? As she analysed it more, the penny finally dropped. The problem was that to Lotta the message signified something much more than a few words. As she stared at them for what felt like an eternity, not knowing why they'd pushed so many of her buttons, she slowly nodded and sighed. Deep down, she knew exactly what was going on; she'd let herself fall in way too deep with Jack and if anything went wrong, she didn't know how she was going to cope.

The microwave pinged, jolting Lotta out of her racing thoughts. She took the mug out, stirred it vigorously, popped it back in for thirty more seconds, and then pulled it back out.

The chocolatey milk sent steamy wisps into the air as she stirred it again and ladled a few dollops of Callala cream on top. She followed it with a healthy sprinkle of brown sugar for good measure, picked up the mug, and walked over to the conservatory and stood by the old vine. Taking in the night's view of the garden, she could hear the waves in the distance and tiny little stars twinkling in an inky black night sky. She shook her head. At least the garden was looking up. She might be worried about the text, but her surroundings were a whole lot better when she'd been ceremoniously dumped by Dan and the app.

As she stood leaning on the conservatory doorway, sipping on her hot chocolate, she ever-so-slowly began to feel a wave of calm come over her as she stood there, watching the goings-on of the garden at night. She closed her eyes and for the first time since she'd received the text, she started to feel a tiny, really tiny, minute bit better.

Once she'd finished the chocolate, she padded over to the library room, pulled one of her favourite old books from the shelves, and returned to bed. She sat there for ages, with her knees up and her little reading light on, lost in the book. Eventually, her eyes began to feel heavy, she double-checked her alarm was set for work, laid down, and with the pink jacket feeling as if it was burned to the inside of her eyelids, she closed her eyes. Even though she was tired, her mind still continued to whizz and buzz as she pondered the implications of Jack's text. She tried desperately to make sense of it all, telling herself it was nothing, but no matter how much she convinced herself, she was unable to come up with a reasonable explanation. After what felt like hours of contemplation, she finally drifted off to sleep, not sure of what was to come.

24

The next evening, with her eyes on matchsticks, Lotta was sitting in the library, glued to her laptop, scrolling through her social media feed and answering comments about her latest book review, when her phone rang from the other side of the room. Without even looking at the caller ID, she had a funny feeling it was Singapore. In the back of her mind, she'd been waiting for more bad news. She groaned inside as she saw that she was right and her mum's partner was calling. This was not going to be good. She answered the call, her voice a mix of concern and resignation.

'Hi, Dave. Is everything okay?' she said, in a tone that was slightly sharper than she had intended but full of concern.

There was a pause on the other end before Dave came on the line. Lotta's unease grew as she heard the tone in Dave's voice. 'I need to talk to you about your Mum. She insisted that I didn't call, you know what she's like.'

Lotta's heart sank, and she felt the familiar anxiety around anything to do with her mum rising in her chest. She had known something was going to happen. She'd felt it somewhere in her bones. What was worse was her mum had done the thing she'd done to Lotta all her life; she'd disengaged even further, if that was possible. From experience, Lotta knew that the disengagement always preceded heavy episodes of drinking. Despite what she might have been told by a doctor, or indeed Dave, Lotta knew inside that after the diagnosis of a mini heart attack, her mum would have turned to the bottle. Lotta had grown up around it and knew exactly the game her mum played all too well. It was like a script just sitting in the wings, waiting to be read. Lotta knew exactly how the script was written and how the play was going to go. She'd tried not to immediately write her mum off and had held onto a tiny bit of hope that a heart attack might change things, but not much.

Dave's voice validated all her thoughts: Lotta had been worried that things were going to get worse, and here was the call. She'd been half expecting it since the first one. 'What's happened?' Lotta asked, her voice barely above a whisper.

Dave paused again before speaking. 'She had another turn at the weekend. She insisted I didn't tell you. She was kept in for observation, but she's out now. They're not sure what it was,' Dave spoke in a low, steady voice with a strange mix of calm and stress at the same time. 'It could have been a stroke, but they don't know.'

'And the drinking?' Lotta asked resignedly. She was positive there would have been drinking.

'It's, well, umm, secretive.' Dave sighed.

No surprise there, Lotta nodded and thought to herself. She'd seen it so, so, so many times before, she wasn't even shocked that someone could have a heart attack and still continue to drink. Now that she was older and more clued-up on it, she was well aware that it was part of the disease.

Dave let out a harassed-sounding sigh. 'She's been drinking, definitely. I still believe she thinks I don't know how much.'

Lotta knew how that felt – she'd been on the end of it many times. She shook her head. None of it surprised her. She didn't really know what to feel, but she did feel as if the wind had been knocked out of her sails. Her mum had struggled with alcoholism for years, even though no one was allowed to talk about it, least of all Lotta. Now, it seemed, the disease had taken a turn for the worse. Lotta had always tried to prepare herself for the moment that was happening now, but it was still horrible.

'Is she going to be okay?' Lotta said, fighting back a combination of anger, sadness, and little pricks of tears right at the corner of her eyes.

'I don't know is the only answer,' Dave said. He paused again. 'Look, I know it's tricky, but well, I think it would be good for you to see her, maybe. I know you've had it tough but...'

Lotta felt a sharp pang of guilt. Even though she'd barely done anything wrong, it was always the same. A horrible guilty feeling that she was somehow a bad daughter, that somehow it was her fault, engulfed her. Her mind flashed back to when she was a child. When she'd let herself in from school to find her mum either absent or lying comatose on the sofa. Or the many times she'd find vodka bottles hidden in all sorts of places. The times when she'd been home alone all night, wondering what was going to happen. How she'd hidden her mum's drinking from the family in the days when the family still cared. How she'd pretended her mum was like all the other mums. Only her mum really never was.

The strange guilt walloped Lotta in the face. Even though Lotta had sent texts and tried to speak to her mum, as usual, her mum hadn't really been interested. On top of that, Lotta had been so wrapped up in her own life, her mind had been full and busy with many other things.

Lotta felt her voice trembling. 'Sorry. What are you saying? Are you telling me to come to Singapore? Is that right?'

Dave's voice was low. 'I know this isn't easy for you. I'm sorry I had to call you. What I'm saying is...' Dave stopped, swore, and then continued. 'I don't know if I'm speaking out of turn, but I have a funny feeling that, well, you know, there might not be…' He paused, searching for the right words. 'I'm saying I think you should come out here, yes.'

Lotta went cold, and her voice was barely audible. 'You must think this is serious enough to ask me to come?' she stated.

'I do. I really do. Sorry,' Dave replied. 'I wouldn't call you otherwise. I know how much of a big deal it is to get here, and well, how things are between you and your mum.'

'Does Mum know you were going to phone me?'

Dave sounded sad. 'She just nodded. I think she knows too. Sorry, Lotta, I don't really know what else to say.'

'Okay, right, I'll speak to you in the morning. I mean my morning.'

'Okay. Yep, speak then.'

As she hung up the phone, tears filled Lotta's eyes. She wanted to be strong, but part of her wanted to curl up in a ball, pull a cover over her head, and wait until it was all over.

Her mind raced with memories. She'd always looked at other people with their lovely families and relationships with their mums. She'd seen other girls at school collected by happy, pretty, smiley mums while she'd walked home alone to a sombre, depressing house. She'd watched her mum's drinking ruin family events. She'd witnessed her mother scream and shout and behave like anything but an adult. She'd sat in silence as her mum had made every single thing in Lotta's life an ache. Now it seemed, even in this, her mum was going to act in the same way. Lotta screwed her face up and put her head in her hands, not wanting to be part of it at all. As ever, she really had no choice.

25

Lotta settled into her seat and felt the fast train pull away from Pretty Beach. As it moved slowly over the tracks, she could see glimpses of the sea and the hills in the far distance. Feeling the carriages clatter underneath her as they pulled further away from the coast, she took her Kindle from her bag and rested it on her lap – at least she would be able to use the journey to see her mum to escape with a book.

She gazed out the window, watching as the countryside passed by in a blur, an odd flash of blue in the distance and a low sun glinting off buildings. Her stomach was twisted into a tense knot as Pretty Beach faded away from her and the outskirts of the little town slowly erased from her view. As the train quickly picked up speed and sped through the countryside, a blur of trees and green whizzed past the window, and Lotta felt her veins swirling with apprehension and uncertainty about what she would find in Singapore. Whatever was on the horizon, she knew from prior experience that it wouldn't be good.

Flipping the cover on her Kindle, she started to go through her new books. As she opened a romcom based in Scotland where a woman had just moved to an island and wasn't quite as enamoured with the grey skies and constant drizzle as she thought she was going to be, Lotta lost herself temporarily in the dreary weather in the book. But as the train got nearer to its destination, she grew more and more anxious. Her chest felt as if someone had tightened it with an Allen key, and her veins were running alive with adrenaline.

The next time she looked up from her book, she realised the train was now slowing, and people were getting ready to leave. As she packed her Kindle carefully into her bag, verified the location of her passport for the hundredth time, and put on her jacket, she took a deep breath and watched as the man opposite her put his laptop into a sleeve and then typed a message with his thumbs on his phone. Lotta checked her watch; she'd need to muscle to get the next express train to the airport, and then she'd be on her way. Her stomach churned as she hurried along, and she felt sick with what might be waiting for her in Singapore, what her mum would be doing, and how she would behave. Lotta had a horrible sense of foreboding. Only time would tell.

Despite her worry about her mum and what was going on with Jack, Lotta had a secret little chuckle to herself when she boarded the flight. Thanks to Jack's involvement in her ticket, she'd totally turned left on the plane. As a smiley, happy woman with the most perfectly applied make-up and immaculate updo ever offered her a glass of champagne, she felt a sudden urge to pop a picture of herself to Dan. Yeah, Dan, how are you getting on? How's the app, my friend? Are you still dealing with that? Yeah, well, matey, you might have left me for dead and with a lot of debt, but yeah, I'm no longer best friends with a bottle of bleach and a whole lot of worry about money.

Yeah, matey, I'm moving in different circles now. Stick that in your pipe.

Instead, she laughed to herself again as she settled into the plush seat and looked out the window at the huge expanse of pink-orange sky beyond the tarmac. She then alternated between watching the passengers file past, putting their things in the overhead lockers, and observing the sun slowly dipping down, making its way towards the horizon. She might be full of worry, but as she sipped on her champagne and scrolled through the entertainment system, her surroundings were definitely helping. Trying to concentrate on what movies to watch, she felt a surging wave of nerves in her stomach at how she was going to be received at the other end.

After noting a couple of films she wouldn't mind watching as the plane continued to load, she opened her Kindle and tried to push aside her worries. This flight and its return leg, for all she knew, might be the one and only time she'd be up the front of a plane – she was going to try and focus on the moment and make the most of it. She looked around her at the other passengers and started to read as the buzz of conversation and movement around her continued.

She was speed reading and well into the first meeting between the protagonist and the love interest on the Scottish island when the captain's voice came over the intercom. As he welcomed everyone aboard the flight and informed them of the weather in Singapore, Lotta felt butterflies about how it was going to go with her mum. Dave's call and tone had unsettled her immensely. That fact alone meant that things were not looking good. As the plane slowly ascended into the sky, she looked down at the buildings and lights of London below and with thirteen-odd hours ahead of her, Lotta settled back into her seat. Closing her eyes, she let her mind wander about what she would be feeling on the way back.

Thirteen hours, a few cocktails, and a lot of reading later, the plane started its descent and Lotta looked down at the cityscape below and marvelled at the beauty of it all. In a flash, in complete contrast to what had happened at Heathrow, she was through passport control, on the other side and in a line for the taxis.

The journey from the airport to the hotel was simple enough, and Lotta had done it enough times that she knew what was what. Dave had said that he'd thought it would be a better idea if Lotta didn't stay in the house – Lotta had agreed with a sigh of relief. She'd been on the end of her mother's fits more than a few times in the past, and it was safer for all concerned, but most of all her, if the opportunity for her mum to suddenly turn and start screaming and spouting venom was minimised. With Lotta in her favourite Singaporean hotel, she could at least come and go as she liked.

She smiled as the taxi pulled up in the courtyard of the lovely old colonial hotel. It was the one place in her life where she'd never been concerned about budget. As the taxi door was opened by the hotel doorman, the Singaporean humidity and thick, intense heat hit her squarely between the eyes. She inhaled the sweet, heavy air as she was greeted by the hotel's bright white and exotic blue façade. She looked up at the ornately decorated building with its intricate coloured tiles, fancy columns, and traditional peaked roof. She sighed in plea-sure. At least the hotel was a place to escape to, no matter what went on with her mum.

She took another deep breath as the heat zapped her from above and inhaled the tropical air filled with jasmine and all sorts of florals of whose names she had no clue. In the short few steps to the lobby, the humidity clobbered her, and she shud-dered when the hotel air conditioning and its perfumed scent nipped at her skin. She smiled at the elegant, shiny marble floor, the old, highly polished grand staircase sweeping down on the right and the concierge desks on the left. Antique furniture, the ticking of a clock and the scent of a subtle combination of cherry blossom, wood, leather, and furniture polish filled the serene air. She might be full of worry, but the colonial hospitality let her shoulders drop just a little bit away from her ears.

With a smooth, efficient check-in from a friendly face, Lotta took the lift up to her room and sent a message to Dave as she pulled back the curtains and gazed out over Singapore's skyline.

Lotta: *Hi Dave. I've just arrived at the hotel. How is she?*

The little buttons flashed for what felt like a long time.

Dave: *She's asleep in bed.*

Lotta: *Right. I'll come tomorrow then.*

Dave: *Yes.*

Lotta: *She didn't seem very happy about me coming over when I messaged her before I left.*

Dave: *Sorry. I don't know what to say.*

Lotta: *She said if I was here I must be dramatising.*

Dave: *I saw the text. Sorry, Lotta. She'd had a fair bit to drink when she sent that.*

Lotta: *I gathered that.*

Dave: *Are you going to be okay?*

Lotta rolled her eyes. Of course, she was going to be okay. She for sure knew that her mum wasn't going to be worrying about her. And what other choice did she have? Lotta always had to be okay around her mother. Always had to keep her mouth very firmly closed. Always had to not have an opinion of her own on anything. Always, always must never mention the drinking.

Lotta: *I'm fine. Don't worry about me, Dave.*

Dave: *Do you want me to come and collect you tomorrow?*

Lotta contemplated for a minute. Her mother had used Dave picking her up as a weapon before. She typed back quickly with her thumbs that she would make her own way over and closed off the text conversation and pottered around with her bag, musing over the messages. From Dave's response, things certainly hadn't changed.

Once she'd put a few things in the bathroom, had a shower, and was about to go down to walk around the mall adjacent to the hotel, her phone buzzed with a video call. Lotta propped her phone on the desk and smiled as Jack came onto the screen. As she looked at her phone screen, the sprawling metropolis of the Singapore cityscape seemed to stretch away in the distance behind her, towering skyscrapers dotted the skyline, and the hum of traffic on the streets below was softened by the hotel soundproofing. As Lotta waited for the lag to catch up and Jack's face all the way back in England to unfreeze, it was almost as if she was in a completely different universe. She'd never felt so removed and *so* alone.

As he fully appeared, her heart thudded. She'd been waiting for his call and was already missing him so much that it scared her.

'Hey,' Jack said, smiling. 'You've arrived safe and sound. How was the flight?'

'It was good. As good as a thirteen-hour flight can be!' Lotta replied, smiling, feeling a wave of happiness wash over her at the sight of Jack's face. 'Long, but uneventful. What have you been up to?'

'Not much. I've just been working.' There was concern written all over Jack's face. 'How are you feeling?'

Lotta totally lied about how she was feeling. Not many people knew too much about her relationship with her mum, including Jack. It was tricky and ugly, and she hated it. She'd told him enough so that he knew what was what, but the actual truth ran deep. 'I'm okay. How are you?'

Jack gave her a rundown of his day since he'd dropped her off at the fast train. He'd just been at work. The image of the bottle of perfume lodged in his desk drawer flashed into Lotta's mind as Jack spoke. She flicked it away. 'Sounds like you've not done much at all.'

'Nope. I'm missing you already.'

It was on the tip of Lotta's tongue to ask him if he missed her enough to tell her who he'd been meeting the other night when he'd accidentally texted her, instead she just chatted. She'd told him brief bits about her mum and explained the gist of Dave's text. Jack had listened and not made much comment.

'It sounds like it's going to be quite tough for you,' Jack noted with narrowed eyes. 'Sorry if I'm out of line to comment, but I can't believe she texted you to say you shouldn't have come.'

Lotta smiled, feeling a wave of homesickness wash over her. It felt odd to have someone who had not only cut straight to the chase and read the situation adeptly but who was also on her side. She nodded. She didn't need anyone to tell her about her mum's behaviour, but she was glad Jack was concerned. All she really wanted to do was bury it all, hop back on another plane, zoom through the front door at Pretty Beach to the Breakers, collapse in the library room, get lost in her books and hope that it would all go away. That was a pipe dream, like a plotline in one of her books. 'I'm glad I've made the effort. At least I know I've done that,' she said.

'Yep. You have. Well done, you.'

Lotta then changed the subject, and for a while, she lost herself in all things Jack. They talked and chuckled and chatted for ages and as Jack made her laugh and she told him about a funny thing that had happened on the flight, for a while, she forgot about her mum.

'What did work say in the end? You only told me briefly,' Jack asked.

'They were fine. There aren't any functions this week in the arcade anyway, well not any of mine. Marie has a few I was supporting, but she said it was no drama. So, yeah, I'm just keeping an eye on it via my emails. There are a few things I have to put together for next month. I did some of it on the plane when I wasn't reading.'

'That's good that they're flexible,' Jack noted. 'You've landed on your feet there by the sounds of it.'

'I know. I'm lucky.'

'Same old story, really,' Jack said with his mouth turned upside down.

'What does that mean?'

'It's not luck, Lott. They want to keep hold of you. Trying to find staff who are firstly, good, and secondly, want to work, is like trying to find a needle in a haystack these days.'

Lotta didn't really know. From her end of the stick, finding a good job had been nigh-on impossible. 'Hmm. I guess so.'

'I know so,' Jack affirmed with a nod.

When they said their goodbyes, Lotta felt a pang in her heart at being so, so far away from Pretty Beach. As she finished the call, she sat staring out at the skyscrapers, lost in thought. She hadn't realised in the slightest how living in the little town had buoyed her and somehow wrapped her up in its protective arms. Now even though she knew the hotel, knew where she was going, and knew what was what, all of a sudden she felt very vulnerable and very alone. As if she was once again on a rollercoaster that was out of control and was about to fall off the tracks.

She was so far away and so worried, she couldn't quite compute what was going on. Her brain seemed both fried and wired at the same time. It was as if the whole thirteen-hour journey had gone by in a split second and had picked her up by her shoulders, given her a great big shake and dropped her in Singapore. Lotta didn't really know whether or not she was coming or going. She did know that all she wanted to do was climb into the perfectly starched, perfectly white hotel sheets, pull them over her head, switch on her Kindle and not look up for air.

26

Lotta had got off the MRT one stop early so that she could walk through Dempsey and past the black and white houses. She loved the old colonial Singaporean-style houses and had done since she'd first set eyes on them when her mum had initially moved out to Singapore. Thick tropical air stuck her linen shirt to her skin and her hair to her head but as she ambled along, she tried to ignore it as she looked at the beautiful old shutters on the stark white buildings.

Putting her umbrella up to shade her from the sun, she strolled along under the palms, surrounded by the idyllic charm of the old houses and squinted at the gorgeous verandahs and the glossy black window frames. As she got closer and closer to her mum's place, situated in a private block adjacent to the black and white houses, she got more and more anxious and her heart began to race.

Surrounded by lush palms and greenery and the air thick with the scent of frangipani and hibiscus, she pushed the button on the intercom to let her into the grounds. Dave answered the buzz, the gate clicked, and she started to walk around the tropical gardens on her way to their front door. As her mind raced, the humid air seemed to get thicker, the flowers brighter, and the sun hotter. Birds so different from those in Pretty Beach, perched up in the trees, chirped away busily, and thick green palms lining the pathway rustled in the wind.

Lotta sighed as she got to her mum's house. How sad it was that her mum had never been really interested in her, always seeing her as a burden. Lotta was the leftover from a person she'd met on a drunken, drug-fuelled night. Lotta pushed down the same old feeling she had whenever she was around her mum. She tried, as she always did, not to dwell on how different her life could have been if her mum hadn't been an alcoholic. How she'd always looked at other people her age with lovely stable mums who did lovely stable things. They, and the people around them, not constantly walking on eggshells of what their mother's mental health and alcoholic state would bring.

She ran her finger along an ornate shutter that adorned the window next to the door as she waited for it to be answered. As she stood there with the humidity wrapped around her, making her clothes stick to her skin, she became more and more melancholic. The heat was the kind of Singapore heat that pressed down like a heavyweight, but it was nothing compared to the weight currently residing on Lotta's shoulders. As she stood waiting, she could hear the cicadas somewhere hidden in the trees and the low buzz of the air conditioning unit hidden behind the louvred doors beside her. Inhaling slowly, trying not to feel anxious, she attempted to steel herself for whatever mood her mum might be in.

Dave opened the door and stood still in the doorway, his expression unreadable. Lotta nervously touched her ponytail to keep it out of the way of the heat, but as she looked at Dave, she could feel her face flushed from the humidity and sweat running down the small of her back. Dave raised his eyebrows, took in a deep breath, and nodded slightly in acknowledgement before opening the door wider and breaking into a small smile. 'How are you? How was your flight?'

'Yeah, it was fine.'

Dave motioned for Lotta to go inside and stepped back to let her pass as she stepped in; she felt the icy cold air conditioning feather over, hitting her damp skin. Lotta lowered her voice, 'How is she?'

Dave shook his head and looked down at his feet and then clasped his hands together. 'She's already had a drink.'

Of course she had. Lotta felt her heart sink. 'Right.'

He pointed to the sitting room. 'She's upstairs. I'll make us a drink. What would you like?' Dave asked, looking at Lotta with weary eyes. He motioned for her to sit on the sofa.

'Anything cold would be lovely. I'd forgotten how the humidity zaps you.'

Dave nodded. 'I'll do a jug of iced tea.'

A few minutes later, Dave was back in the sitting room with a glass jug full of ice, lemon, and tea. He poured out two glasses and handed one over to Lotta. The glass felt cool in her right hand, and she rested it on the wrist of her left hand to cool her down. 'How are you?'

'I'm okay. Look, just be prepared. I know it's been a while since you've seen her, what with what's been going on in the world. She's, well, she's not looking her best.'

Lotta had to stop herself from shaking her head. Not having seen her mum for a long time was not just about the global health situation. Her mum hadn't really wanted to see Lotta. It was as simple and as cut and dried as that. 'Right, okay.'

'She's lost quite a bit of weight from when you last saw her,' Dave stated. 'I know it's hard for you. I wish I could say something a bit more, well, a bit more, umm, helpful or something.'

'Thanks, Dave. It's fine.' Lotta's voice caught in her throat, but she would be darned if she was going to cry. She gulped a mouthful of the sweet tea and as it went down, she pushed down the emotion threatening to bubble up in her chest and overwhelm her.

Lotta had to stop herself from exclaiming when her mum hobbled into the sitting room. She looked at Lotta with barely concealed disdain. 'I really don't know why you bothered. Always making a drama out of everything. You didn't need to come.'

Lotta didn't really hear what her mum was saying – she was too busy taking in the fact that her mum had halved in size. No wonder Dave had told her to come. Despite her mum's usual make-up, her cheeks were gaunt and her eyes appeared hooded. Tears pricked at the corners of Lotta's eyes. She blinked them back and stood up. Her mum seemed to rattle and held her hand up. 'I don't need help! Don't touch me.'

Lotta's heart sank. She had known it was a possibility, but hearing her mum's tone, she knew it wasn't going to be a good visit. When her mum was irritated by Lotta's very presence, it never ended well. Lotta sat back down and didn't say a word, and observed her mum and quietly sipped on her tea. Lotta had to stop herself from frowning; her mum was so thin, yet her stomach was distended.

'I'm looking old, yes,' Lotta's mum almost snarled.

As Lotta watched her mother ease herself onto the sofa, the full weight of the situation came crashing down on her. Lotta's mum squinted and screwed her mouth up so that tight lines formed above and below her lips. 'You don't need to look at me like that,' she said.

Lotta swallowed, all at once transported back to the kitchen in their house when she was a young girl. Her mum had fallen over drunk and hit her head on the sink. When Lotta had tried to help her, she'd snarled and told her to keep away. It was as if the years had been wiped away in a second. The snarl was still the same, the look of disdain still there, the winced-lined lips still as nasty.

It had been many years since Lotta had had to endure the same house as her mother, but Lotta could spot the signs that she'd had a morning drink. Lotta inwardly sighed but kept her mouth firmly closed. If there was one thing she'd learnt, it was how to play the game. She'd learnt the hard way when she didn't. The less she said, the more she nodded and let her mum spout off, the better everyone would be.

Lotta felt her breathing increase, her throat tight with emotion, and she felt herself gripping the iced tea like a vice. She could tell her mum had been drinking, there hadn't really been too much of a surprise in that. What she hadn't expected was how her mum looked. She was only just in her seventies but appeared as if she had aged overnight.

Lotta continued to sip on her tea and not say much. Her mum started with a few words about the hospital and doctors and then quickly changed the subject to family. Lotta felt a little bit of her die inside. She'd been here before. If her mum was talking about family, the best thing Lotta could do would be to get out as quickly as she could. As Lotta heard her mum droning on about how the family had disowned her, Lotta knew things were bad. It was the subject her mum always banged on about when she was feeling low.

Focusing her eyes just above her mum's eyebrows and appearing as if she was listening, she contemplated what to say for the best. When her mum was in this mood, Lotta was never quite sure what to say. Her mind whirred as she took in her mum's appearance. Part of her had wondered if Dave was being a bit over the top when he had called. Another part of her had been in denial, hoping that it would all go away and she wouldn't have to deal with more of her mum's problems. But now that she was sitting opposite her mum, she was in no doubt about Dave's concern.

Lotta was jolted out of her thoughts as she heard her mum ask a question about the flight. At least she'd stopped talking about family. Lotta dared not tell her about business class. Her mum would not like that in the slightest. 'The flight was pleasant, thanks,' Lotta said noncommittally.

'You're in the same hotel? I did tell Dave it would be better if you weren't here. As I said in my message, the last thing I need is you here upsetting me.'

Lotta nodded, gripped her glass, and stared down at the lemon floating amongst the ice in her drink. She took a sip, trying to keep her composure. 'I just want you to get better,' Lotta whispered. By the looks on her mum's face, Lotta instantly realised she'd said totally the wrong thing.

Her mum couldn't quite manage a screech, but she wasn't far off it. 'Here we go! Here we go. All about you. Always was and always will be.'

Lotta swallowed and forced herself not to cry. From her side of the room, it had never, ever been about her. And by the looks of the situation in front of her, that was not about to change anytime soon.

27

Lotta had been back to see her mum a few times. The second and third times, her mum had tried and failed to conceal her drinking, and Lotta had spotted her mum's state right away. She'd walked in, read the room, and counted down the minutes until she could go.

Lotta had an uncanny knack of knowing all about the alcohol intake. She'd learnt, and fast, all sorts of things as markers; the look on her mum's face, the overpowering stench of perfume to cover the smell of drink, the mug of supposed peppermint tea by her mum's side. All of them pointing in the same way.

There were so many other signs Lotta had learnt to read over the years. Depending on the stage of her cycle of drinking, her mum would have done her hair, applied lots of make-up, would be dressed, and would be constantly one after the other popping mints. All of it contrasting so ironically with what would ultimately happen – her ending up on the floor.

The fourth and fifth times she'd visited hadn't been much better, and her mum had remained in the bedroom and refused to come out. Dave had made up an excuse, telling Lotta she was having a nap. Lotta knew better.

After more visits and more upset, Lotta had decided she couldn't take much more of it. It was clear to all involved that she was really very much wasting her time.

About a week after she'd arrived, she sighed as she walked away from the hotel. She knew all the whys and wherefores of what was going on; that the disease was one of isolation and secrecy. She was well aware too that along with all the other things, the denial was part of it. But it didn't make it any better.

Lotta had been through all the emotions through the years; up, down, round and about, and back again. Now here she was again on the end of it. But this time, a new feeling was accompanying her. In the past she'd been sad, then furious and everything else in between, but this time she was just so very tired. Tired of having it in her life.

The humidity cloaked her as she walked along looking at the beautiful old Singaporean buildings and made her way to a coffee shop she had visited every time she'd been to stay. Waiting at a set of lights, she crossed over and got in the queue snaking along the pavement outside the old colonial pink building.

People-watching, she smiled as the customers in front of her came away with their coffees in funny little plastic carrier bags for one. Thoughts of her mum's refusal to see her raced through her head as she got closer to the counter and watched the barista deftly pouring liquid through the coffee sock.

A few minutes later, she was sitting at one of the funny little low marble tables, looking at the old-fashioned tiled walls and art deco pendant lamps flanking the ceiling. A long, wide teak mirror hung from high up on the wall, bouncing light around and little carved teak stools were clustered around the tables. Around her, paintings of Singapore's past with traditional scenes and idyllic fishing villages were fixed haphazardly on the walls, and next to her, postcards tacked up with drawing pins offered a glimpse into Singapore's past.

Shelves stretched from floor to ceiling were lined with tall stacks of brown paper coffee sacks. Dried beans of every kind were neatly stacked and labelled and sat in between huge Mason jars filled with spices. All of it jumbled around her, releasing a heady, fragrant mix of coffee, spices, and cinnamon into the air.

Lotta gulped it all in and took out her Kindle as she gazed around as she waited for her order; a group of teenagers in school uniform, some with laptops, sat chatting and soaking up the atmosphere, and a tiny baby sound asleep in a pram, snoozed alongside the table beside her. The sound of the coffee machine hissed rhythmically and as she opened her Kindle, she started to drift away and get lost in her book.

Alternating staring out the window with reading her book and being lost in thought, Lotta sipped on her coffee and watched as people hurried by in the mid-morning sun. Her phone buzzed from her bag, jarring her from her thoughts. She answered it, seeing that it was Jack.

'Hello?'

'Hey.'

'Hi,' Lotta said with a small smile and felt a twinge of pleasure at hearing his voice. He sounded familiar and kind and as if he cared for her, all at the same time. She relished in how that made her feel.

'What's going on? Any further news?'

'Nope. Nothing else. She was in bed again this morning when I went there.'

'Oh, okay. So she didn't want to see you again?'

'She did not.'

'That's tough. I'm so sorry, Lott. I didn't really realise it was going to be like this for you.'

Lotta squeezed her eyes together, willing herself not to cry.

She was fine dealing with her mum most of the time, but when someone else noted how tough it was, it knocked her out of kilter. Talking to Jack made her feel both better and worse at the same time. She did, though, feel a wave of gratitude wash over her that he was in her life. She took a sip of her coffee and let out a long, dramatic exhale. 'Thanks. I'm still trying to wrap my head around it all. It's nothing new for her not to see me, but, I don't know, she just looks sick. She always hid it so well before. She's lost so much weight.'

'How's Dave doing?'

'He's doing okay, I think. It's just so awkward having to pretend and skirt around the drinking issue. I don't know. To be honest, I don't even know what to think…' Lotta said, not finishing the end of her sentence. 'At least I came.'

Jack didn't say anything for a bit, and a moment of silence passed between them. 'How do you actually *feel*?' Jack asked.

Lotta hesitated. She never really told anyone the real truth about her feelings. Liv knew bits and pieces, but the best way she'd learnt to deal with her mum and the emotion was to lock it all up in a nice tight little box. She had been avoiding her real feelings the past few days and just telling herself it was her mum's disease that was doing the talking. Or, more appropriately, not doing the talking. She sighed again and went to say that she was fine and then in a split second changed her mind. 'I'm… I'm, you know, honestly, I'm not okay,' she said. 'I mean, I'm okay, but I don't know. All of a sudden, it's become really real. I've had this on my radar in the distance for so long, and now it's happening. She really is not very well, by how she looks.'

'Yeah, it doesn't sound good.'

'Nope,' Lotta said, her voice wavering. She pressed her thumb and forefinger into the corners of her eyes. 'I've been trying not to think about it, but I just keep going back to the fact that despite what's happened, not only is she still drinking, but she's still keeping up this ridiculous farce. It's on my mind all the time. I've been... I've been struggling a lot. I just want to come home, to be quite honest.'

Jack's voice was serious. 'You don't have to pretend as if everything's okay. It's clearly not. Sorry, Lotta, but she doesn't sound nice. I don't care what's wrong with her.'

The simple act of Jack acknowledging that made Lotta feel lighter, as if a weight had been lifted from the bricks sitting stacked up on her shoulders. 'I know. I just... I don't want to do the wrong thing. You know?'

'And what would the right thing be?'

'I don't know. Be a good daughter...' Lotta let her sentence trail off and sighed.

'From what I've seen, you are a good daughter,' Jack said firmly.

Lotta's stomach lurched, and tiny warm tears spilt out over her lids and ran in warm streams down her cheeks. She wiped them away quickly. 'Thanks. It helps to be able to talk about it.'

'I'm here if you need to talk,' Jack said. 'I'm not sure what help I am.'

She smiled, thankful for his support. 'Thanks.'

On top of everything else that was going on right at that second, the pink jacket landed front and centre in Lotta's mind. Jack was being so supportive and kind, it was hardly the time to start questioning his loyalty. She pushed the thought down and sighed. 'What have you been doing?'

'Working, that's it. When are you going back to your mum's house?'

'I really don't know. Tomorrow, I suppose.'

'Look, Lott, tell me to mind my own business, but maybe it's time to come back home. If she's not willing to see you and she's being, to be quite frank, nasty, is it worth it? All that upheaval and emotion, and she doesn't want you there anyway.'

'I know.' Lotta sighed.

'You've made the effort now, and you've been there, what, a week, and now she doesn't want to see you? I mean, sorry, but I'm calling it. That's really pretty horrible.'

Lotta nodded. 'It's just the disease. It's always been that way.'

Jack sighed. 'Maybe so, but you have me here now. I'm in the Lotta corner, and I am telling you that I think perhaps it's time to look after you. Time to call it a day. What is the point in you being there and being upset?'

'True.'

'What has Liv said?'

Lotta thought about her conversation with Liv. 'More or less the same. Maybe not quite as forceful. She knows what Mum is like.'

'Yes, she obviously knows a bit more about it than me,' Jack noted.

'Yep, she does.'

'What about the rest of the family?'

'Mum fell out with them years ago. It was all take, take, take from her end. It got quite nasty in the end. No one has anything to do with her nowadays.'

'And this hasn't changed anything?'

'Well, Liv's dad, my uncle, was Mum's brother, but he passed away a few years ago and his wife won't have anything to do with Mum. Mum has also said she doesn't want anyone to know about her drinking so, umm, it's all really tricky.'

'Phew, families!'

'I know.'

'Look, you just need to make sure you're okay. I know I haven't been around long, but I'm here to stick up for you,' Jack said.

Lotta felt her heart swell. 'Thanks. I'd better go,' she said eventually.

'Okay, well, let me know how you get on today. Phone me anytime. Love you.'

'Okay, thanks Jack, will do. Love you too.'

As Lotta put her phone in her bag, she sighed. Maybe Jack had a point. Maybe it was time to call it a day and get home.

The next day, Lotta was sitting in a quiet corner of the lobby of her hotel in Singapore, her laptop open in front of her. Liv looked out from her computer screen, and they were discussing the situation with Liv's mum. Liv's face was like thunder. 'Sorry, Lott, I know she's your mum, but she really is so flipping ignorant and arrogant. You've gone all that way, and now she doesn't want to see you! Ahhh!'

'I know. It's always been the same, you know that.' Lotta sighed.

'You've done *nothing* wrong. You never have. Grr, it makes me so furious. I'm not even telling Mum this. You know how she feels about the situation.'

'To be fair, she said she didn't want to see me in the first place. It was Dave that said I should come,' Lotta tried to reason.

'There is nothing, and I mean *nothing*, fair about this situation!' Liv exploded. 'She's so bloody selfish! I don't care if it's the disease speaking. Sorry, Lott, it has to be said.'

'I know,' Lotta said, her voice wavering as she spoke. 'I am glad I came, though. She looks terrible. Dave was right on that call. At least I've done the deed.'

'At least there's that then,' Liv replied, her voice softening. 'I can't believe she didn't want to see you at all yesterday.'

Lotta sighed, a wave of emotion washing over her. 'I can. It's because she knows I know the truth and can see precisely what's going on,' she replied. 'Dave is only a few years into this. He's not quite as experienced in the cycle of it as I am. He doesn't know the signs quite as well.'

'I'm so sorry you're having to go through this. She can't even think about you,' Liv said, her voice heavy with empathy. 'I feel helpless here, too.'

Lotta shook her head. 'There's nothing anyone can do, anyway. From what I've gathered, it's a waiting game.'

Liv nodded, a solemn expression on her face. 'It's so hard to be so far away when something like this happens. I wish there was something I could do to help. I should have come with you.'

Lotta smiled sadly. 'What, and have two of us here who she won't see?' She let out a little ironic chuckle.

Liv smiled back. 'Yeah, that would have been a bit of a waste of time.'

Lotta nodded, her heart swelling with emotion. She was so grateful to have Liv in her life. 'Thank you,' she said, her voice full of appreciation.

Liv nodded. 'What has Jack said about it? Have you filled him in on the truth?'

Lotta felt tears sting at the side of her eyes. 'He thinks I should come home. He didn't quite understand it, which isn't surprising for anyone who doesn't get it.'

'Or he's thinking about you, as *she* should be,' Liv stated.

Lotta nodded, a small smile forming on her lips. 'That's one way of looking at it.'

'What are you going to do?'

'I don't know. I think I may book a flight back. There's no point in me staying here if she doesn't want me to. Plus, I have a new job to think about. Jack is right, really. I have to think about myself for once.'

Liv nodded in assurance. 'You really do, Lott. It's about time, to be honest.'

'I know. I think I'm going to come home tomorrow. There are loads of flights, so that's no drama.' Lotta sighed and flicked her eyes upwards. 'Also, I know this is odd right in the middle of this, but I can't stop thinking about the message and the pink jacket.'

Liv screwed up her nose. 'Oh, crikey, yes. I thought you'd decided to leave that and not worry about it.'

'I did decide that, yep. Easier said than done, though. I can't get it off my mind.'

'I can see why. I really don't think he's up to anything, though. Come on, think about it. He's been so good through this, he sorted the flight, he's been involved…'

'Ahh, he has. I am not rational at the moment, though, Liv! You are currently looking into the eyeballs of the human embodiment of an emotional nightmare.'

'A funny one at that! Do you really think he'd have paid for your flights and be calling you and supporting you if he had someone else?'

'No, but then that is my point. You never do know.'

'I suppose not, but no, Lott. I think you're barking up the wrong tree with this. Just let it lie. There will be a simple explanation. I'm positive.'

'Yes, yes,' Lotta said quickly and turned the subject to something else, but as Liv continued, she kept on seeing the perfume and the pink jacket, and she seemed unable to do anything else but let it lie.

28

The next day, Lotta was back on the plane, coincidentally in the same seat but going the other way. The whole trip had not been her idea of fun. She was emotionally, physically, and mentally spent.

Settling into her seat, she attempted to get comfortable, and with a deep sigh, she tried to force herself to relax. The dull roar of the engines filled her ears, and she found herself anything but relaxed as her mind raced. All she could think about was that her mum was still the same, even after a heart attack. It ate away at Lotta that she might have changed things in her life in terms of her job, her boyfriend and her house and her life might overall be on the up, but where her mum was concerned, nothing had changed. Bottom line was that Lotta felt as if she would always be alone.

She went to the loo and peered in the mirror at her reflection. So much for a glow-up and a break in Singapore. The woman looking back at her was jaded and grey. In addition, the woman was sporting complimentary bags under her eyes, and they were rimmed with a particularly fetching shade of tired red. She didn't really need her reflection to tell her that she was exhausted though, her bones were giving her a good enough indication of that as it was. As she sat back down and ordered a cocktail, the crew member then brought it over, put it down on a little mat, and smiled.

'How are you?'

Lotta automatically responded with her staple answer. 'I'm fine.'

'Business or pleasure?' the woman asked, nodding to the cocktail.

Lotta scrunched up one side of her mouth. It certainly hadn't been pleasurable, that she knew for sure. 'Neither, actually. My mum is...' She paused for a second. What even was it? 'Poorly.'

'Aww, sorry to hear that.' The woman leant on the back of an empty seat. 'My family lives in Melbourne. It's tricky when someone gets sick. Even worse when families don't get on, and then there's the time difference on top of it all. I feel your pain.'

Lotta smiled; it felt nice to hear someone saying some of the things she felt. Though she was pretty sure this woman didn't have a mum who didn't like her. 'Yeah, it is.'

'There's not much you can do about it, I suppose. You just have to get on with it.'

'Yes.' Lotta nodded. There was no change there. She'd always had to do the same.

The woman tapped alongside Lotta's screen. 'Now you let me know if there's anything you need, and I'll get it for you. At least I can help to make this part of your journey as nice as possible.'

Lotta was a tad taken aback by the kindness. 'Thank you. Thanks so much.'

As she sipped on her cocktail and opened her Kindle, a funny feeling washed over her as she thought about her mum, Jack, Pretty Beach and her new job. The feeling was that she wasn't going to let any of it get on top of her. She'd crawled up the mountain, there was no way she was going to slide back down.

She thought about what the woman had said about just having to get on with it. She nodded emphatically and swigged the cocktail. She was determined to pull on her big girl pants. This was just another challenge. She would move forward with aplomb. She would not let anything get in the way of her new life and her new start in Pretty Beach. This Lotta was strong.

Her mind mused her mum and her behaviour. Lotta was not going to let this latest episode, as she had in the past, infiltrate every area of her existence and stir up its usual mix of guilt and shame. She would, rather, take the reins of her life and make sure that she took care of herself. Lotta was going to take control of everything, keep her ducks in a nice little row, and forge on.

Attempting all sorts of positive self-talk, she stopped thinking about her mum and moved to Jack. She went over and over the Jack situation and the pink jacket. By the end of her third cocktail, she'd decided that despite everything, she'd back off just that little bit from him. She wouldn't let him actually realise that though. He didn't need to know about her doubting or her wondering about the pink jacket. She would just step back, put a little ring around her heart and ensure it was protected. Easy enough, she told herself. Easy peasy. Yes, she nodded to herself. She had a plan, and she would stick to it.

Half a day later, Lotta stepped off the plane and into Heathrow to continuous beeps from her phone. The top notification was from Dave.

Dave: *I hope you had a safe trip. Just to let you know, we've had a few more results back. Everything is as good as it can be.*

Lotta swallowed. As good as it can be until the next episode. If her mum wasn't going to stop drinking, it was going downhill and fast. Dave didn't need to know her views on it, though. Lotta thought about her reply as she headed to the immigration counters. She was determined to put herself first in the situation.

Lotta: *OK. Thanks for letting me know, Dave. I've just landed, and the flight was good. Let me know if anything else happens. I will text Mum also.*

Lotta put her phone in her pocket and after going through passport control, she headed for the train with resolve and a tight look on her face. She was damned if she was going to let anything get her down; not the pink jacket, nor the heart attack, nor the bottle of perfume in the drawer. Lotta Button was on a mission for one thing and one thing only – herself.

29

Lotta had been home from Singapore for a good few weeks. She'd put all the plans she'd hatched on the plane into place; she continued to text her mum but had put herself first, she'd cracked on with her job and reading account, and she'd pulled back a little bit from Jack. She'd assumed that Jack hadn't noticed that she'd said no to a few things and had sealed a nice tight little circle around her heart. It was better to keep herself safe.

The quiet stillness of the library room enveloped her as she sat on the sofa, fussed to make sure the bookshelves behind her were perfectly styled and got her phone ready for another sponsored live. In the short time since her first DM regarding sponsored posts, she'd had all sorts of requests about work and was building up quite the nice little bit of work and side income. It was never going to buy her a Caribbean island, but it had not taken her long to work out that if she put in the hours and continued to grow her account, the debit on her credit card would go down sooner rather than later.

She gazed over to the far corner of the room, where the

large window overlooked the garden and she could see the sea in the distance. The evening light was fading and the room was filled with a warm glow. Lotta breathed all of it in and sighed. It felt so very good to be at home and in charge.

She was nervous with anticipation as she logged onto her account. She'd had a lot of interest from her followers about the newly released book she was about to review, and she wondered how it was going to go. All of it felt a bit strange; she had these connections and relationships with women all over the world who she didn't actually know from Adam. Once she'd sat down and thought about it and chatted to clients about sponsored posts, she'd realised that she'd internet-known and engaged with some of her followers for a long time and now they were here, all logging in for this next part of her journey.

She gulped as she saw the vast number of people joining the live. Thank goodness for make-up, it was doing a very good job of making her appear a lot more glowed-up than she felt. In real life, on the library room side of the screen, she had so much blusher on that she looked positively clown-like.

As she sat waiting and as people continued to join in droves, she felt a flurry of nerves in her stomach. She'd been expecting a few hundred viewers, but as she scrolled through, there were many, many more ready and waiting. She cringed and winced a bit inside – it was far beyond her expectations, and even more, it was much more than the publishing house who were paying her was hoping for. She crossed her fingers on her lap that it would go well.

Filled with a mixture of emotions, she got ready to start. The irony of the years she'd spent desperately working in publishing was not lost on her. All that time she'd been quietly squirrelling away, growing a huge following of people who were just as obsessed with reading and getting lost in a book as she was. Most of it still surprised her every time she logged on. She felt strangely humbled, surprised, anxious, and excited, all at the same time.

She watched herself as people logged on, and she smiled warmly, greeting her viewers, and once the time clicked over, she was off. 'Good evening, everyone! Welcome,' she heard herself say. 'I'm so excited to share this with you all.' She pushed the book in front of her screen. 'Out today, and I know most of you have had it on preorder. I have to tell you, as I always do, there were parts of it I loved.' She paused for a second. 'And parts of it I really *didn't* love. As ever with me, it's warts and all.'

She stopped for a minute and read the screen as love hearts flurried up the side and people left their comments.

'It's time to dive in. I'll be reading a few passages, then I'll tell you what I thought, and then we'll talk a bit more, and I'll take questions. You know how I roll. Here we go!'

Lotta picked up the book and began to read. She juggled the book with the notes beside her and a timeline she'd noted on her iPad beside her. After she'd read the first chapter and had pulled out quotes she liked, she paused and looked at the comments. So far, so good.

Once she'd reached the end of her prepared section, she was flooded with comments and questions. She couldn't quite believe how well it was going. Her mind was racing as her phone also flashed up a message from Liv, who was watching and told her she was doing well, and the client who was pleased with the numbers and the engagement.

By the time she'd gone through the many questions and replied to comments about the actual book, she started getting lots of questions about the library room. On a whim, she flipped her camera around and toured the room. As comment after comment came in about how lovely it all was, Lotta nodded to herself. There was now no doubt about the fact that the library reading retreat idea was a good one. In actual fact, Lotta was more or less certain that it would take off. As she continued with the live, her mind whirred. All she had to do was get her act together, focus, and get on with the next part of her plan.

The next day, Lotta was feeling upbeat. She'd been flabbergasted to call her mum and not only get an answer, but her mum had sounded okay. She'd also had a text from Dave to say that he thought she was cutting down on her drinking. Lotta wasn't going to hold her breath, but she took the news and ran with it.

Following her extremely successful sponsored live and the overwhelmingly gushing response to her tour of the library room, she was on a mission to get the boathouse building up and ready. She felt as if fate had dealt her a run of a few cards, and she was going to maximise it as much as she could.

With a cup of tea in hand, she walked out to the garden, down the path, and opened the door to the boathouse building. She felt a pang of guilt about Jack as she looked around. It had been he who had been the driver on the turnaround of the room. He'd done a tonne of the work, and now here she was, pulling back from him. Not that she'd made it obvious, at least she'd hoped she hadn't. As if he was reading her thoughts, her phone buzzed.

'Hi,' she said and smiled.

'Hey. I'm just dealing with a few emails at work. I'll be a bit later than I said I would be.'

'No worries,' Lotta trilled as the pink jacket went through her mind. 'Are you staying over?'

'Yeah, if that's okay.'

'Of course!' Lotta said. She knew she was doing the casual, nonchalant thing Timmy and Liv always accused her of doing when she was trying to pretend she didn't care.

'Lott, is something wrong?'

Lotta pretended she was fine. 'No, nothing's wrong. Of course not!' she said.

Jack didn't sound convinced. 'Are you sure?'

'Yes, I'm sure,' she replied, trying to sound not bothered.

'You're being, I don't know, sort of odd. You keep doing that funny voice.'

'What funny voice?'

'You sort of singsong or something. I don't even know what it is,' Jack replied. He didn't sound particularly happy.

'I'm just tired, that's all. The trip took it out of me. I'm still recovering.'

Jack sighed. 'Okay. Look, just tell me if I've done something wrong.'

'No, no.'

Jack exclaimed. 'The penny has dropped! You're doing the same voice you did after the ball.'

'Jack! Honestly, I am *fine*.'

'I'm not convinced.'

Lotta hesitated. She wanted to blurt out about the perfume, the pink jacket, and the text, but she also wanted to stick with her plan about pulling back from him. On top of that, there was no way she wanted to sound either desperate or overly bothered. 'All good.' She changed the subject, moving the conversation away from her feelings. 'I'm looking forward to you coming over. I've got a nice bottle of white in the fridge.'

'Me too,' Jack said.

'See you later, then,' Lotta chirped.

'Yeah, and we'll talk about what's going on. Don't think you can change the subject and flick me. I'm not stupid,' Jack replied, his voice gruff.

There was a long pause. Lotta felt a wave of nerves wash over her. She attempted to lighten the air. 'Don't be ridiculous, Jack. Rightio, I'm down by the boathouse. I'll see you for some more DIY. Love you!'

'Yeah, see you soon,' Jack replied.

Lotta slipped her phone back into her pocket, picked up her mug, and walked back to the kitchen to make another cup of tea. As the water boiled, she looked out the window at the garden and mused her conversation with Jack. She'd thought she was so very clever with her big girl pants and determined ideas to keep her heart protected. It seemed, though, that she wasn't quite as clever as she thought. She added milk to her tea and stirred. Maybe she should just come clean with Jack after all.

~

By the end of the day, progress in Lotta's reading retreat had moved on vastly. Jack had worked at a pace she'd hardly been able to keep up with and she'd spent the day on her feet working hard. She had also spent nearly all the time trying to bring up a way to voice what was on her mind. It hadn't worked in the slightest.

After clearing up and showering they'd walked down to the Smugglers pub and were sitting at a table in the corner with a couple of drinks.

Jack held up his glass. 'Locals Only beer isn't too shabby,' he said with a grin.

Lotta beamed but her mind was elsewhere. Feeling like it was now or never, she tentatively opened her mouth to mention the pink jacket and then she closed it again. Ever since Jack had arrived earlier that day, she'd clammed up every single time she'd gone to say anything about what was on her mind. It was as if whenever she went to speak she didn't want to mess up the bliss between her and Jack. The bliss marred by the location of a bottle of perfume and a few misplaced texts.

Jack watched her, a frown crossing his forehead. 'Everything okay?' He asked, concerned.

Lotta looked up, meeting his gaze. She felt a lump form in her throat. All the words she wanted to say were jumbled up inside her, a jigsaw of emotions and feelings. 'Yep, couldn't be better.'

Jack reached his arm out and laid his hand on hers. 'Want to talk about what's wrong?'

Lotta bit her lip, her gaze dropping to the table. She was silent for a few seconds, gathering her thoughts before she drew in a deep breath and incredulously she heard her chirpy singsong voice coming out of her mouth. 'Nothing's wrong!'

Jack nodded and then took a sip of his beer. 'Right. Yeah, you've said that a few times.'

Lotta nodded. 'I've been thinking about what you said earlier,' she said, trying to hide the shaking in her voice.

Jack nodded again and squeezed her hand gently. 'Go on.'

'I know I've been a bit distant and there is a reason.' Lotta squeezed her left hand into a fist. 'I've not been quite myself - I'm putting it down to the emotion of everything in Singapore.' Lotta nodded as if trying to convince herself that she hadn't just totally lied through her teeth.

Jack didn't really smile. His face was a blank void. 'Okay.'

Lotta nodded, the lump in her throat growing by the second. 'I just need a bit of time to get over it all. You know what with the journey on top of it and everything.' She heard her voice singsong. She now knew for sure she was doing her cheery trying-to-be-casual voice.

Jack picked up his glass and sipped his beer. 'Yep, it was quite the trip.'

Lotta felt herself blinking rapidly and doing a strange wince-like smile. Here she was again with the pink jacket as if it was on the back of the chair beside them but just as every other time, she couldn't bring herself to actually make its presence known. 'So, yeah, anyway, I'll be fine.'

She couldn't really read the look on Jack's face, but she could tell that he was more or less not convinced. She picked up her glass and nodded towards the window and mentioned the view, changing the subject like a pro. She'd leave the pink jacket right where it was on the chair and deal with it another time.

30

Lotta strolled along next to Timmy and Giles on an unmade road on the far side of Pretty Beach and watched the funny little funicular railway carriage going up the side of the cliff. All three of them were silent for a minute as they observed the train stop at the top and then slowly begin to descend again. Its clattering and rumbling filled their ears as they got closer and closer to the booking office at the bottom.

'Ooh, this looks fabulous, darling!' Timmy exclaimed. 'So quaint and gorgeous. Love. It.'

Lotta chuckled as Timmy clapped his hands together in excitement. A post about the Pretty Beach Funicular Railway had caught her eye on the Pretty Beach community page. The post had detailed spots for private train rides only open to residents that were booking out fast. Lotta had liked the sound of it, so she'd read more, clicked on the website, and learnt that the Pretty Beach Funicular Railway Society facilitated special events involving private cliff rides and all sorts of functions. She'd scrolled through the details with a smile on her face, knowing that it would be right up Timmy's alley, and had booked tickets accordingly.

A few days after she'd booked, an email had come through from the Pretty Beach Funicular Railway Society. The email was signed off by a woman named Barbara Barnutt, and it had detailed all sorts of information about the history of the railway, how private events were run, and had informed her that when her party arrived they were to look out for Gary, the stationmaster.

Lotta smiled as they got closer to the little building at the bottom of the cliff. 'It's going to be fabulous up there. The views are supposed to be brilliant. You can see for miles, apparently. The pictures on the website alone were amazing!'

Just as the three of them were standing outside gazing upwards, Holly and Xian from the bakery, a tall handsome man, Suntanned Pete, and a couple of what Lotta recognised as bakery staff piled out of the booking office door laughing. Holly waved and stooped.

'Hello!' Holly gushed, pointing up to the top of the cliff. 'We've had so much fun. We missed the LO rides last year. There was no way we were not going this year. Ooh, you're booked in for the twilight rides. Lovely.'

Lotta smiled and peered up. 'I've read it's amazing.'

'Yep. A nice bottle of bubbly and the view. It's all you need.'

Xian, who was standing next to Holly, grinning, butted in and raised a bottle with amber-colour liquid in it. 'Or you can take some of this up there with you.'

Holly pushed the bottle away. 'No way. They are not taking that disgusting stuff with them.'

Lotta gestured to Timmy and Giles. 'I have these lovely guests down from London. This is Timmy and Giles.'

Holly shook hands and then turned to her left. 'My son, Rory.'

Lotta swallowed and looked up. Rory was rather, ahem, nice. 'Hi.'

Rory shook her hand, and Holly continued, turning to Rory. 'Pretty Beach to the Breakers,' she said in explanation.

'Ahh, yes, I've heard.' Rory smiled. 'How are you getting on with it?'

Lotta nodded. 'Very well, thanks. It's coming along nicely, and I never thought I would hear myself say that.'

'What about the reading retreat idea? How is that going?' Holly asked.

'I'm nearly done with the actual building. I'm just waiting on a few things – the plumbing and the like.'

'Sounds like you've been busy,' Xian noted. 'You must be close to ready to go.'

'Ahh! I wish. The garden is still a real mess, and seeing as the boathouse building looks out to the back section of the garden, it will need to be sorted.'

Xian nodded. 'Good luck with it all, then.'

'Yes, thanks.'

'What have you got on for the rest of the weekend?' Holly asked.

'I have a Sunday full of doing said garden ahead of me,' Lotta replied. 'I'm hoping to at least break the back of it.'

'Sounds busy. Cheerio, then,' Holly said. 'We're off for dinner now. Have a lovely night. Enjoy the ride and the lights,' she said, peering back up the cliff.

'Thanks. Nice bumping into you guys. Have a good evening.'

Giles pushed open the door to the booking office, held it for Timmy and Lotta, and they all stood in the old-fashioned waiting room. A glass-partitioned office sat in the corner alongside a noticeboard, and a huge brass bell with a white rope hung from the ceiling. A few minutes later, as a party of passengers left from the far side, a man in a train conductor's hat smiled.

'Afternoon or evening. How are we all?'

'Evening,' Lotta replied. 'We're good, thanks. You must be Gary. Is that right? The email said to look out for you.'

'Yep. That's me alright.' Gary nodded and tapped on a computer. 'By the looks of this, I have two more parties after you, meaning you must be Lotta, if I'm not mistaken.'

Lotta chuckled, now more used to the quaint ways of Pretty Beach where people made it their business to know your name, but you weren't quite sure how. 'Yes. Lotta Button and two guests. It was meant to be three, but my partner couldn't make it.'

'Oh, that's a shame. Righto, take a pew, and I'll be with you in a minute.'

Lotta sat down on a beautiful, highly polished old timber bench whilst Timmy and Giles stood peering at posters on the wall depicting pictures of the railway from days gone by. Lotta quietly observed as Gary checked in another party of four. He then slid the partition window on the ticket desk across, pulled a brass latch over on the door of the booth, stepped into the waiting room, and adjusted his station master's hat. He looked over at Lotta with his eyebrows raised. 'Rightio, all set for you three. I hope you're ready for it. The views up there this evening are phenomenal,' Gary said with a grin. 'We've had all the colours today – reds, oranges, yellows, then purples, and now dark blues.'

Timmy beamed. 'We're champing at the bit to get up there! This is fabulous.'

Lotta, Timmy, and Giles trailed behind Gary, who led them through a timber and glass door, leading to a tiny platform nudged into the rock cliff. Gary clunked a gate shut and then slid over a brass catch on the carriage door, and as the four of them stepped in, the carriage wobbled and the old floor creaked.

'Okay, let our journey begin,' Gary joked, gesticulating his hand upwards, as Lotta sat down at the front on a bench seat running all the way along the far side of the carriage. Gary then pulled an old-fashioned brass lever towards him, there was an accompanying clunking and whining sound, and with a rumble and a judder, the carriage slowly began to move away from the bottom of the cliff. As the train rumbled and clattered, Lotta craned her neck at the front and looked up the steep rock cliff. The train creaked and clanked and Timmy and Giles stood on the other side near Gary, who was pointing out things as the magnificent view slowly came into sight. Timmy pointed to the lighthouse. 'Wow, this is amazing! Everything is getting smaller as we go up.'

Giles turned back to Lotta. 'Thanks for this. It really is a sight to see. Fantastic!'

'You wait until you get up to the top,' Gary added. 'The colours out there this evening are banging.'

The train slowly made its way further up the steep incline, winding its way towards the top. Lotta gazed out the window, taking in the stunning views; the sea shimmered, the lighthouse shone, Pretty Beach seemed more picturesque than ever, and the little town was showing off as never before. As they climbed higher and higher, the carriages rocked and swayed, clanged and banged, and finally stopped with a judder at the top. Lotta got up and all three of them stood looking at the view as Gary pushed and pulled the brass levers.

'You okay?' Timmy asked as they waited for Gary to open the doors. 'You're very quiet this evening, Lott.'

Lotta followed Timmy's gaze to the waiting room. 'Am I? No, no, I'm fine.'

'You are. It's a shame Jack couldn't make it,' Timmy noted.

Lotta waved her hand in dismissal. 'He had a family thing.'

'Right.' Timmy nodded. 'You didn't want to go?'

'I didn't want to miss this.'

Once they'd disembarked and watched the train descend back down the cliff, the three of them had followed Gary's instructions and were sitting on a tartan picnic blanket, looking out over the magnificent view. Lotta sat next to

Timmy, a champagne bottle beside them, and a wooden platter with cheese and biscuits placed in front of them. The view stretched endlessly away, the lights of Pretty Beach starting to glitter and twinkle as the purples and blues Gary had mentioned got darker, and Lotta leaned back on her hands and crossed her legs out in front of her. 'Remember when we used to sit up at Primrose Hill on summer evenings looking over the city?' Lotta said with a wistful smile on her face. 'This reminds me of that.'

Timmy laughed. 'Those were the days. Young, free and single, eh?'

Lotta looked at the view and took a sip of her bubbles, a wave of nostalgia washing over her. 'They were. The days before apps, ha ha.'

'And Dan. The days before he ruined everything,' Giles added.

'I rue the day I ever met him, if I'm honest,' Lotta said, shaking her head.

Timmy flicked his hand. 'All behind you. Water under the bridge. Don't even dwell on it ever again, darling.'

Lotta waved her hand. 'Yep.'

'You now have Just Jack.' Timmy winked. 'Even though he couldn't make it tonight, which is a shame.'

Lotta injected cheeriness into her voice, not wanting to focus on the pink jacket situation. 'I do. Yes, it's a shame he couldn't make it.'

Timmy's head snapped around at Lotta's voice. 'I thought I imagined it earlier, but now I'm positive. You're doing the voice. The casual I-don't-care voice. What's happened? Something's up with you.'

Lotta let out a huge sigh. 'Ahh. Am I really that transparent?'

'Yes, you really are. What? What haven't you told me?' Timmy persisted.

Lotta waved her hand again in dismissal. 'It's nothing. I told

Liv, and then I decided to just bury it and then my mum and Singapore and everything.'

'What did you bury?' Timmy insisted.

Lotta sighed. 'It's probably nothing, which is why I didn't tell you. I don't really want to get into it…'

'Doesn't sound like it's nothing if you're doing the casual voice. Start at the beginning,' Timmy instructed.

'I found a bottle of perfume,' Lotta said and blinked slowly. She then relayed the whole story to Timmy and Giles, who both sat there, taking it all in and not really saying much.

Timmy frowned as he looked out to sea. 'I really think you might be making a mountain out of a molehill here, Lott.'

'Liv said the same. The thing is, it's made me realise that I don't want to be as serious with him.'

'Pah! Darling, you're kidding me, right? What a load of twaddle, if ever I've heard it! I could tell from the night after the ball that you were serious. Don't even fool yourself that you're not serious. Absolutely ridiculous, darling.'

Lotta sighed. 'Exactly. And I don't want to be serious. I need to be…' Lotta paused and searched for a word for a moment. 'Independent. I'm not getting myself into that situation again. No way. No, no, no.'

'Sorry, but you're being ludicrous.'

'I'm not. I've just cooled it a bit.'

'Right,' Timmy said with his eyebrows high.

'What do you think about that?' Lotta asked.

'I think it's pretty low, if I'm honest, darling,' Timmy said, his voice serious.

Giles chimed in, nodding gravely. 'I'm with Tim. We're not kids here, Lott. You've cooled it a bit. What does that even mean? I wouldn't want to be going out with you if you did that.'

Lotta sighed. 'I just, I don't know.'

'Just bloody well get it out in the open, darling! Stop pussyfooting around. Honestly! Did you learn nothing from Despicable Dan?'

'This is different,' Lotta said.

'How? Tell me how this is different,' Timmy insisted.

'I don't know. I have so much to lose this time,' Lotta stated despondently. 'And, well, yeah, I want to make sure that doesn't happen again.'

Timmy raised his eyebrows, screwed up his lips, and shook his head. 'Well, you're going the right away about it if you carry on acting like this.'

Lotta turned to look at Timmy, a twinge of alarm in her chest. 'You don't think I should cool it?'

'No, I do not!' Timmy added. 'This is the man who did the whole Pretty Woman thing at the wedding.'

Giles agreed. 'You can't knock him for that.' He sighed. 'Gosh, that was so romantic.'

'I suppose not,' Lotta replied. 'I just need to keep myself, I don't know, safe.'

Timmy tutted and rolled his eyes. 'You're going about it the wrong way, darling.'

'And then there was the bedroom makeover thing,' Giles noted. 'That was something else. And you're cooling it? No, sorry, just no. At least have the decency to tell him what's going on. Sorry, Lott. You need someone to tell you you're being an idiot and not a nice one at that.'

Lotta gulped. She didn't want to think about it too much. She'd now been told by all of her best friends – Liv, Timmy, and Giles – that she was going about the pink jacket thing the wrong way. She so didn't want to admit it. She just wanted to bury it all. She changed the subject. 'Let's have a toast,' she said, reaching across and picking up the bottle of champagne.

'Changing the subject, but yes, sounds good,' Timmy said, his eyes lighting up. He pointed to the view. 'Quite the spot for toasting.'

'To the view, and to us,' Lotta said, raising her glass towards the sea.

'To us,' Giles and Timmy echoed, and they clinked their glasses together.

Lotta smiled as the bubbles tickled the back of her throat. She looked out at the view of Pretty Beach below. Her life had been a lot worse. It was so good to be sitting with Timmy and Giles in Pretty Beach. She reached out and squeezed Timmy's arm. 'Thanks for coming down. Thanks for being, well, err, for being harsh but truthful. Maybe I needed to hear it.'

Timmy nodded. 'No worries.' He looked out towards the lighthouse. 'We love it here. That train is the best thing ever.'

They all sat for a bit in silence, sipping their champagne and looking out at the view. Lotta let out a little sigh and tried not to think too much about Jack.

After a few hours, a lot more chatting, and further dissection of what was going on with Jack, Timmy finally got to his feet and stretched.

'We should be getting back,' he said, nodding down towards the lights of Pretty Beach. 'It's getting late, and I've had enough champagne and cheese to last me a lifetime.'

Lotta sighed. 'I suppose so,' she said, reluctantly getting up.

'Come on,' Timmy said. 'We don't want to miss Gary's last trip down the cliff; it's a long walk home otherwise.'

Lotta smiled. 'Nope, I don't want to take on that walk in the dark. Thanks for tonight, by the way. I needed someone to talk some sense into me.' She hugged Timmy, and he chuckled.

They stood there for a moment, and then Timmy held her away from him and raised his eyebrows. 'You, my friend, need to sit down, have a good old think, and work out what you are going to do. Do not let this one get away because you've been burnt in the past. Ask me how I know.'

'Thanks.'

'You need someone to knock some sense into you,' Giles reiterated.

Lotta nodded and let out an exhale through her nose. If there was one thing she'd learnt in all the years she'd been friends with Timmy, it was that he was more often than not, right. And a little voice inside was telling her that she so needed to run with that.

31

The day following the funicular ride, Lotta was sitting in the library room with a warm cinnamon bun and a cup of tea. She'd already done a live on her socials, had worked on her week's posts including outlining a sponsored one, and she'd checked on a couple of things at work. She'd also tried to call her mum, but as usual, had not had a reply.

Jack was due to arrive at any time, and after her discussions with Timmy and Giles the night before and a long text conversation regarding the same topic with Liv, she'd decided to stop beating around the bush. She was going to take the bull by the horns and talk to Jack about the pink jacket. That was the plan, anyway.

After making another cup of tea, she checked the time and decided to call Dave. She'd been messaging either him or her mum every few days since she'd been back from Singapore, and it seemed as if her mum was maybe not drinking as much. Lotta knew all the signs of her mum's drinking and its cycles, and she hoped this one would last. Her feelings had been all over the place regarding her mum. When she'd first got back, she'd thought it wouldn't be long before the next problem with her mum's health. What had actually happened was that after more tests, her mum was stable. No one had been more surprised than Lotta. She was relieved that her mum seemed to be taking heed of her health, but she still couldn't help but worry. One thing was certain in the world of Lotta's mum; she had been here before, and Lotta would not be holding her breath.

As she pressed Dave's number, her stomach did the usual thing it did and swirled full of anxious butterflies. She took a deep breath and wondered whether or not he would answer.

'Hello,' she heard him say as if he was wondering who was on the other end.

'Hi, Dave. Just calling to check on how things are. I've tried Mum a few times, and it usually just goes to voicemail,' Lotta said, trying to keep her voice cheerful.

'Good to hear from you. How are you?' Dave asked, his voice nowhere near as chirpy as Lotta's and sounding tired.

'Not too bad. How's Mum doing?'

'Hang on a minute,' Dave said, and Lotta heard him open a door and from the sound, he'd clearly stepped outside. He lowered his voice. 'Fingers crossed, she's doing better every day. She's not had a drink much. That's not to say she's not drinking, but, well, yeah, she's up and about more.'

Lotta felt a surge of relief. She wasn't sure whether she believed it or not – her mum was an absolute master at concealing her drinking, but it was a start. 'That's good news.'

'Yes, hope so. She's even been following the diet plan they gave her. I've never seen her eat as much.' Dave sighed. 'Yeah, it's good.'

Lotta smiled. 'I hope it lasts.'

Dave sighed. 'She needs to take it easy and eat well, and hopefully...'

Lotta nodded. 'Yep.'

'I don't think we're out of the woods yet, though,' Dave warned.

213

Lotta didn't need to be told that. She thought about how ill her mum had looked and the fact that her mum's drinking went up and down. 'No. Let's hope so, though.'

'One day at a time.' Dave sighed.

'You'll let me know if I need to come?'

'Of course! Look, I'm sorry this is all a bit, umm...' Dave searched for the right words. 'Awkward.'

Lotta felt empathy for Dave. 'It's fine. I'm used to it is all I can say.'

'Yes, yes, I suppose you are. Thanks for calling. I'll pass it on,' Dave said, sounding grateful.

Lotta nodded. She was certainly used to the way her mum was with her. She certainly wasn't happy about it. 'See you then. By the way, how are you coping?' Lotta asked, knowing full well Dave wouldn't be drawn.

'All good,' he said, his voice tight.

Lotta took his cue. 'Right. Well, see you later.'

'Take care, Lotta,' Dave replied.

'You too. Call me if I can help with anything. I'll continue to text Mum. She can reply when she feels up to it.'

'Okay, cheerio then.'

Lotta put her phone down and felt somewhat more at ease with the situation with her mum. She was relieved to hear that her mum was doing well. Perhaps she was somewhere close to starting a journey of recovery. As she looked out the window, she knew one thing for sure, where her mum was concerned, you really could never tell. And for Lotta, the best thing about being an adult and having lots of experience behind her was that she was aware of that. Gone were the days of false hope and ridiculous ideas that her mum would one day stop drinking. Lotta now knew the ins and outs of the disease only too well.

∾

Lotta was standing by the hob in the kitchen with a pan of bacon and mushrooms on the go, mulling the Singapore situation over in her head, when she heard Jack letting himself in the back door. She'd cooked a full English, and everything was about ready. She'd set up a table in the conservatory with a linen tablecloth and placed a little blue Mason jar full of flowers from the garden and a jug of orange juice in the middle. Putting the spatula down she walked towards the back door, where Jack hugged her hard and then they stood chatting in the kitchen as Lotta pottered around finishing off the breakfast. As she cracked a few eggs into the frying pan and started to make fried bread, Jack looked over at the hob and the pan where the tomatoes, mushrooms, and bacon were sizzling.

'This smells and looks delicious,' Jack said, inhaling deeply. 'I'm ravenous. When you said don't eat, I took it literally.'

'How was last night?' Lotta asked, referring to Jack's family event.

Jack nodded. 'Yep, good. How about the train ride with Timmy?'

Lotta swallowed, thinking about how a large proportion of her night had been discussing the problem that was eating away inside of her. She thought about asking him about the pink jacket and went to broach the subject. In an instant, all of her earlier resolve was gone and instead, she heard herself doing her casual, cheery, I-don't-care voice. 'Gorgeous. I'm sorry you missed it.'

Jack smiled. 'Plenty of time for that.'

Lotta nodded and let his words compute through her brain. These weren't the words of a man who was up to something with a pink jacket, were they? Surely not? 'Yep.' she replied, her voice still faux-cheery. She smiled, then turned and reached for the pepper grinder on a nearby shelf. 'Okay, we're nearly done with this.'

'Good. I'm ready! And then we get to spend the day working in the garden,' Jack bantered.

Lotta smiled as fat spat from the pan, and she moved the mushrooms further to the side. 'You don't have to if you don't want to.'

Jack frowned. 'I was joking.'

'Okay.'

'Lott, is something wrong? I'm asking again. I know you said no before, but you're... You're odd.'

Lotta poked the mushrooms and felt as if someone had stuck her tongue to the roof of her mouth with a gigantic dollop of high-strength glue. 'I'm fine.'

'You're not. You've been weird since you came back from Singapore.' Jack's voice had changed – it was tight with an underlying tension.

Lotta started to spoon the contents of the pan onto a warmed platter. Her brain continued to hold the pink jacket and the bottle of perfume tight, not letting them communicate with her voice. 'Nup, I'm fine.' She dismissed what he had said and nodded to the salt and pepper. 'Grab those and the teapot.' Balancing the platter in her hands, they walked out of the kitchen, the smell of breakfast trailing behind them as they made their way into the conservatory. As they sat down, the sun shone through the glass panes, and Lotta put the platter into the middle of the table.

Jack seemed to be content not to continue about what was wrong with Lotta, and he tucked into the breakfast and then looked out to the garden where the sunshine made the colours pop. 'So, once the garden is done, and the plumbing and bits like that are complete, it will be ready for your peeps and the retreat.'

'Yep.'

'How are you feeling about that? Excited?'

Lotta grimaced and scrunched up her lips in contemplation. 'I don't know now! It's sort of scary.'

'Mmm. You'll be fine.'

'I'm going to start it off as a daily thing, I think. Baby steps and all that.'

'Yeah. With me here, you'll be fine too. I can keep an eye on everything.'

Lotta felt her heart do a full tumble on the balance beam. This was not a man who was cheating. Was it? 'Yep, thanks. That's so kind of you. '

Jack put his fork down. 'You see, this is what I mean.'

'What?'

'You're distant and chirpy at the same time.'

'I'm not.'

'You are. What even is that thing you do?'

'No, no. Honestly.'

Jack didn't look happy. There was confusion in his eyes. 'Frozen, that's it. Perkily frozen. And like you locked something up.' Jack's voice was tight. His eyes looked angry.

Still, Lotta couldn't blurt out her thoughts and come clean with what was wrong. 'No, I'm not,' she chirped. And being the master that she was at changing the subject, she gesticulated outside to the weather and the sunshine and was grateful when Jack seemed to move on.

Once they'd finished and Jack had cleared up and loaded the dishwasher, they had just walked out into the garden when there was a sharp rapping from the side gate.

Lotta wrinkled her nose and frowned. 'Expecting someone?'

Jack side-eyed. 'Nup.'

Lotta re-did her hair, twisting it into a bun on the top of her head as she walked towards the gate. After fiddling with the latch for a second or two, she yanked open the old gate and frowned to see Holly, Xian, Suntanned Pete, a tall man in shorts, and a woman in jeans and a black t-shirt.

Holly beamed and trilled, 'Hello, hello, hello. Working bee! Here for your pleasure.'

Lotta frowned and squeezed her eyes together. 'Sorry?'

Holly, with a white paper bag over her arm, pushed on past letting herself in. 'You're witnessing the Pretty Beach way right here, right now.' She swung her arm around. 'I think you know everyone.' She pointed to the woman in the black t-shirt. 'This is Clemmie. She may look as if she just walked off the Paris catwalks, but she's a grafter worth her weight in gold.' She then nodded. 'Ben Chalmers, also gold, and whose lads will be here shortly.'

Lotta was astonished as she stepped aside and gestured for the rest of them to come in, and Jack joined the party standing by the gate. 'The Pretty Beach way,' she repeated back to the group, not really knowing what to say.

Xian wearing a pair of shiny purple ankle-length welly boots shuffled past. 'Yep, let's be having you then. You know, the Pretty Beach way by now. Right. Who's doing what? I haven't got all day. I'm on the phone to New York later.'

'Wow, thanks!' was about all Lotta could muster to say, her voice ringing with delight.

Xian shuffled down the path, her eyes widening at the sight of the overgrown garden. Lotta followed her gaze as if seeing the garden again for the first time. Despite her initial work on it, it had grown fast; weeds had taken over the flower beds, and the grass was long and wild. The fruit trees were looking healthier and the path she'd cleared when she'd first moved in, wound its way through the tall grass. But beyond that, it was hard to make out what was what. Standing there looking at it as Xian was, the job seemed vast.

Pete stepped up to stand next to Lotta and whistled. 'That is quite the job.'

Lotta chuckled. 'It is indeed. I did tell Holly that.'

Lotta had to stop herself from shaking her head, and she

chuckled as Jack took charge and started instructing everyone what to do. Deciding that a cup of tea was in order, she went and made a pot, and came back with mugs on a tray. As everyone took a mug, Holly opened the paper bag full of cinnamon buns, and they all stood around chatting. Lotta looked on, amazed. This place she now called home? The Pretty Beach way? It really was something else.

Four or so hours later, Lotta waited for another pot of tea to brew. After getting mugs ready on a tray, she stood in the conservatory with Jack, looking out towards the garden. The working bee had performed nothing short of a miracle. The garden had been turned around. It still had a long way to go but the back of it had been broken; the lawn was mowed and edged, the flower beds no longer contained a bevy of weeds, and trees and hedges had been trimmed. Xian had spent her time with her headphones clamped to the side of her head jet washing the terrace, and Holly, in sparkly gardening gloves, had cleared the little area outside the retreat building.

Lotta whispered as they looked out at the garden. 'Look at it, Jack.'

'I know.' Jack replied with an edge of bewilderment.

'This Pretty Beach way thing. It's, I don't even have the words.'

'It's got me too,' Jack said, sounding stumped.

'You have to laugh at the sparkly gardening gloves.'

'And Xian with the jetwash. I don't know where she gets her energy from.' Jack chuckled.

'Nope, but I know I need some of it.'

'She's gone through like three of those flasks. Every time I looked over at her, she had the jet wash in one hand and was swigging with the other.'

Lotta burst out laughing, 'I did the same!'

'Too funny.'

Lotta shook her head back and forward. 'How in the name of

heaven am I ever going to repay this? What can I do as my contribution to the Pretty Beach way?'

Jack made a funny little sound as if he had no idea. 'Good question.'

'I don't think they'd be interested in my reading,' Lotta stated jokingly.

'Mmm, tricky one. I'm sure something will come up. You could loan me out for DIY duties.'

'Yeah, no. No one is having you, ha ha. Okay, the tea should be ready. You take the biscuits out, I'll bring the tray.'

The members of the working bee all stood around the little area outside the boathouse. The patch of grass was mown, the old roses going up and over the door looked healthy, and a vintage sun umbrella in the Pretty Beach pastel colours stood in the middle of a small timber table setting.

Xian stood beside Lotta with a mug of tea in her hand. 'Not a bad job, eh?'

Lotta nodded gratefully, 'I should say so. I'll never be able to repay you all.'

'Ahh, don't even think about that. It'll come soon enough. That's how it works.'

'Thanks.'

Xian nodded. 'I wouldn't mind sitting out here with a book or two on a nice sunny day. It's a little suntrap.'

Suntanned Pete butted in, 'Facing south and out of the wind. Nice spot for a bit of sun, yep.'

Xian cackled. 'I don't think you need any more sun by the looks of you, do you?'

Lotta giggled as she looked up at Pete's orange face and he frowned. 'Always in need of a bit of sun, me. In fact, I'm going to my sister's up in the hills later to sit in her garden.' He inclined his chin over towards the sheltered spot and the brick walls. 'It's the same as this, surrounded and sheltered out of the wind and facing the right way. Like our own little microclimate down here.'

Xian nodded. 'Yeah, it will be a nice evening up in the hills. How is Betty, by the way? I haven't done a bread round up that way for ages.'

Pete nodded. 'Yep, she's the same as ever. Her life consists of the shop and flying off to the sun.'

'Can't be bad,' Xian replied as she took out a silver flask and glugged its contents into her tea. 'Well, I'm cream crackered after all this. The old bones are feeling it.' She looked around. 'It really has come up roses.' She nodded to Lotta. 'You'll be able to rent this out for holidays, let alone reading retreats.'

Lotta nodded. 'Hmm, it's looking that way. All I need now is to get the plumbing sorted and then think about some sort of a kitchen.'

Pete gestured around. 'Today has broken the back of it.'

Lotta felt ridiculously grateful. 'Thank you all so much. I can't believe you turned up to help me out.'

Xian cackled. 'Ahh, we like you.'

Pete joined in the laughter. 'Yeah, you'd be watching your back if we didn't. Nah, joking, it's just nice to see the old house alive again. I used to ride past this place on my bike on my way to school. Those were the days.'

'Yes.' Xian agreed, holding up her mug. 'Here's to Pretty Beach to the Breakers and future reading retreats.'

Lotta lifted her mug in response. 'I'll drink to that. Here's to this lovely old house, and my new life on the coast.'

32

Time had flown by since the funicular railway ride and the working bee, and despite everything that Timmy had said and further discussions with Liv, Lotta had still not mentioned the pink jacket, the hidden perfume, or indeed the text message to Jack. She might not have mentioned it, but it did fill her brain for many of her waking hours. And there was no question that Jack knew something was wrong with her, he just didn't know what.

Lotta walked slowly along the beach, mulling it all over. The sun was setting, and the sky was filled with pink, purple, and orange streaks. She felt the sand between her toes, the cool sea breeze on her skin and the fresh air filling her lungs. She'd had a long week at work and not much time to think about anything, but there was no doubt that Jack had got wind of her feelings and her pulling back from him. Her mind whirred with it all. She'd never felt a connection like the one she'd had with him before, and here she was pushing him away. The chemistry from her end was electric, as was the jumping around of her heart. It was what ruffled her feathers the most – the deepness of her feelings – and as much as she wanted to be close to him, she was scared.

She thought about it as she watched the waves lap onto the shore. The part of her that had been burned by Dan and the app years was exponentially hesitant about getting too close, of trusting someone too much. The pain of the aftermath of Dan was still all too evident in her mind. Sighing, she tried to work out what she was going to do as she paddled along in the water, and her brain flicked between thinking about him and thinking about not being with him. He'd zoomed into her life, and she'd almost forgotten what it felt like not to have him there. She wondered what it would be like if he decided, like Dan had, to call it a day. She stopped, sighed and gazed out at the horizon as if looking at it would somehow tell her what to do.

Once she had finished her walk on the beach, she headed for the shops and was strolling down the laneway in the sunshine. She'd stopped to look in the window of the florist, had stood and read through the whole of the menu outside the curry house, and was making her way over towards the bakery to get supplies. A Saturday afternoon in the library room with books, tea, and LO cinnamon buns was calling.

She strolled along as the pastel bunting flapped above her, and as she was walking towards the bakery door, Holly and Xian were coming the other way, laden down with white paper bags.

'Yoohoo!' Holly called out. 'Lovely day for it!'

'It's beautiful. Long may it last,' Lotta replied, cheered up by Holly's friendly smile.

'What are you up to?'

'A long-awaited day off,' Lotta said.

'Lucky duck! How is your mum now?' Xian enquired.

Lotta sighed. It was tricky telling people about her mum. How did you tell someone you and your mum didn't have much of a relationship? How did you tell someone you'd always been unwanted? How did you put it across that you'd gone all the way to Singapore to see someone, and they'd barely been able to give you the time of day? As she always had done, Lotta left out that part. She felt embarrassed that despite messaging her mum every day and calling multiple times, she'd hardly spoken to her at all. She had had updates from Dave though, and despite everything, further tests on her heart had shown that she was okay. 'She's doing okay,' Lotta heard herself say.

'That's good. So, you're not needed for a bit over there?' Holly asked.

Lotta shook her head. Not needed and not wanted – that was about the bottom line of it. 'Not at the moment, no.' Lotta breezed. 'She's on the mend.'

'What a relief that must be,' Holly noted and touched Lotta lightly on the elbow.

Lotta considered the comment for a minute. It was a huge relief and when Dave had told her the latest test results, she'd felt as if a dollop of worry was taken away for a bit. What hadn't changed though, was the stark reality that her mother just wasn't particularly interested in her. And it had always been the same way. The latest trip to Singapore had batted her with that in the face. No one wanted to hear that, though. 'Yes.' She nodded. 'Thanks for asking.'

'Of course!' Xian said as she quickly nipped from a silver flask.

'What have you ladies been up to? You have a lot of bags with you.'

Holly cackled. 'We are off to our new bakery. The fit out isn't even finished yet.' She held up the bags. 'We're bribing people with these to speed it up.'

'Locals Only cinnamon buns will do the trick.' Lotta chuckled.

'Hope so,' Holly said, the diamonds in her ears sparkling.

Xian lifted her head up and raised her eyebrows. 'How's the

love life?'

Lotta squirmed inside. Another thing she wasn't quite going to tell the truth about. 'Lovely.'

'Right you are. We haven't seen him around and about as much.'

Lotta stopped herself from shaking her head. How in the world did these two know Jack hadn't been in Pretty Beach quite as frequently?

'Jack's, umm, been busy with work and all that.' Lotta flicked her hand back and forth. 'You know what it's like.'

Xian nodded, lugged her flask, screwed her lips up and then sighed. 'Yeah, nice one that one. Don't make many like that these days.'

Lotta laughed. 'Aww!'

'I'm not joking. I know I've only just met him, but I have an old woman's radar for these things.'

Holly rolled her eyes and shook her head. 'I wish it wasn't true, but she does.'

'You see—' Xian started to say something, but then Holly interrupted her.

'Don't start on with all that gobbledegook stuff, Mum. Really, no one is interested.'

Xian tutted. 'I know my stuff.'

Lotta's eyes widened. 'Really?'

'Yup. I can tell you a good man, a good woman, or a good anything for that matter, just by looking at them.'

Holly rolled her eyes. 'You so cannot.'

'It's the aura, see,' Xian added.

'Right, and what sort of aura does Jack have?' Lotta chuckled.

Xian held her head to the side. 'You'd be thinking he might be a bit on the aloof side at first glance. I'd possibly even put him as grumpy. I would even go so far as to say not to mess with him. But by that golden aura around his head, there's one thing I'd be doing if I was you, Lotta Button.'

Lotta swallowed. Xian's voice had suddenly gone very serious. 'What's that?'

'You, my friend, need to keep him close. He's gold. Keep him close, and never let him go. Well, not literally.' Xian winked and swigged again. 'But you know what I mean.'

Lotta swallowed. It was as if Xian was cementing things she'd earlier thought as she'd stood looking out to sea. She really did need to stop being an idiot. Everyone had now told her. Push really had now come to shove.

33

It had been a few weeks or so since the garden working bee, and things were going well in Lotta's life. Her job was good, and she was gearing up to launch the dates of her first reading afternoon to her followers. Her mum's condition had stayed the same, and she'd actually started talking to Dave about her drinking problem. In the Jack department, though, Lotta had still not said anything about the jacket or the premise that she was keeping a little bit of her gymnastics performing heart under lock and key. In actual fact, despite everyone's advice, she'd decided not to do anything about her concerns at all. So much for confronting her fears. She'd ignored everyone's advice on the matter and resorted to plan A, which she'd hatched on the plane back from Singapore. Plan A meant she was safe. She liked how that made her feel.

She'd hoped that Jack hadn't noticed too much, anyway. Despite his noting of Lotta's behaviour, both of them had been busy; Jack had been away on business a few weeks in a row and was wrapping up a deal he was working on in Texas, and Lotta had been busy at the arcade.

There was also another little thing – even though she'd told herself she'd cooled it and tried to kid herself that there was a nice, locked circle around her heart, in reality, she hadn't really. Because Just Jack had proved quite hard to resist. Even when he'd been away, she'd spoken to him every day, sometimes multiple times, and she'd seen him every weekend. She continued to tell herself that she'd cooled things and that her heart was locked, but deep down, it couldn't have been further from the truth. She was in, big time. She loved Jack deep and hard.

Jack, though, had still clocked that something was going on with Lotta, and he had brought up the subject again and had asked her a couple of times if she was okay. When they'd discussed it, Lotta continued to convince him she was fine and everything was hunky-dory. She proceeded to feel as if her tongue was stuck to the roof of her mouth when discussing the subject. Inside, she'd decided she would just trundle along with the relationship and see how it all panned out.

She just needed time to get used to the whole him and her thing. At least that's what she'd told herself and Liv anyway. Liv had tutted and told Lotta she was dreaming if she thought it was the right way to behave, and Timmy had continued to tell her she was bang out of order. Lotta continued to stick her head further and further into the sand and thought she'd known better, and had decided to ignore them both.

Tucking her Kindle with a newly loaded book into her book bag, she got in the car, hooked her phone to the system, and pushed the button to play an audiobook. As she drove along on her way to meet Jack's sister for the first time, she wondered what his sister was going to be like. She'd heard a lot about her and as much as she could gather, Lotta had ascertained that they were fairly close. She shook her head a few times as she slowed down to approach a set of traffic lights. So much for cooling it. She was meeting his family and all sorts. Who was she even kidding thinking that her heart was safe?

Once she'd arrived at Jack's house, she reversed parked onto the drive, checked her make-up in the mirror, locked the car, and stood on the doorstep in anticipation. Jack opened the door with a grin, put his arms around her waist, and kissed her. She consumed the Jack smell, inhaling deeply. 'Hi.'

'Hello, Lotta as in hotter,' Jack said with a straight face.

'Just Jack, how are you?'

'I'm good. You look beautiful, as usual,' Jack said. 'How was the traffic?'

'I didn't really notice it. I had a book playing.'

'Ahh, course you did, the humble power of the audiobook,' he said as he led her into the open-plan kitchen at the back of the house. She sat down at a long marble island and nodded as he offered her a drink and accepted it gratefully.

'Long week?' Jack asked as he handed her a glass of wine.

'Yep, I've had four conferences this week; Tuesday, Wednesday, Thursday, and Friday. Now I know why it's not recommended for one person to be lead across those like that.'

'That's how it works, is it? What, so you second behind someone some days, do you?'

'Yeah, I'm mostly with Marie. It's a good system. It helps if there are problems, which there invariably are. Plus, it's tiring being over the conferences on your own, four days in a row. Not that it's about the tiredness. Everything is so meticulous, they never want a ball dropped – so they want you to be sprightly.'

Jack nodded. 'I assume that's why it's so successful.'

'Guess so.' Lotta put her wineglass down. 'I really do love it there. I feel like I landed on my feet. It's all so flexible too. As long as you put the work in, of course.'

Jack's face was straight, but he joked, 'Does that extend to me? Do you feel like you've landed on your feet with Just Jack?'

Lotta chuckled. She tried not to let it happen, but she felt her heart pull its competition leotard on and prepare to do a double back. Jack was joking, but she was serious. No matter what she told herself about being cool, she so totally was not. Her heart was so far from being safe it wasn't even funny. 'Yup.'

'Good. Same on my end.'

'Mmm.'

'I was going to ask you something,' Jack stated with a straight face.

Lotta frowned. 'You were? Sounds ominous. Like what?'

'Like, do you fancy coming over to the States with me for this next business thing?'

Lotta swallowed. Accompanying him on a business trip was serious. Wasn't it? Business trips to the States were not mini-breaks or overnight stays in hotels. Or little flits here and there. Business trips to America made everything very real. She wanted to say no and stick to her plan, instead, she heard herself saying yes. 'Love to, as long as I can sort it out at work. I already went to Singapore. They're fine about stuff like that, as long as I don't have conferences on. I can work from anywhere other than that.'

'Yeah, I thought that. It'll only be a long weekend, really, anyway. A quick business trip.'

'Will I be in attendance at a ball? Will there be prawn vol-au-vents present?' Lotta giggled, referring to the ball she'd attended with Jack on a fake date where she'd got food poisoning from prawns.

'I hope not, but if I know the Texan lot, you'll need a nice dress. You'll need to be sparkled up by Holly from the bakery.'

Lotta suddenly thought about the bottle of perfume in Jack's drawer. It was now or never. She picked up her wine and took a gulp. Just as she was about to launch into it, the doorbell went. Jack laughed. 'It's a miracle! She's normally at least half an hour late. She's clearly trying to impress. Don't worry, it won't last long.'

Lotta listened as Jack's sister came in full of laughter and loudness. She'd heard from Jack that they were like chalk and cheese. As she came into the kitchen, Lotta was hit by a strong perfume. Lotta slid off her stool, and not sure whether to be too familiar, she held out her hand. Jack's sister grinned. 'I'm Natasha. I've heard so much about you.'

'Same here,' Lotta replied, taking in Natasha with her fair hair and very well-turned-out appearance. Lotta smoothed down her top as she settled herself back down.

'Wine?' Jack asked as Natasha put a huge tote back down on the floor under the island bench.

'I might have a gin and tonic, actually,' Natasha said and then turned to Lotta. 'How are you? It's so nice to meet you at last. We keep crossing paths and missing each other.'

'Yep, seems you have a busy life.' Lotta smiled.

'Ahh, yep, don't we all?' Natasha said, plonking herself down and slipping the backs of her shoes from her heels.

Lotta was trying to take everything in at once. Natasha was bright, loud, and very confident. In a short-sleeved silk shirt, she also smelled amazing and had really good hair. Lotta felt herself touching her hair self-consciously. 'I hear you love a book,' Natasha said brightly.

'Oh, gosh yes. I'm a total bookworm. What about you?'

'I wouldn't say a bookworm, but I like a read before bed. And I love a good book about fashion.'

Lotta was always fascinated by what people read. Books about fashion though weren't really on her radar. Each to their own. 'Oh, right, like what?'

'Biographies, stuff about people in fashion. You know, Blahnik and Chanel and all that.'

Lotta didn't know, but she nodded and played along. 'You like, umm, designer things then, do you?'

Natasha contemplated for a second. 'It doesn't have to be a designer, as such. I don't know, I've just always been into clothes and bits, haven't I, Jack?'

'Yep,' Jack agreed.

'And fragrance and stuff,' Natasha said.

Jack finished pouring tonic into Natasha's gin. 'Speaking of clothes.' He walked to the end of the island and opened a door, turned around, and held up a pink jacket. 'This has been in my office for ages.'

'Ahh! I couldn't find that anywhere! I didn't even dare tell anyone. I mean, who loses a Chanel jacket? Only I could do that,' Natasha exclaimed and laughed.

Lotta stared at the pink jacket Jack was holding in his hands. She swallowed a huge lump in her throat and felt herself feel a bit sick. She grabbed onto the edge of the worktop, feeling the kitchen spinning. Natasha was chattering on; she leant over the island, took the jacket, and then picked up her huge bag from the floor. She rummaged around and turned back to Lotta. 'See, I say I like fashion and fragrance, and I'm a walking embodiment of that.' She started to pull out bottles of perfume, two make-up bags, and a cardigan and bandied them around and put them on the worktop. 'Seriously, I could dress someone from my handbag. I'm like Mary Poppins!'

Jack pointed to one of the perfumes. 'There's a bottle of that in my drawer at work, too.' He rolled his eyes. 'Duh, I meant to bring that too. It's been there for ages.'

Lotta couldn't have made it up if she'd tried. She felt so stupid, she just sat there not saying anything.

Jack frowned and looked over at her. 'Lott, are you okay? You've gone very quiet.'

Lotta nodded. 'Oh yes, I'm marvellous. Never been better in my life.'

Jack side-eyed. 'Right. Sure?'

Was she sure? Oh yes. She was very sure. Very sure indeed.

34

Lotta double-checked the picnic basket, and that she hadn't forgotten anything. Cheese, quince paste, pickled onions, fancy crisps, a chilled bottle of wine, cordial, a flask, teabags and milk. All of it was present and correct. All she needed to do was stop at Holly's for a baguette and she'd be done.

Hooking the picnic basket over her arm, her book bag on her shoulder, and a tartan picnic rug in her hand, she hurried through the house and deposited her stuff in the boot of her car.

All she could think about was her stupidity over the pink jacket. It had filled her mind every single minute since Jack had given it back to Natasha. She'd wasted so much of her emotional currency on worrying about it, it was ridiculous when all along it was totally Jack's sister's.

As she got in her car and drove through Pretty Beach and pulled into a parking space on the laneway, she shook her head. She'd been so scarred by what had gone on in her old life, she'd lost sight of reality; the jacket and the perfume had both had perfectly reasonable explanations just as both Timmy and Liv had said they would. Lotta felt embarrassment and foolishness smooshed into one all over her body. She'd wasted so much mental energy on it, she felt absurd.

Crossing the road, the sun was shining on Pretty Beach, promising the beginnings of a beautiful day. The pastel bunting fluttered in the breeze, the ferry horn sounded in the distance, and huge palms rustled in oversized white pots. A couple of seagulls circled overhead and the air carried a smell of the coast; seaweed, salt and warmth mixed into one glorious, heady inhale.

Lotta was surprised to see only one person in the bakery and not the usual queue snaking out the door. As she stepped in, Holly emerged from the back.

'Morning, Holly!' Lotta said brightly as she breathed in the scents of the bakery.

Holly smiled. 'Good morning! You're full of the joys. What can I do for you on this bright and lovely day? We're having a run of sunshine that's for sure.'

Lotta leaned against the glass counter at the back of the shop and grinned. 'French stick for me please.'

Holly whipped a French stick from a huge basket on the wall behind her, deftly wrapped it in paper and placed it on top of the counter. 'You're looking gorgeous. Where are you off to?'

'Off out for the day. I've packed a picnic, hence the French stick. I may have a book and a nice chilled Sauvignon Blanc with me.'

'And you'll have Jack with you, will you?' Holly laughed.

'Yes, I'm picking him up from the ferry.'

'Where is your picnic taking place?' Holly joked.

Lotta considered for a second. 'I was going to go down to the beach huts here, but then I remembered your mum and Pete mentioning the hills the other day. I thought we might go there, seeing as the weather is so nice. They said it's lovely walking through the woods and stopping at the pub.'

Holly's eyes lit up. 'Ooh, that sounds nice! It'll be lovely up there today. Park behind the old rectory and stroll up the bridleway there.' She nodded as if agreeing with herself. 'Yep, just the day for it.'

Lotta smiled, opened her phone and frowned. 'The old rectory, right, yeah, I saw that on the map.'

Holly nodded, 'Yes, there's a public footpath running down the side of the rectory which leads to a bridleway. That eventually veers up and takes you through the woods and up the hill there. You'll love it.'

'Okay, right, I see.' Lotta said, expanding the map on her phone, and squinting.

Holly nodded and held her hand up. 'One sec.' She came back with a white paper bag. 'Buns. New recipe. LO, but don't tell anyone. Perfect for a picnic in the hills.'

Lotta chuckled and took the bag. 'Thanks. Jack will be pleased. He's become addicted to your buns.'

Holly cackled. 'I like it!'

'So you think a walk on the bridleway is the best place to go in the hills?'

Holly nodded. 'To be fair, you can't go wrong. There are plenty of nice areas up there. I was only thinking about it yesterday when I was delivering to Betty in the shop. Suntanned Pete's sister, that is. It's all lovely up there. Have a little stroll along the main street if you get time.'

'It runs right through the middle, doesn't it?' Lotta asked.

'Yep, with a pub on each end. Both of them are good. Harriet at the Golden Lion is lovely.'

'Right, thanks.'

'Your best bet is what I said, it's gorgeous up through the woods there. It's a lovely spot, with a stream running alongside, and at this time of year it'll be full of wildflowers. Once you get up to the top, you can see for miles right to the lighthouse too.'

Lotta smiled and nodded. 'Done. Thank you so much for the advice. Rightio, I'm all set.' She thanked Holly again, grabbed the French stick and waved her hand as she walked towards the door.

As Lotta made her way out along the laneway, she felt a little hum of excitement. All she had to do now was clear up the text message situation and her life would be back on track.

When she arrived at the ferry wharf, the sun shone down bouncing off the glistening water lapping at the feet of the old wharf. Salty sea air filled Lotta's nose as she stood looking out to sea. She spotted the ferry just as it chugged around the corner and watched almost mesmerised, as with seagulls soaring above it, it boobed up and down churning up the water.

The wharf buzzed with activity, with people bustling around waiting for it to arrive. When it finally pulled in bumping the timbers, Lotta could see Jack strolling up the wharf with a jumper in his hand and sunglasses on his head. She swallowed at the sight of him. He greeted Lotta with a smile.

'Hi,' Lotta said, hugging him.

Jack smiled. 'How are you?'

Lotta was ecstatically happy to have the pink jacket behind her. She positively buzzed. 'Really good.'

Jack frowned and side-eyed. 'You're *very* chirpy. What's happened?'

'Oh, no, nothing at all. Just full of, you know, all this,' Lotta replied, gesturing around to the wharf, the sky and the ferry.

Jack laughed and bantered, 'Yeah, it's certainly a very nice day to go out with a bookworm.'

A few minutes later, Jack and Lotta weaved their way through the laneway. The sunshine had brought Pretty Beach locals out of the woodwork, and a throng of people bustled here and there. As they got to her car, Lotta looked up at the sky, dotted with puffy clouds. 'This is what it's all about. A perfect day for a picnic in the hills, isn't it? I just spoke to Holly when I went to get the French stick, and she said it will be gorgeous up there today.'

Jack smiled and nodded in agreement, and the two of them got into Lotta's car. 'Works for me, Lotta as in hotter. Works for me.'

About ten minutes after they left Pretty Beach via lanes weaving in and out of fields lined with hedgerows, Lotta and Jack arrived in the little hamlet she'd looked at on the map. She slowly drove through the main street where terraced cottages butted up to the pavement, hanging baskets filled every available space, and pastel bunting layered from left to right.

Jack chuckled, 'And we thought the town was nice.'

Lotta sighed as they passed an information sign and she read aloud, 'Pretty Beach Hills is a small hamlet conservation area mentioned in the Domesday Book of 1086.'

'Nice. Got to love a bit of the Domesday Book,' Jack deadpanned.

Lotta pulled into the public car park alongside the old rectory just as Holly instructed, and Jack pointed over to a public footpath sign nearly hidden by a vast laurel hedge. He squinted and peered down to the end of the car park. 'That must be it, there.'

Lotta nodded, turned off the ignition, and they proceeded to take the picnic basket and rug out of the boot. They made their way slowly along the public footpath until it emerged onto a wider bridleway where a mossy timber sign informed them of the way. Lotta gasped at the prettiness of it all on the beautiful spring morning. The hedges seemed to glow green in the dappled sunlight and flowers danced along the bottom of the hedges. Wildflowers sprinkled a fresh sweet scent through the air, and a breeze whipped around the edges.

Jack smiled as he looked around. 'What a beautiful day,' he remarked. 'You still seem full of it, too.'

Lotta smiled wryly to herself. The owner of the pink jacket was helping with her mood, that she knew for a fact. 'It certainly is,' she agreed.

They continued down the path, taking in the sights and sounds of the countryside, passing the backs of lovely old houses and gardens, until they got to the stream Holly had mentioned. 'Holly said it was lovely up here. She was right. Look at that. So pretty.'

'Yep.'

After standing and staring at a lovely old house with stables and a paddock, they took a rickety old bridge over a stream and the path started to incline through rippled light in a patch of woods. Jack looked around, taking in the beauty of the place. 'The air is magical up here,' he said. 'Or am I imagining it? It's sort of sea-ish but country-ish.'

Lotta smiled. 'I know. Weird right? It really is.'

After the path narrowed then widened again, and then again got so narrow that they had to walk in single file, it eventually cleared and they found themselves in a small park area. A couple of picnic tables were lodged on the far side, a map board looked out over the hills and down towards the coast, and an old couple was sitting on a bench looking out over the view.

After choosing a spot on the edge overlooking the hills, Lotta laid the tartan rug on the ground, propped up the picnic basket, and sat down. As she put the cheese on a little board and undid the French stick, Jack took out two glasses and poured the wine. 'My kinda picnic, Lott. I could get used to this. It sure beats a working bee pulling tree branches all day.'

Lotta followed Jack's gaze to the deep green of the hills, a patchwork of fields, and the coast in the distance laid out in front of them. She could just about make out the stream turning into a river, snaking its way through the countryside, and the lighthouse way out on the cliffs. She looked around as she cut a piece of cheese, popped it onto some bread, and marvelled at the view. 'This has bookworm all over it.' She giggled.

'No doubt we are travelling with at least one Kindle.' Jack chuckled, nodding over towards Lotta's book bag.

'There might be. I don't go out without one. As you know.'

They sat in comfortable silence, soaking in the beauty of their surroundings, with the cheese being washed very nicely down by the wine.

Lotta smiled and grabbed Jack's hand. 'I need to talk to you about something.'

Jack's face didn't crack. 'It's about time.'

Lotta wrinkled up her nose. 'What does that mean?'

'You've been acting strangely since you came back from Singapore. I've been waiting to see what's going on. Did you bring me up here to dump me? To tell me that it's you and not me, is that it?'

Lotta grimaced, ignoring the banter. 'I'd hoped you hadn't noticed.'

'Yeah, right, of course not.' Jack's face turned serious. 'I've told you more than once I've noticed. You just decided to keep changing the subject.'

Lotta winced. 'Sorry.'

'I've racked my brains, but in the end, I decided it was to do with your mum. I imagine it was a very emotional trip.'

Lotta nodded. It had definitely been emotional, but she was more than used to it where her mum was concerned. She coughed and started to say something and then stopped.

'What?' Jack frowned. 'Just tell me.'

Lotta sucked air in through her teeth. 'I, well, I don't know what I thought, but I saw Natasha's perfume in your drawer at work and her jacket hanging on the back of the door...' she stopped and Jack's whole face seemed to cloud. 'Then there were...' She let out an enormous sigh. 'The texts.'

Jack shook his head in bewilderment. 'Texts? You're going to have to give me a little bit more than that to work from.'

'Ages ago there was a text from someone called Sam.'

Jack's forehead wrinkled into deep creases. 'Err, that would be Sam, yep.'

'He sends you kisses at the end of texts, does he?' Lotta said, only half-jokingly.

'He would be Samantha.'

Lotta swallowed. 'Right.'

'He would also be my cousin.'

'Oh.'

'Anything else to run by me?' Jack said, his face straight.

Lotta let out a sound between a cough and a laugh. 'When you said you were having an early night.'

Jack squinted. 'What? I don't even know what you're talking about.'

Lotta had started rambling, her words tumbling out at a hundred miles an hour. 'And then you said see you later and accidentally texted me.'

Jack squinted his eyes as if trying to recall what Lotta was saying. 'If it's the text I'm thinking you're referring to, Natasha was picking something up for one of my nieces for a fancy dress day at school.'

'Right.'

'Lott, have to say, I'm not really liking where this is going. Not at all. Are you, in fact, accusing me of something?'

Lotta had to laugh to herself, with his answers, it wasn't going anywhere and she was glad to see the back of it. Jack didn't seem that happy. 'No, no. It's fine.'

Jack rolled his eyes, 'Oh, god, don't start the cheery casual voice again. That, I can't stand.'

Lotta swallowed, not sure what to say. Jack continued, 'I'm so not interested in anyone else. I thought that bit was quite obvious.'

'Hmm.'

'Do you really think I run around the countryside arriving at random weddings dressed up in a morning suit for any old bod who takes my fancy?' Jack asked, rolling his eyes.

Lotta couldn't speak. Jack was not best pleased.

'Do you think I am interested in clearing out buildings and taking part in working bees with orange men and funny women in sparkly gardening gloves? That would be a no. Bloody hell, I could have just paid someone to do the whole job...' Jack let his sentence hang in the air.

'I see.' Lotta's voice was very small.

'If I didn't want to be here, or wanted to see someone else, I would.'

Lotta's mind raced as she computed what he was saying, and at the same time tried to work out how she was going to backpedal her way out of the situation. None of it worked. She just swallowed and fiddled with the edge of her napkin. 'Okay.'

Jack shook his head in a mixture of irritation and confusion. 'So are you telling me that's what the oddness has been about? A text from my cousin, a fancy dress costume and a pink jacket? Really?'

Lotta's voice was barely a squeak when it came out, 'And a bottle of perfume.'

'I'm not even going there.'

Lotta's heart stood on the side of the Olympic gymnasium's floor. Its sparkly red leotard caught the light as it presented at the end of its routine. 'I think, I umm, yeah, I think there may have been a little bit of overthinking involved on my part.'

Jack's eyes widened incredulously. 'Just a bit.'

'Yes.'

Jack's face changed and Lotta let out an inward sigh. 'I think you might have to do a lot of sucking up to me,' he said.

'I do?'

'Yes.'

Lotta didn't really know what to say. He'd turned very serious, his tone was almost scary. 'What would you like me to do to suck up?'

Jack's face still looked serious. 'It's going to take a bit of work to get you out of this. I can't believe you would think that of me.'

Lotta gulped as she realised that she'd read just about everything wrong, and that Jack was more than annoyed. She went to speak but Jack interrupted with an eye roll and a chuckle, 'I'm joking, you muppet.'

Lotta let out a huge sigh. 'Ha!'

'You were obsessing about all that? Really? I do not need anyone else in my life. Got it?'

Lotta nodded, not able to speak.

'I'll spell it out for you, shall I? I love you, Lotta Button. The end.'

Lotta took a huge breath in. 'Right back at you, Just Jack.'

'Now, let's get on with this bottle of wine. You have a lot of sucking up to do. And please, don't go snooping around and looking at things and turning them into something they are not.'

Lotta beamed and looked out towards the coast. She'd come a long way. What with beginning a new job, the situation with her mum's health, moving to a new place and starting again, her emotions had taken a battering. It was no wonder she'd questioned everything and obsessed over things. But here she was, sitting on a picnic rug with a man who made her heart somersault, telling her he loved her. She flicked all the other things off and nodded to herself. It really didn't get much better than that.

Find the next part of bookworm Lotta's story at Amazon.
The Pretty Beach Life.

Want to read more about the Pretty Beach hills?
My new novella series has arrived!

THE PRETTY BEACH LIFE

The brand new book from the author of The Boat House Pretty Beach.
(Lotta Button Book 3)

One lovely seaside town. One gorgeous bookworm. Will there be one big happily ever after?

Since Lotta Button hit rock bottom she has certainly been through some ups and downs. But in her new happy place in Pretty Beach and her utterly fabulous old house she's finally beginning to love the fact that her climb up the mountain of life is going well. With her amazing new job, great relationship, and setting up her own small business in reading retreats, she's doing quite nicely indeed. In fact, there aren't many blips on the seaside horizon at all.

As she sails along on top of the water and enjoys all the delights of the best little town by the sea, she's so happy she doesn't quite know what to do with herself. All is splendid in her world until bam, something decides it might like to give her just one more little incy-wincy test...

SPRING IN THE PRETTY BEACH HILLS

A Polly Babbella.

A beautiful spring day. A chance meeting. A love story in the
Pretty Beach Hills.
Get ready to fall in *love*. You're going to utterly adore it.
Jam-packed with all Polly's much-loved unique trademarks - a
divine coastal setting, **gorgeous female characters** you'd just love
to chat with and liberally sprinkled with a healthy dose of
Polly's special blend of *escapism by the sea*.
'Polly really is like my secret best friend in a book. I knew I was
a goner by the end of the first page.'

∽

Fancy a trip to my new happy place?

You'll love it in the Pretty Beach Hills.

Spring in the Pretty Beach Hills is the first of four books based
in the hills of Pretty Beach. And you thought the town was nice.

;) We have a new character to fall in love with, there may be a shirtless man on a bike (oh. my. gawwd.) and the house is utterly swoon-worthy. Then there are the two pubs, the stream, the hills, and let us not forget the cottages and the window boxes.

If you're a Babbette (if you know you know) you are going to die.

Love Polly x

READ MORE BY POLLY BABBINGTON

Spring in the Pretty Beach Hills

The Pretty Beach Thing
  The Pretty Beach Way
  The Pretty Beach Life

Something About Darling Island
  Just About Darling Island
  All About Christmas on Darling Island

The Coastguard's House Darling Island
  Summer on Darling Island
  Bliss on Darling Island

The Boat House Pretty Beach
  Summer Weddings at Pretty Beach
  Winter at Pretty Beach

A Pretty Beach Christmas
  A Pretty Beach Dream

READ MORE BY POLLY BABBINGTON

A Pretty Beach Wish

Secret Evenings in Pretty Beach
    Secret Places in Pretty Beach
    Secret Days in Pretty Beach

Lovely Little Things in Pretty Beach
    Beautiful Little Things in Pretty Beach
    Darling Little Things

The Old Sugar Wharf Pretty Beach
    Love at the Old Sugar Wharf Pretty Beach
    Snow Days at the Old Sugar Wharf Pretty Beach

Pretty Beach Posies
    Pretty Beach Blooms
    Pretty Beach Petals

OH SO POLLY

Words, quilts, tea and old houses...

My words began many moons ago in a corner of England, in a tiny bedroom in an even tinier little house. There was a very distinct lack of scribbling, but rather beautifully formed writing and many, many lists recorded in pretty fabric-covered notebooks stacked up under a bed.

A few years went by, babies were born, university joined, white dresses worn, a lovely fluffy little dog, tears rolled down cheeks, house moves were made, big fat smiles up to ears, a trillion cups of tea, a decanter or six full of pink gin, many a long walk. All those little things called life neatly logged in those beautiful little books tucked up neatly under the bed.

And then, as the babies toddled off to school, as if by magic, along came an opportunity and the little stories flew out of the books, found themselves a home online, where they've been growing sweetly ever since.

I write all my books from start to finish tucked up in our lovely old Edwardian house by the sea. Surrounded by pretty bits and bobs, whimsical fabrics, umpteen stacks of books, a plethora of lovely old things, gingham linen, great big fat white sofas, and a big old helping of nostalgia. There I spend my days spinning stories and drinking rather a lot of tea.

From the days of the floral notebooks, and an old cottage locked away from my small children in a minuscule study logging onto the world wide web, I've now moved house and those stories have evolved and also found a new home.

There is now an itty-bitty team of gorgeous gals who help me with my graphics and editing. They scheme and plan from their laptops, in far-flung corners of the land, to get those words from those notebooks onto the page creating the magic of a Polly Bee book.

I really hope you enjoy getting lost in my world.

Love

Polly x

AUTHOR

Polly Babbington

In a little white Summer House at the back of the garden, under the shade of a huge old tree, Polly Babbington creates romantic feel-good stories, including The PRETTY BEACH series.

Polly went to college in the Garden of England and her writing career began by creating articles for magazines and publishing books online.

Polly loves to read in the cool of lazing in a hammock under an old fruit tree on a summertime morning or cosying up in the winter under a quilt by the fire.

She lives in delightful countryside near the sea, in a sweet little village complete with a gorgeous old cricket pitch, village green with a few lovely old pubs and writes cosy romance books about women whose life you sometimes wished was yours.

Follow Polly on Instagram, Facebook and TikTok
@PollyBabbingtonWrites

AUTHOR

PollyBabbington.com

Want more on Polly's world? Subscribe to Babbington Letters

Printed in Great Britain
by Amazon

39735276R00145